# ARIADNE

by

## June Rachuy Brindel

ST. MARTIN'S PRESS

*New York*

Grateful acknowledgment is made for permission to use the following copyrighted material:

From *The Greek Myths* by Robert Graves: Used by permission of Penguin Books. Copyright 1955 by Robert Graves.
From *The Masks of God: Occidental Mythology* by Joseph Campbell, Viking Compass Edition, 1972. Used by permission of Viking, Penguin, Inc. Copyright 1964 by Joseph Campbell.

Special thanks to Joseph Campbell, Gail Godwin, Jayne Berland, Jane Bonham, Tom Bracken, Alice Cromie, Pamela Painter, and all those others who encouraged me to keep shining a light through the dark labyrinth, especially my editor, Karen D. Johnsen.

Library of Congress Cataloging in Publication Data

Brindel, June Rachey.
Ariadne

1. Ariadne—Fiction. 2. Crete— History—
Fiction. I. Title.
PZ4.B85815Ar [PS3552.R483]     813'.54     80-14013
ISBN 0-312-04911-0

*For Bernard, Beth, Paul, Jill, Bill,*
*Noah, Sarah, Amy,*
*and Louis*

# Author's Note

SOME TIME BETWEEN 1800 and 1400 B.C., the last matriarchies in the Western world were crushed. With them died a system of belief that regarded childbirth as the primary miracle, all women as intrinsically holy, and the Great Mother Goddess as supreme deity. Thousands of people who had devoted their lives to this worship died also, as well as hundreds of priestesses who would henceforth be damned as servants of evil and dozens of queens who would never again be assured of their divine right to rule state and church. One of these queens was the Lady of the Labyrinth, the last Matriarch of Crete—Ariadne.

In the most popular myth, Ariadne's story has been rewritten, her voice almost obliterated. Yet she was the legitimate head of church and state in a country regarded as the cradle of European civilization. Ancient Crete in its prime ruled the Mediterranean, thriving on the export of its crafts and the exploitation of relatively uncivilized tribes in the Aegean area. Among those "barbarians" were the ancestors of Plato and Aristotle.

Those readers who wish to refresh their memory of the traditional version of the myth of the labyrinth should refer to the summary provided in Appendix I.

For an understanding of the historical events upon which the labyrinth myth was initially based, as they can be reconstructed from contemporary research in archaeology and anthropology, I am most heavily indebted to Robert Graves' *The Greek Myths* (see Appendix II for a relevant excerpt), to Joseph Campbell's *Masks of God,* and to Jane Ellen Harrison's *Prolegomena to the Study of Greek Religion.* For readers who are interested in pursuing the subject further, a supplementary bibliography is provided in Appendix III.

*"To the Lady of the Labyrinth: A Jar of Honey."*

(LINEAR B TABLET FROM KNOSSOS)

# I

*Men are not awake; they resemble those who are in deep sleep, or they may be likened to the drunken; they are like children or like the beasts.*

HERACLITUS

# 1

A HAND TOUCHED MY FACE and I woke instantly, my heart charging against my ribs. The old woman's enormous eyes stared down into mine. I could barely see her other features in the dim lamplight. She was whispering. It seemed as though she had been whispering forever and that I had just awakened to hear it. "Come, come. It's time." She pulled me out of bed and through the hushed corridors of the palace into the silent outer darkness. I went without question.

She knew her way up the dark mountain path with no need of a torch. At night she lost all her years and clambered over the rocks as easily as a wild cat. I stumbled sleepily behind, hanging onto her cloak. She moved without sound. Even her interminable whisper was stilled until we reached the old broken shrine on the cliffs rising toward Iyttos. There she stopped and stood rigid as rock. I could not stop shuddering. Perhaps it was the cold of the mountain wind or the chill trickle of water. It seemed more than that. Merope put her cloak around me and drew me close to her legs, and we waited in the slow dawn.

"The sun is the Mother's child," Merope whispered. "Each night he dies and goes back to the Mother. Each morning She gives birth to him again. He is your grandfather." I felt him stirring in me. A humming began somewhere in the ground and rose through me, filling my head with the voice of the Goddess or with the whisper of Her old priestess. It was all the same for me, Goddess or nurse—the whisper came as if from the center of the earth.

"In the start of time, splendor appeared," Merope was chanting. "It was the Mother. She was all that was. She divided the sky from the sea and danced upon the waves. A wind gathered behind Her from Her swift dancing. When She rubbed this wind between Her hands, it became the Great Serpent. She took him to Her and loved him, and a great egg grew within Her and She became a Dove. The Dove-Mother brooded over the egg until it was ready. Then out of the egg came all things—sun, moon, stars, earth, mountains, rivers, and all living creatures. The splendor of the Mother flowed through everything—through sun and sea, through the veins of the earth into root and leaf, into grain and fruit, into all women and all men. And each birth became forever an acceptance of splendor and each death a gift to the Great Mother."

She was moving back and forth now as though the whispered chant swayed her body through the air. Her voice grew stronger with the growing of the light. "Through it all moves the queen, Vessel of the Goddess, the Bearing One, a constant revelation to all people so that no one can forget how at the end of pain will be glory."

Merope chanted it. The walls of the palace displayed it. Pasiphae, my mother, moved in gold through rows of bowing men, her breasts shining. When she danced in the ritual, the sky came down to her and the earth rose. Doves descended upon her hands, carrying blessings. The Serpent of life and death curled up out of the Great Mother's womb and encircled her arms. And from her mouth came the voice of the Goddess, repeating the promise.

Suddenly Merope grew stiff and seemed to choke. "Then this new Minos came!" she gasped. "A consort should not rise above his office!" The words came in fierce bursts from her black hood. "Pasiphae has forgotten her duty, and the world is breaking." She bent over and her legs shook. I clung to them, my eyes closed tight. I thought the sky would break instantly and shatter down upon us. But it was still. Gradually Merope, too, became quiet, and that quiet seemed to spread out around her. The doves were motionless upon their nests. Even the spring water seemed not to move.

Through my eyelids I could see that the sky was brightening. Merope took deep breaths and held them as if she were afraid to let them go. She held me tightly too, and this seemed to me a sign of hope. Just as the great red eye of the sun crept up out of the earth, I opened my eyes. Rays of blue and green shot across my vision as if the sky and the grass were intertwining. Suddenly all the doves lifted up and flew into the sun.

"They are the spirit of the Goddess," breathed Merope.

The birds spread out like a web and blended into the sunlight as if they were knitting the earth to the sky.

Merope raised her arms shoulder high and began to chant a prayer. I followed her. As we turned round and round in the dance, the sky, sun, and earth seemed to move with us.

How many times the old woman took me to that shrine in the darkness and waited for the sunrise, whispering, whispering. Every time she would collapse into terror and then gradually quiet again into hope, so that I grew accustomed to the sequence and welcomed the delicious chill of fear because I knew it would be wiped away by birds and sun. One morning another kind of terror appeared.

We were returning from the mountain shrine, and I had gone on ahead, leaving Merope far above, pecking among the rocks like a quick black bird. The sun was already hot. The doves had long ago risen into the light. Then one returned. I had been watching her from far off, a spot coming through the clouds, growing larger. All around me was the sound of bees, of grass rustling, of the mountain breathing. The dove descended through the sun, alighted upon her nest, and sank down with ruffling noises. Only her head peeped over the rim, eyes alert, darting to one side and the other, head turning, listening. Leaves screened me, and I stayed quiet as the sun crept through my cloak and skin, entered bone, drove deep downward, chaining me to the earth.

In the distance, I saw two men creeping noiselessly over the rocks, their brown torsos gleaming with oil, lithe and graceful as lions stalking. Nothing else moved. Even the dove's eye was still as a target. Suddenly a rock sliced through the air. With a lift of wings, the dove started to rise, then stopped as if painted on the sky, broke open, wings and feet askew, red tumbling out of her feathers, and dropped like a stone. The men rushed to the dead bird. One picked her up and flung her in a high arc into the ravine. The other took the eggs, splattered them against the rocks, and pulled the nest into fragments.

[ 5 ]

The sun pressed against my eyes. The men were red shapes dancing in it. I could not see them clearly, but I seemed to know them. I think they were my brothers. Perhaps I cried out, because knives came up in their hands, and their eyes looked directly at my hiding place. But all at once they turned and ran off down the path.

Merope's black head poked up over the rock above, her sharp eyes looking, looking. When she saw the shattered shells, her hands went out like the dove's feet. She moaned and fell upon the ground, writhing as if she were trying to enter it. Her clothes were smeared with the yellow hearts of the smashed eggs. Leaves and dirt matted her curls. A spider stuck to her hair. Her dress soaked in a puddle of stagnant water caught in a crevice.

I was still hiding, but the rustle of branches must have told her I was there. She grabbed my arm and started moaning again, and then she pulled me down with her to the rock, the water, the broken eggs. When at last we left, she held my arm pinched against her and bent her mouth into my hair, whispering, "Who were they?"

I did not answer.

"Were they men?" She shook me.

"Yes."

"What men?"

I could not name them. I thought, "The sun blurred my vision. It might have been someone else." Yet I never really doubted that it had been my brothers. I could not tell which one had thrown the stone, but it was Androgeos who had picked up the dove and flung her away. Over and over the action played against my eyelids. The lithe, handsome figure leaping onto the rock, bending down in one graceful movement and throwing the bird as if she were nothing but a stone. I can still see his arm complete the curve and descend smoothly to his side, and his black hair drift gently down to curl against his neck. His back was to me. I could not see his face as the bird fell. But I could see that of Tauros.

I hardly ever saw my brothers now that they lived in the men's palace, but when I was very small, before Phaedra was born, we played together. Once they tossed me back and forth from one to the other as if I were a toy. I loved it. I felt as if I were flying. But then Merope came in and screamed and they had to stop. How we all laughed together when she left. How I loved Androgeos then. No one was so beautiful as he, or so skillful. He could dance against the fiercest bulls and outwit them. And when he did he would shout up to me and laugh as if it were the easiest thing in the world and he had done it just for me. I could not understand why Merope disliked him, or why she was so glad when my mother finally sent him—and Tauros—to live away from us with the men in Minos' palace.

But I did not like Tauros myself. He was ugly, yet he was always preening himself. I hated the way he looked at me sometimes. His lips would drop suddenly out of a brilliant smile into—not a frown, but an expression of complete indifference, as if he cared for no one. That same look was on his face as he crushed the eggs. But Androgeos stood against the sun like a boy god.

"What men?" Merope shook me harder.

"The sun blurred my eyes."

"They'll be cursed, whoever they are." Darkness settled into her face. "The Goddess will pull them into death."

I could feel the Great Mother reaching for their feet. A sharp pebble would point up out of flat stone and pierce their soles and they would go hurtling off into chasms, their bodies breaking against the cliffs. The dove's eye hung in my own and grew until the black of its center swallowed all other vision.

"They think it will show their courage to tempt the Mother!" Merope's breath was as sour as the water in the crevice. "They're fools, like all men."

I pulled away and ran down the steep path. At the turn I saw the men again far below, leaping from rock to rock. Were they really my brothers? I decided that if they fell, they were not. I waited to see. One of them shouted something, I could not tell what. The other laughed. And they disappeared behind the brush, the laugh echoing in the still air. I was certain that in a moment it would turn into a scream. Instead, Merope's hand descended again upon my shoulder and her whisper drove into my ear. "They must be killed. A queen must see to it. Remember that, the Goddess wills it." I listened through her hiss for the screams of falling men, but they did not come.

When we reached the spring shrine south of the palace, we could see soldiers coming. From a distance, they looked like strange beasts, men and horses molded together in single bodies as the goldsmiths blend them. Merope cursed them as they approached. They were Minos' troops, foreigners, with arrogant faces. They did not see us at first. One, two, maybe five of them rushed past as we cringed against the wall before there was any sign that they had heard Merope's scream, though it seemed to me louder than the sea.

Finally a horseman stopped, dismounted and bowed, waving for the others to do so. They all did then. The man who had stopped first abandoned his horse to someone else and scooped me up onto his shoulders. All the men dismounted then and bowed as he carried me into the palace. Merope hobbled along at his side, her voice still raging. But now she seemed remote to me as I rode above her on the broad shoulders. On every side, people moved aside and bowed, setting down their pots and woven goods. I rode higher than a queen, almost touching the beams overhead in the long corridor. I was as high as the frescoed face of the very first Minos, walking among the lilies in a time before time. He was even more beautiful than Androgeos. No wonder the Mother had chosen him to head the long line of consorts. As we passed, I reached out to touch the feathers of his crown. But it was just cold wall.

My mother was laughing in the Great East Hall. Her voice floated down the stairs around pillar after pillar. My carrier climbed as though pulled toward the sound. Suddenly we saw her, with heaps of saffron cloth piled around her and the sun shining full on the huge bronze double axes, the symbols of a queen's power. She was dancing but not as in the ceremony. She was whirling like a barbaric slave, in no pattern, and laughing as she turned.

Minos stood at the side watching her, shouting now and then, tossing rings and jewels at her from a great golden bowl. The jewels and the robes swirled the sun about the room as though it too were dancing there. Minos with his gold belt and his huge muscular arms seemed powerful as a bull. No one else was present except

Daedalus, hunched in a corner, watching silently and turning a seal over and over in his hands. None of them noticed us. My carrier paused. Even Merope was quiet. We watched. Minos spilled out all the jewels at my mother's feet, stopped her dance, and kissed her breasts.

My carrier swept me down to the floor then and left. But Merope dashed across the room, pushed Minos aside, took my mother's face and held it in her hands, all the while crying out the story of the men killing the dove of the Goddess. She spoke so fast and with such agonized intensity that I did not think they could understand her, but my mother seemed to know what she was saying. She brushed away Merope's hands and her words were sharp. "Later, later," she said. "It's not important. I will take care of it. Later." She turned back to Minos, laughing, and bent his head down to her. Merope suffered a moment of defeated silence and then she was at it again, her words flapping out fast and urgent and her hands sticking out at her sides. Minos stamped off into my mother's inner chamber, her *megaron.*

"Go away!" My mother screamed at Merope and ran out after Minos. Merope stood bent and awkward, arrested in an unfinished gesture. Daedalus was watching it all in silence, his eyes moving from face to face. The sound of Minos' deep voice came from the *megaron,* followed by my mother's laugh. At that, Merope grabbed my hands and pulled me down stair after stair and across the court to the pillar shrine deep in the palace.

We prayed to the Goddess. The old woman's voice had quieted now to a mumble. From time to time, she looked at me as if her eyes were swallowing my face. I thought she might weep, but her cheeks were dry. For a long while we were silent there, our arms encircling the pillar. Far away I could hear the sound of laughter and of horses. But it was a thin sound next to the deep insistent murmur coming from the stone. All through my years I have heard this double music.

The sun had already passed its peak before we left the pillar shrine. I was trembling with hunger, but Merope would not let me stop to eat. We climbed directly back to the Great East Hall, past chattering ladies lounging in the anterooms and slaves bustling about with fruit and wine. The hall was empty. It looked cold now—the light no longer entered directly and the jewels were gone. Only a few robes remained, one of them thrown carelessly upon a double axe. Merope clucked in disgust and removed it.

A passing slave told us my mother was in her *megaron*. Abruptly Merope dragged me away from the food and through the dim passageway. Chione, my mother's woman met us at the door, motioning for quiet. "She is asleep," she whispered. Chione was tall and bore herself like a queen, but she was no match for Merope. My old nurse had been chief priestess in the palace since long before my mother was born, and few could oppose her. She brushed Chione aside and dragged me with her into the queen's *megaron*.

A moving light played upon the walls, probably the shadow of leaves against the sun in the light well. It made the dancing ladies on the walls move as if through water. My mother lay sleeping on her bed, more beautiful than any of the dancers. She had taken off all her clothes. Only a white scarf lay across her. Her lips were open; the kohl had smudged under one eye. Even Merope did not dare to wake her directly. We sat on a bench near the light well and Merope made noises—coughs, grunts, loud yawns. Presently my mother stirred and turned over without opening her eyes. "Go away, Merope," she mumbled. The old woman would not budge. Again she started the story of the killing of the dove. My mother sat up then and threw the scarf at her, draping it over her head.

"Chione, make my bath," screamed Pasiphae. Chione came in at once with two slaves and there was much bustling about as they went in and out of the *lustrum*, bringing towels and fragrant oils. All the while Merope continued her story, but I could see that my mother was not listening. She seemed as remote from us as the mountain. She did not stop Merope, but there was no sign that she heard. Merope followed her about through the bath and the dressing, talking, talking, her old voice trembling with anger, and my mother was serene through it all as though the old woman were no more than a butterfly.

When we returned to the Great Hall, Minos was there. My

mother went to him and put her arms around his neck. Minos said something, but I could not hear what it was. Merope seemed to, though. She stiffened. When my mother laughed, Merope jerked me fiercely from the room. "Ignorant!" she mumbled. The soft folds of her neck shook and the cords stood out. "Ignorant!" Her lips tightened and vanished.

"Pasiphae is air," said Merope. "She has forgotten the earth. She walks as though there are no caverns under her feet, as though the mountains will not tremble again, as though the barley does not need feeding. She neglects the ceremonies. She is spellbound by Minos, happy to be drugged with perfumes, bathed in oil. She has surrounded herself with beautiful things, but she has forgotten what she must do." Her face became as sharp as a broken rock. I was afraid it would cut me as she drew close. "Minos is evil," she hissed. I had heard her say it before, but it frightened me now more than ever. "He has violated the sacred law. Pasiphae is ruler here, remember that. He can never be more than consort. He should have yielded his place in the ninth year, but he fooled the people with his laws." Merope spat. "He has bought her," she said, "with jewels and slaves."

It was much later that day. I was playing with Icarus in my courtyard, running in and out between the pots of anemones. Merope sat disapproving in my inner chamber. She did not like Icarus. Every few moments she would interrupt the game and call me over to see the skirt she was embroidering. "It will be yours when you are older," she said solemnly, ignoring Icarus' existence. "When you go down to the Goddess and pour libations. Then you will wear a golden serpent and a golden dove."

I cared nothing for it. I was happy to play with the gentle boy. When Merope left the room, we decided—I decided—to play another game. There was a *pithos* in my quarters that held scented oil. It was a huge urn—as high as my waist—and I loved to jump over it, pretending it was a bull. I could do it well. It felt like flying. I thought this must be how the doves feel. But Icarus was not a good bull dancer. He did not judge how high he had to fly to clear the *pithos* and he knocked it down with a great crash. It shattered and the oil spread over the tiles, making them shiny and fragrant. Merope came dashing back into the room so fast that she slipped on the oil and sat down hard on a broken fragment. I could not help but laugh, though I should have known it would make her angrier. "Wicked Athenian!" she shouted at Icarus. He was terrified.

"His mother is a Cretan," I said, but it only fanned Merope's fury. She scrambled to get up, thrashing out her arms in all directions, and accidentally pulled the new skirt from the bench down into the slippery oil. "Monstrous Athenian!" she screamed. I loved Icarus and I wanted to run to him, but Merope was in between, raging.

At that moment, Daedalus limped up to the door. He was holding a new toy, a little priestess swinging between sacred horns. I had seen him working on it and I knew it was for me, but when Merope saw it, she snatched it from his hands, threw it onto the oily tiles, and crushed it with her feet.

Daedalus and Icarus disappeared then, and I was left with the raging woman. She dashed about my room grabbing all the toys Daedalus had ever made for me, threw them on the floor, and crushed them. By now I was terrified too. I stood numbly watching her. Then she swept all the fragments of toys into the ruined skirt, and holding it out from her body as if it were poisoned, she dragged me with her to the shrine at the underground spring. As we entered there was the sound of an owl from the darkness. Merope took the broken toys and offered them all to the Great Mother. "In return for your life," she hissed. The pool swallowed them. They sank down and down until we could not see them any more, and Merope said that the Mother had accepted the offering. Then she tied knots in my hair and washed my hands and made me pray with her again for hours. In between the prayers came warnings: "Daedalus is evil, you must not forget that! He is Minos' tool. Minos uses him to destroy the old belief. You must never again take his dolls! Don't you know that only a believer can make the image of the Goddess? This is sacrilege. And Daedalus means it to be. It's as bad as killing a dove! Stay away from men. Stay away from Daedalus! And Icarus, too. You must know this. You must remember this. Because Minos is evil. He has cast a spell on your mother. He has broken all the laws. The Goddess cannot accept him. He must be killed!"

When she stopped speaking, the owl murmured as if in agreement. I was shuddering again as at the mountain shrine, feeling the breaking of the earth. This time the sense of quiet did not follow.

# 2

How the old woman whispered. I still hear the steady hiss of her voice. "In the earliest time, when there was no Minos, no blood was spilled in anger . . ." Even then I did not see how it could be so. Merope's eyes were great wrathful circles, and her hands were bent like claws. She had been my mother's nurse. "I know how to raise a queen," she would say, her voice rising imperiously. Yet she raged at my mother's actions. And though she said the Goddess was everywhere in the palace, in walls and pillars, under the floor and shining through the frescoes in the corridors, I knew there was also fear.

We did not go to the mountain shrine again for a long time. Merope had other things to do. Every night someone came to see her in my room after she thought I was asleep. Sometimes it was a man, but mostly they were women. They talked in whispers. I kept my eyes closed and listened, but I could not hear what they were saying. Merope seemed to give them orders.

Once, Merope's voice was clear. "She will not kill him."

I opened my eyes then. No one noticed me. There were two women staring at Merope. They held their hands across their mouths. Merope's face had the hatchet look. "Tell them!" she hissed. The women covered their faces and left. I wanted to ask about it, but Merope looked so angry I was afraid.

Then came the night I woke and found someone carrying away my old clay tablets. I was frightened. Merope was not there. I sat up and called to her. At this, the figure turned to me and raised her hands as if I were very holy. I was suprised because no one made this gesture anymore except during the ceremony. I didn't know what to do.

"Bless her," came Merope's voice from the doorway. It was her warning tone.

So I extended my arms in the blessing. The woman clutched the tablets as if they were gold. Then she bowed and left.

Merope stood looking after her.

"Why does she want those old things?" I asked.

She put her hand over my lips. "You must not speak of this," she whispered. Then she looked at me as if she had never seen me before. "Now you must listen. And you must say nothing of what I tell you." I wondered what could cause such a trembling in her voice. She put her face close to mine. "Your mother, Pasiphae, has offended the Goddess, and the Goddess has withdrawn Her voice. Now She will speak only through you. That is why this mountain priestess is taking your tablets. Your words are sacred."

"But didn't you read them?" I asked. "I just wrote down some dreams I had and things I thought about when I was alone. They're not important. They're silly. They don't mean anything."

She put her hand across my lips again. Then she stumbled backward into a bow.

I couldn't believe that it was happening. Merope bowing to me! And not even in the ceremony.

Now she was whispering again. "Every word the Goddess puts into your mind has meaning. She speaks to you in dreams whether you are sleeping or not. You must catch the words. You must write them down."

Some strange thing seemed to be happening to me that I could not see, though Merope could. And so I began to let my words run out on my tablets as if they were breath. If Merope were right, I needed to clear the way for the Goddess to speak through me. Often the words seemed silly. But when I wrote that once, I became afraid.

Then another strange thing occurred. When I danced, I began to feel that the Goddess was touching me. Her breath seemed to come out like a snake and coil around my arms. Her mind entered mine like a dove. As I whirled, arms floating toward the sun, head touching the sky, my feet seemed to take power from the earth and pull it upward. I felt the Goddess both above and below me. I was filled with her.

Merope was very excited when I told her. At first she said it could not happen yet, that before the Goddess entered fully there would be a breaking and blood would anoint me. But later she came back and said, "Even though you are too young, the Goddess is speaking." She began to insist that I tell her all my feelings when I danced.

Meanwhile Daedalus was changing the palace. My mother's throne room now had griffins on the walls. Merope hated them. She said they were not alive like the old frescoes blessed by the Goddess. The old ones were disappearing. Daedalus made new designs and the artists painted them everywhere.

One day my mother asked him to build a dancing floor for me. Merope said he was building it to trap my feet. "The Goddess will never come to you on that floor," she said. "You must never use it."

And so when Daedalus finally announced that the floor was finished and my mother said I would try it the next day, I went running to Merope in terror. The words seemed to turn her to stone. Finally she spoke. "You must dance on it," she said. "If you do not, it will create suspicion, and we are not ready for that."

"But what if my feet are trapped?"

Merope was immovable. "You must dance on the floor," she insisted. I wondered whether she had gone mad.

It was a splendid floor, the maze outlined in blue and saffron mosaics. My feet knew exactly how to follow the pattern. Everyone came to watch my dance—Minos in his best helmet and my mother gleaming in gold. My brothers came too, Androgeos flashing new plumes and Tauros playing with his dagger. I studied them, remembering the dove, but there was no sign that they thought of it. They were proud of living in the other palace now that they were grown, but one could see that they liked to come and strut at ceremonies. Even my little sister Phaedra was there, plump and shy, hiding behind her nurse.

But the old Sibyl from the Dhikti mountains would not come down to pour the libation. My mother was smiling, but Merope's face was fierce. As I whirled I caught her eyes and so I did not dare to do the holiest dance. Daedalus was watching, too, but Icarus was not there. I did not feel the Goddess.

Every night Merope's visitors came. They took my tablets, whatever I put on them. Once I wrote nothing but "Ah-ah-ah-ah-ah-ah." They shook their heads over that, whispered a while, then bowed and hustled away, carrying the clay scrawls with infinite care. They could not read the tablets when I wrote in the new script. Neither could Merope. Once in a while she would say, "Write only in the old script, the Mother's language." Usually I did. But I wondered why all languages were not the Mother's.

Abruptly one morning Merope announced that she was going back to her village for the Anthesteria—the spring festival when the land would be purified. She told me that there it was not contaminated by Attic customs.

"No men can witness it," she said.

"Not even the consort, the Minos?"

She looked as me so scornfully that I was ashamed of my ignorance. I begged her to take me along, but she said I must stay and take my part in the palace ceremony, for without me it would mean nothing. "When the time comes," she said, "I will take you to my village where there is an ancient sanctuary in the mountains, presided over by a priestess so old there is no counting the moons she has lived. She will purify you of all the evil that has come into this house, and then you will return the country to the Great Mother and all will be well: the barley will flourish, the sheep foal. Trees will return to the barren mountainsides. Lilies and roses will grow again in the low places. The ocean will be at peace; the ground will not tremble." She put her hands on my shoulders. "The people are all praying for your strength, Ariadne. You must live well and endure, for the sake of all of them."

But when she had gone, I felt abandoned. My mother did not come to my quarters. Nor did Minos. I saw almost no one except Lyca, a woman from Merope's village who had come to serve me in her absence. Lyca spoke with a strange accent and seemed to be half-afraid of me. She was always bowing and bending. It became tiresome. It also frightened me a little.

Even Phaedra was out of sight. Her nurse was quite young and very timid. Most of the time she kept my little sister in her own quarters and now more than ever. Merope had always disapproved of Phaedra's care, but my mother waved it away with a laugh. "She will not need so many of your lessons, Merope," she said. "She will not be a queen. Let her be happy."

Most of all I missed Icarus. I never saw him now. I thought that Merope must have given orders to keep him out after the breaking of the toys. But it seemed possible that he was ill or had been sent away. No one would say where he was. I had thought I might take him as my consort when I became queen. Merope scoffed at that. She said he was a barbarian and not worthy to be more than a toy, but I knew that only I could decide that. Only the Goddess could decide. When the Goddess came to me fully, then I would know. But I also knew that if I took him as my consort, he would have to die in the ninth year. Merope said it was the law.

For days after Merope left, Lyca kept me in my quarters until it seemed to me that the walls had moved inward. Sometimes I could feel them shake. Perhaps that is a message from the Goddess, I thought. But suddenly they seemed too close and I wanted to break them. I was tired of writing on my tablets. What was more, I knew Lyca could not really stop me from going out, because she was afraid of me.

And so I went past her into the palace, which seemed strangely empty, and then past her again into the sunshine. I went alone. I ordered Lyca not to follow me, but every time I turned, there she was, trembling. Merope must have threatened her not to leave my side.

It was glorious on the hillside, looking down to the sea. If I am to receive the Goddess, I thought, it must be outside, my head bare to the sun. I took off my sandals so that I could feel the murmur of the earth. Almost always it was there. Not everyone could feel it, but it was there for me. Merope said that it was the Great Mother's voice, which I must translate.

I walked for the joy of it all the way to the ocean. I could see Lyca following me, dodging from one wall to another, trying to hide from me as she followed. It amused me that she was so childish and so earnestly obedient to Merope's orders. I could easily have lost her, but I let her think I didn't see.

The harbor was almost empty. All the big ships were gone. An old man sitting on the dock said that Minos had taken them to sea, that they had been gone for days. "The young prince, Androgeos, went with him for the first time. They said they were going to the Attic games." The old man shook his head. "Those games won't take place for months. No. They're out after something else." He nodded knowingly. "The royal ones always lie. They never let us know what's going on."

I realized that he had not recognized me. I wondered whether I should tell him how little some of the "royal ones" knew. It was very strange that I had not known they were gone. It was even stranger that they had gone so soon before the spring festival and that nothing had been done to prepare for the ceremonies. There was no sign in the streets that the Anthesteria approached.

As I returned to the palace, I saw one of Merope's night visitors. I startled him as I came round a corner. He started to bow, thought better of it, and looked wildly around until he spotted my poor dodging Lyca, hopelessly exposed in the sunlight. A signal passed between them. From that moment on, I had two followers.

Lyca was distressed at my outing and fluttered about in my room that night trying to show me how awful it was that I had done it. At the same time, she was frightened of me and ready at any moment to fall down flat in worship. When I asked her where Minos and Androgeos had gone, she seemed terrified. How I wished that Merope would come back.

Finally the day of the festival came. It was a paltry ceremony, thrown together at the last moment by the palace women. My mother hardly took any notice. The old Sibyl from Dhikti did not come. The worshippers were mainly children; only a few men straggled along the route. My mother barely made it to her place in the procession of women. She was laughing and still adjusting her hair. She had on her richest robe, though, and so much jewelry one could hardly see her skin. My brother Tauros came laughing with her down to the Path of the Great Goddess and would have slipped into my place if the priestesses had not stopped him. When they did, he smiled and raised his hands to me in the ceremonial fashion and went down to his position at the side. The priestesses exchanged glances and I saw Lyca put her hands over her face. But my mother only laughed.

The bull dance was a half-hearted affair. No one paid much attention. The animals were the runts of the lot, and the dancers seemed tired. The wind was hot and carried dust into my eyes. A slave brought my mother drinks that she would not share with me, saying I was too young. But she gave some to Tauros, which was against the tradition. And both of them laughed. The priestesses stood stiffly, frowning. Phaedra cried and was taken away. Some of the people left when the word spread that we would not go down to the Sacred Mound. They did not even wait until the dancing was over.

Merope would have wept. The Goddess was not there.

More and more I felt abandoned. Without Merope's presence, the Goddess would not come to me when I danced. The frescoes looked flat. The palace, though there must have been many people walking through it, seemed empty. My mother moved through the rooms without seeing me. She had never really tried to know me. Her mind was like soft wool draping about the things it touched. She did not send it out to search above and below. Now, in Minos' absence, she seemed to be aware of no one but my brother Tauros. When she was with him, her eyes glossed over me as though I were not visible.

At night I lay awake staring into the dark. When I tried to sleep, dreams flew into my mind like attacking birds and wakened me. I sent for a lamp then and began to write them down. There was one I have never forgotten. A little priestess was cloistered with a murderer. He had gone down a long winding passageway until he came to her door and she opened and received him. Seven old women sat in the Great East Hall, stitching a gray garment. "Another row," they said, "another row." For some reason, the dream made me cry. Lyca came and stared at me with her fatuous eyes, but I felt more alone than before.

Of all those left in the palace, it seemed that only Daedalus could really see me. I tried to avoid him, but he was everywhere, changing things, watching. I had not spoken to him since the day Merope broke his dolls, but I felt him looking at me. Even though I wanted to know where Icarus was, I was afraid to talk to him. One day, it became unavoidable.

Daedalus had made a miraculous carriage for my mother and she had called everyone to see it. It was of bronze in the shape of a cow with golden horns, encrusted with amethysts. The eyes were crystal, cut in such a way that all colors flashed from them in the light. It was an enormous beast with an opening on the side through which one entered. The inside was filled with bright-colored cushions upon which passengers could recline. There was room for two.

Daedalus was having it brought to the north entrance as I came up, and my mother met him there, Tauros at her side. She was very excited, laughing and exclaiming about the figure of a beast, half-man and half-bull, embossed on a bronze blanket over the back of the cow and forming the upper part of the door. She ran her fingers over the creature as if fondling it, and Tauros put his hand over hers and did the same. They laughed as if at a secret. Then both of them climbed into the carriage and the slaves drove them away.

At that moment I felt Daedalus' eyes. Even before Merope's warnings, his eyes had frightened me. Nothing was hidden from them. I started to go, but he touched my shoulder. No one else was still around except Lyca, cringing in the distance.

"Why did you break your dolls, Ariadne?" he said.

It was as if he had sliced my voice. I wanted to say how evil it was to mock the Goddess, but nothing would come from my mouth except a childish cry, "Merope says—" Then I remembered how Merope had said we must be secretive, and I broke into tears. I hated myself for doing that in front of Daedalus. I hated being weak so that people could handle me. There was no one to help me. I could see Lyca with her hands against her face, but she would not come near. Then Daedalus said, "Does a princess listen to a stupid slave?"

I jerked away from him and ran down the corridor to my room. Merope had said that Daedalus' mind killed things, that it was a blade carving new gods. He would not be afraid to say that, I thought. Perhaps he is himself a god. I was terrified.

That night another dream came. I was going down a long tunnel into blackness. It kept getting smaller and smaller. Every few feet there would be a mouth, with great jagged teeth above and below, and I would have to go right into it. Although I could not turn around, I knew there was someone at my back pushing me forward. The tunnel got smaller and blacker. Presently something rose out of the air and floated toward me, a hood over her head, her face gray and with no eyes—only hollow spaces. There were snakes coming from her mouth. Then it was Daedalus coming, but he had no head. In its place was a knife. I could not move.

I woke screaming and Lyca fell on the floor and covered her face. She would not touch me though I ran to her. She only kept bowing and praying. Finlly someone brought another lamp and some warm water in a basin. My mother's woman, Chione, came and bathed my face and sat by me. But I could not go back to sleep. She held my hands, but she would not get my mother.

The next day I went down to the pillar shrine alone. I looked for my mother, but she had gone off with Tauros in the bronze chariot, which she loved. As I walked down the corridor, I could feel Chione's eyes, but she turned away when she saw me looking. Lyca would not come near me without bowing.

From then on I had twelve lamps burning in my room all night. Dreams came whenever I closed my eyes.

Finally Merope came back. At once she took me down to the pillar shrine. "The Great Mother will protect you," she said. "We are all dolls in the Mother's hand, but you are Her voice." Merope slept with me and gave me warm mead when the dreams came. She said I did not have to write them for a while.

# 3

FOURTEEN TIMES THE MOON had swelled and died since Minos left. My mother grew large with child. Merope said it could not be Minos'. "Perhaps its father is the north wind like mine," I said. Merope shook her head. "Pasiphae has not been down to the Goddess for many years. The ceremonies in the palace are nothing. They are for show, for those who do not believe, for the barbarians."

The people were uneasy. "They would not care about the child if Minos were dead," said Merope. No word had come from him since he had sailed away with Androgeos. Perhaps they are both dead, I thought. I did not care. I had loved Androgeos once, but now the dead dove hung over his face.

I did not love my brother Tauros either, though at that time he was raising his hands to the Goddess in the Great Hall every morning. The Goddess never entered his soul. I could see his face from where I stood beside my mother. Once his glance strayed when he was supposed to be lost in the ecstasy and he looked directly into my eyes. He started as though he had been found out. Perhaps he had forgotten that I would be there with clear eyes, still too young to drink the consecrated wine from the *rhyton*. My mother saw nothing. Her eyes seemed to be drawn inward to the Goddess' heart, but perhaps she was only drugged. Merope said the rite was deformed, that the true knowledge of the Mother came not from the *rhyton* but from within.

Tauros was always whispering with my mother and fondling her hair. Merope said he wanted to be her consort, that he longed to walk in the crown of lilies. We often saw him in his striped red and blue loincloth with the golden girdle of which he was so proud, walking with my mother in the garden or riding in the bronze chariot.

"It would not be unlawful for him to be Pasiphae's consort," said Merope, "if Minos were dead. The people would accept him." I could tell that she was tempted to accept him too, though I had told her how his eyes went at the altar. I had even told her about his breaking the eggs of the dove, but I could see that she did not believe me.

I felt as though we were all waiting. Sometimes the palace was so still it was as if no one were breathing. The visitors did not come to my room anymore, though I saw them in the corridors. They talked to Merope, and sometimes to Tauros. Merope went somewhere almost every night. Once I tried to look for her. Lyca was sleeping in my outer chamber, but I crept by without waking her. The corridor was dark. Only one lamp burned at the turn. The shadows of the owls carved above the portal streaked out on the ceiling, huge and pointed like teeth. I ran back to my bed. No one saw me.

My dreams were coming again. One night I was in the tunnel with mouths and the hooded figure flew at me and covered my face so that I could not breathe. I don't think I screamed, but I must have made some noise, because when I woke Lyca was there staring at me and then she bowed. I could not seem to catch my breath. Finally she dashed out and came back with Merope who stayed with me the rest of the night. I could not sleep and she wanted to know every detail of the dream. But when I asked her where she had been, she would not say.

There came a night when I learned the answer. I woke and found Merope gone and Lyca sleeping heavily as before. I took a lamp and crept by without waking her. The shadows of the owls on the portals in the hall fluttered as if they were alive and moved with me as I walked. There was no sound. At the turn I almost fell over an old servant. He mumbled in his sleep and turned over. I hid behind a pillar and waited until he snored. Watching him settle down fussily like a partridge took all the fear out of me. I set down the lamp behind the pillar and crept through the darkness toward my mother's room. No one stirred, but I could hear voices somewhere.

Presently a guard came down the corridor. I flattened myself against the wall behind a *pithos*. He could have seen me if he had looked, but he was rubbing his eyes and rolling from side to side as he walked. Just as he turned into another corridor, he passed a foul gas and grunted.

At the stairs I hid again because there were footsteps above and a voice that sounded like Tauros'. Two hooded figures rushed silently past me and out into the court. Again I waited in silence. As I started up the stairs, I heard a low sound, almost a moan. It was repeated once, twice, and then in steady intervals as if in a chant. I crawled up the stairs in darkness. There was light coming from somewhere beyond, probably from my mother's inner chamber. The chanting continued and was joined at times by other voices, a woman's and a man's. It grew louder as I came close, but I could not make out the words.

Then I saw them. In attitudes of prayer, with their hands upon their foreheads, were Merope and Tauros. Up on the dais, my mother leaned against the bed, her face lifted, her eyes looking up as though through the ceiling. She was chanting, "Gaea! Gaea! Mother of all!" over and over. The other two joined at intervals in a half-whisper. Their eyes were closed, but my mother's were turned upward so that I could see only the whites.

I dared not move. I knew it was a mystery I was not supposed to share. There was a tension that I had never felt when my mother performed ceremonies in the Great Hall. She was dressed in a purple robe that covered her whole body. Her arms were raised as if she were about to dance the ritual. Instead, they began to tremble and her body swayed back and forth. Her voice became hoarse. The words came in gasps. Merope and Tauros lay down on the floor and pressed their foreheads on the tile. My mother's hands came together at her breast, fumbled with the ties of her robe, and opened it, spreading it out to the sides like wings. Her breasts were swollen and beneath them appeared the great round orb of her belly, the navel stretched out flat and mottled with blue. "Gaea, Gaea," she kept saying.

I was afraid the Goddess would strike me. I didn't know which ritual movement would placate Her. It seemed as though the cries of the others, soft as they were, would pull the world inward into the room and crush us. I went down upon the floor and began to moan. Those in the room did not appear to hear me, but I could feel the Goddess speaking in the vibrations of the floor.

Suddenly my mother started to shriek. Tauros and Merope lay still as stone, but my mother's head rolled from side to side. I knew it was wrong for me to be there. I scrambled to my feet and in my haste knocked over a lamp. Before I could get away, Tauros turned. I ran down the stairs and through the corridors, making no sound though my breath was coming in gasps after great intervals in which I seemed not to breathe at all. Shadows came at me and I went right through them. I did not go directly to my room but wove around past Phaedra's to confuse any who might be pursuing. I think another guard glimpsed me as I passed the main corridor, but he only grunted in a questioning voice and did not follow.

Lyca was still asleep, but my movements must have disturbed her. Just after I got into bed, she stirred and sat up. I lay as still as I could. She came over and looked at me. I do not think she could see my eyelids flicker in the dim light, but if she had put her hand on the bed she might have felt the crashing of my heart. Perhaps she heard it. She seemed to listen intently for a long time. Then there was a sound outside my door and Merope appeared. They whispered together and Merope came over to look at me, but she did not touch me either. Finally they went away.

My mother called me for a ceremony in the Great East Hall at sunrise. Tauros' movements were perfect. Not once did his eyes stray. But afterward I found them studying me whenever I turned.

What distressed me most was that Merope was drawing away. I think she was afraid of what she had told me, now that my mother seemed to be returning to the Goddess. More and more she left me alone. More and more my dreams absorbed me and I wrote them out on my tablets in detail:

"It is a sea of blood. I have come down to the shore to watch the approach of a boat, a great carved vessel adorned with many heads and hands. Around the mast is coiled a giant serpent. In the prow of the boat (which moves without wind by some unseen force) stands a huge woman with flat sagging breasts and a flap of skin at her belly that hangs down to her knees. Her eyes are round without lashes. Her hair coils and moves as if separately alive. Her mouth is open, her long tongue protruding. In her hands is a bowl and she is about to drink. It is blood. I know that it is mine. I look down and see that my hands have been cut off and blood is running from them into the sea."

Every morning now there was a ceremony. My mother's voice and hands trembled, and she often forgot the words. Merope helped her, and the people did not seem to know the difference. I knew all the words, Merope had seen to that, but I would not say any speech except my own during the ceremony. Afterward, when we were being disrobed, I went through all the parts where my mother had stumbled, as if practicing. When I did this, she covered her ears.

Merope did not often come to my room now. She was always with my mother. Chione had disappeared. My tablets were still being taken away. Sometimes I read them to Lyca first because it was amusing to see her eyes swell and her mouth fall. Then she would lie face down spreading her arms toward me for blessing. I blessed her.

Another dream: "I am raising the *rhyton* to sprinkle blessings upon all the people who are lying prostrate before me. Someone comes and takes my arm. It is a man without a face. He lifts the arm with which I am holding the vessel and forces my wrist to turn so that the holy water spills over his head. A face appears then, but I cannot see whose it is."

My mother appeared now only at the ceremony. She walked carefully as if she were balancing. She did not speak to me except in the ritual, but she looked at me as though she would tell me something if we were alone. We were never alone. Always Merope and Tauros were there, fussing about her, holding her arms as she mounted the dais, helping her kneel. Everything about her had grown large and round like the waxing moon. Her eyelids were puffed so that she could scarcely see. Her cheeks swelled out and her lips protruded. Even her nose had grown round. She looked at herself in her mirror sometimes for a long time. She is sad to have lost her beauty, I thought, or perhaps she is afraid of what Minos will do when he sees her. I could tell that she was trying to return to the Goddess, but there was something in the way. Merope did not seem to know how much she was struggling. It occurred to me that perhaps the old woman was stupid, as Daedalus had said.

I did not like to think of Daedalus. I saw him now and then from a distance, and he always looked at me curiously as if to observe a change. Icarus was still absent. I had asked about him, but no one knew where he had gone, not even Merope. Could Daedalus have killed him, I wondered. They said he had killed his nephew in Athens and had had to flee from the tribunal. But Merope said it was our minds that he killed.

One morning after the ceremony, my mother took me with her to her room and sent the others away. They did not go willingly. Merope conceded, but only after much fussing about cushions and baths. At first, Tauros ignored her request. He even laughed. When my mother's voice rang out sharp, he bowed in a mocking way and left but returned immediately. My mother spat at him. His face settled down like a mask, and he turned without speaking and left, but not before he had looked at me again with such hatred that I shivered.

At last my mother took my hands and talked to me as she never had before. She had been reading my tablets—only the latest ones, I could tell. The Goddess was speaking to me, she said, and through me, to her. I must help her now because there was darkness ahead. I must tell her all my dreams, every day, and we would learn what the Goddess is saying. Doesn't my mother have any dreams, I wondered. I didn't dare to ask.

I told her my dream of the hooded figure in the tunnel with mouths, because I had that dream almost every night, but she was not interested in it. She wanted me to tell about the faceless man who made my hand turn to sprinkle the holy water over his head. What did he look like, she wanted to know. I described him as well as I could—cinched golden belt, a luxurious robe, as if he were a consort, but the dream always ended before his face became clear. She questioned and questioned me about him as if the Goddess' message lay in his identity, but I could go no further.

From then on, she demanded my dreams every morning. Sometimes I could not remember one, so I made something up. At first I was afraid to do it, but my mother did not seem to know the difference. Perhaps it doesn't matter, I thought. Maybe the Goddess can speak through me, awake or asleep. No matter what I wrote on my tablets, Pasiphae wanted me to leave them with her so that she could study them. But when there was a man in my dreams, she was most interested. She wanted to know who it was and could think of nothing else until I had described him in detail. Usually I did not know who it was. That made her angry. Sometimes she shook me. Sometimes she cried. Often she said strange words as if in a different language.

One day Chione, my mother's woman, came back, looking as if she had been ill. She and Merope were close now. They stood outside my mother's door and listened as we talked about the dreams. I knew they were there. Sometimes I could hear them, but my mother did not seem to notice. She had given orders that Tauros could not come to her room. He was angry and argued with the women. Once he brushed by them and came in. My mother started screaming. Merope came in and held her, and Chione brought guards who took him away. After that, guards stood at her door day and night. She wanted me to stay in her room all the time, but Merope told her that then my dreams would not come, so she let me go.

Another dream: "It is as if I have just come back from a journey on the sea. I have been wounded in many places. But the harbor here has been prepared. As my boat docks, the land comes out to surround it. They are now joined as if one. I go into a house with bare walls. Frescoes appear on the walls as I approach. The frescoes change constantly. There is always a detail that is different. They are like promises. As each appears, brought in by scarcely visible hands, there are other hands (scarcely visible) taking some part of it away. I feel safe and cared for. But someone whispers that there are other journeys, other wounds ahead, that I must prepare for them, that this is my warning. I dash into my room and close and bolt the door with relief, only to discover in a flash behind me, standing, a lion man, immobile. He tells me—but I cannot remember what he tells me."

My mother was wild when I told her about the lion man. "Is it Tauros?" she wanted to know. I could not be sure. She was ready to beat me, but she was so clumsy that she could not get up by herself and I got over to the door just as Merope came in. I wished that I did not have to tell my mother those dreams. I decided to make up something pleasant:

"I am standing in the apiary among the hives. The sun is warm and the earth fragrant. Bees are all around me. Their wings reflect the sun. I hear a voice from somewhere, though I see no one. It whispers, 'Your body is pollen. The journey is forever. Be still.' And then I am not sure whether it has been a voice or just the sound of the bees."

My mother loved the bee dream, as I had known she would. Merope had told me long ago that the bees were the pets of the Goddess, shining forth Her Being and Her creation—showing everyone that as the bees serve their queen, so do women and men serve theirs.

I had to tell the dream to my mother over and over. "Yes," she said. "There it is. See?" I pretended to understand because it made her feel so much better.

It seemed odd to me that this dream, which I did not really have, was the one that soothed her. To be sure, I had had a dream about bees, and their hum had seemed like a voice. But the rest of it I made up as I was writing. Can the Goddess appear in that fashion, I wondered. I did not dare to tell anyone about it.

There was a guard at my door now, too. I was not sure whether his loyalty was to my mother or to Tauros. Or whether there was really a difference.

Again I had the dream about the lion man, and I woke up screaming. Merope came at once and made me write it down in the middle of the night and brought it to my mother. The next morning she was wild again, even during the ceremony. She forgot the ritual and Merope hissed at me to fill in, so I had to. Later my mother questioned me over and over about the man. It seemed to me that he was the same one who had forced me to pour the libation on his head, but I could not see clearly who he was. It might have been Tauros, as my mother seemed to think, but it might have been someone else. She wanted to know what happened to him after the libation was poured, but I did not know. The dream ended. When my mother became wild as she did then, I was terrified.

Then the black news came, and there was nothing but wildness. Androgeos was dead. Early one morning, before the sun rose, a messenger came running all the way from the dock. "Minos is returning with his son's body," he gasped. "The ships are on the way."

My mother screamed. It seemed to me it was the scream I had been waiting for since the killing of the dove. So the Goddess had pulled him down, after all. Merope had been right. I felt numb; it was the first time someone I knew had died. My mother continued to scream and throw herself about as if she had no control. "The Raging Ones possess her," Merope whispered. She could not come to the ceremony in the Great Hall, and so, for the first time, I performed it alone. Tauros was so nervous he stumbled against the dais.

Afterward, he called all the palace guards to the courtyard. I watched from a balcony.

"The Athenians have murdered a prince of Knossos," he said. A shocked murmur ran through the crowd. Some of them had not heard.

"The queen's son, Androgeos, is dead."

It was a moan now. Tauros paused, looking at the guards. He had never spoken to a crowd before that I could remember. I could see how he studied their faces. They seemed to be his, if he wanted them. Moved by the catastrophe—the killing of a fellow Cretan, of the queen's own son—they were ready for retribution.

"The aging consort, Minos . . . " there was a stir of protest in the line of guards, " . . . has fallen into a trap!" Silence. But Tauros went on as if they had cheered. "The judgment of an old man cannot be trusted!" he shouted. "The welfare of the country is threatened when its protectors have become enfeebled!" The guards looked at one another. "Why else have the rains not appeared as they did of old? Why else have the grapevines wilted? Why else have the barley grains shrunk back into the stalk?"

Tauros had touched a nerve. All of them were disturbed by the drought. None of them could say why it had happened nor where it would lead all of us. I could see that Tauros was exhilarated by their response this time. He drew himself up to his greatest height and raised his hands. They listened intently.

"The Goddess demands . . . " He was almost whispering. You could see the men straining to hear. "The Goddess demands a new leader at the end of each Great Year!" he shouted. They were hushed. "Yet the Great Year has ended." He was whispering again. "One hundred times the moon has swelled and died, swelled and died, and the old consort remains!" Now they were disturbed. There was a great deal of murmuring along the rows. One or two of those in the back left the courtyard, but Tauros did not appear to notice. He was swept into himself now. His eyes were not even looking at the men. "The Great Goddess demands a new leader!" he shouted. A few of the guards nodded, but most of them only looked silently at each other.

Then I saw someone else standing in a doorway, listening. Daedalus.

My mother had been screaming since the word came of Androgeos' death. The birth had started. Servants had been sent to the mountain to gather dittany to ease her pain. I was summoned to her room to chant a prayer for delivery. I don't think she even knew I was there. She lay on her bed and her head went from side to side. The screams were hoarse. She could not talk. I prayed alone. She seemed to be shrinking now, except for her enormous belly. Her face was dark and flat, her lips stretched against her teeth. Merope said it would not be a good birth. "Something is wrong; it should not be like this." I decided I would never have a child.

People were weeping for Androgeos' death, but it just made me feel cold. I kept thinking, "Is he like the dove?"

> Gaea, Mother of Destiny,
>> Come to the house of the woman in travail,
>> Have pity upon the one in travail.
> Gaea, Mother of Destiny,
>> As thou brought forth women and men,
>> May the mother of the child bring forth
>> by herself.

It was a new prayer Merope had taught me. I had to go to my mother's room whenever the servant came for me and chant it for her. I hated to go, but at least it gave me a chance to see what was happening in the palace. Otherwise I was confined to my room, with Lyca and my guards. There were two of them now. Once they brought Phaedra but took her away immediately. Merope and Chione were with my mother all the time, and many guards stood outside her door. The corridors were hushed. Almost no one moved about. Some of the palace people were praying in the Great Hall. In every shrine, offerings were being made to the Goddess. The palace guards, except for the ones at my mother's door and mine, were peculiarly absent.

I saw Tauros again as I passed the courtyard. He had put on his finest clothing and was carrying his ceremonial sword with the crystal pommel. He was surrounded by guards and was talking to them urgently. I also spotted several of Merope's visitors here and there about the palace. They were hooded and silent.

The last time I went to my mother's room that day, her screaming had stopped. She was lying still and flat. Only the monstrous bulb of her belly rose above the level of the bed. Her breathing was rough as if the air were pulled through brambles. Her eyes were half-open, but she seemed to see nothing. I chanted all the prayers. Before I had finished, she appeared to wake. She screamed once and jerked her legs, and blood came from her onto the coverings. Then she lay still again.

Merope went with me to the pillar shrine and we said the prayer for the dying. The Goddess was not there.

# 4

MINOS CAME BACK. And after him a long procession of men carrying a black stench that they said was Androgeos. They set it down in the Great East Hall and Minos ordered that everyone in the palace be summoned. Even Phaedra was brought, though she hid behind her nurse. Merope whispered to Minos about my mother, but he seemed not to be surprised. I think he knew everything. As I carried the *rhyton* to bless Androgeos, Minos took my arm and helped me lift it. (As in my dream!) His hands were huge and there were black hairs curling on his fingers and arms. He smelled of sweat and horses. The muscles in his arm moved as he helped me. He said nothing. Only that touch on my arm.

When I was through with the blessing of the dead, he turned to all the people and his voice was low and strong as the rumbling of the earth. He told how the Athenians had betrayed his trust, how fifty of them had ambushed Androgeos in revenge for his having beaten them in the games, how they had murdered him and thrown his body upon a heap of refuse, how he, Minos, had been told of this while sacrificing to the Ancient Ones, how he had continued the sacrifice, but without flutes or flowers, and how when it was over he and his men had descended upon the Greeks with the fury of the Great Mother in their arms, had ravaged Athens and brought it to heel.

Here a voice ripped out from the crowd, a high and challenging voice, shouting clearly, "He lies! He has betrayed the Great Mother and brought death into the House of the Double Axe!" It was Tauros, standing on the dais, his head covered by the ritual feathered helmet used in the sacrificial dance. He was brandishing his sword above his head. Suddenly all over the hall, hoods fell back and helmets appeared. Blades went up. With hoarse yells, Tauros' followers started slashing at Minos and his men.

Guards closed in around me, but for a while I could see between their bodies. I had never before seen the clean slice of a sword on human flesh. It is like the slaughter of a partridge. The eyes turn to stone and the mouth falls. The blood does not come instantly. Nor do the hands know at once. Like the wings of a partridge, they reach and reach before they learn. Minos' face was above me, a terrible mask, mouth drawn tight. One hand raised a dagger. The other gave some kind of signal. At once, more of his men appeared at every portal, from behind every pillar.

I could see very little now. The guards pressed close around me as I hid behind my brother's corpse. There were screams and cries and a surging back and forth. The body of Androgeos rocked on the litter. Suddenly there was a kind of howl, and everything became silent. I felt Merope's hands tight on my shoulders. The guards stood like a wall around us. Above them we saw Minos climbing to a balcony, carrying a limp form in his arms—it was Tauros. His eyes moved from side to side; his face streamed blood. Both arms dangled as if broken. Minos stood on the balcony and raised the body of Tauros into the air over the balustrade and let it fall. I could not see it strike the tile, but I heard the scream and the thud. The crowd was still silent. They pulled back from Minos as he came down to the altar where I stood. The guards retreated. Even Merope fell back. Then Minos bowed like a suppliant before me, saying softly, "Bless me." When I looked at Merope, she averted her eyes. Perhaps it is only a dream, I thought. I'll wake soon. Let me just get through this. And so I took the *rhyton* and filled it again and sprinkled the sacred water upon Minos as I said the blessing.

Minos stood up, and again as if at a signal the crowd opened up and in came more of Minos' warriors, swords drawn, leading a procession of captives chained neck to neck, seven maidens and seven boys, Athenians. They were lined up in a row behind Androgeos' body. I could see Tauros now, lying on the opposite side of the hall, motionless and silent. A few of his followers huddled in chains among the warriors. Many bodies were being dragged away. I could feel the Great Mother reaching for their feet.

Minos spoke again but I could not hear him. The dove's eye grew inside me and swallowed everything.

I made myself think only of the Athenians. They were very young, little older than I myself. Some of them had light hair, but they did not look very different from us. One of them looked so much like Icarus that for a moment I stopped breathing, but it was not he. When Minos was through talking, he made them all bow to me, and again I had to perform a blessing, but this time it was the blessing given to victims intended for sacrifice. I had never thought about the meaning of the words before. Now they fell from my lips like daggers. I knew then what Merope had meant. This was how it felt to be Minos' tool.

After the blessing, Minos took my arm and led me to my mother's room. The guards stayed at the door. Chione retreated to the outer chamber, but Merope stayed. My mother still lay on the bed, flat as a shadow except for the bulge of her belly. Her breathing was loud and uneven. Sometimes it seemed as if she were strangling.

Minos stood looking at her, holding my arm so tight that it ached. He made me say another blessing over her, and then he went away.

Merope was whispering hurriedly to the other women. I noticed that the guard had been changed. She nodded briefly to them and went with me to my quarters. My old guards were still there. Also Lyca, carrying a cloak which she put around me at once. Then all three of us, with the guards, went silently down the dim stairs to the lowest level and into a black corridor I had not known existed. It was paved for only a short distance; then it became slippery underfoot as in an underground cave. I could hear water trickling somewhere. It was cold and I was very tired, but they would not stop. Finally a guard picked me up and carried me. It felt so good that I may have dozed for a moment, in spite of my excitement. I was full of questions, but they would not let me talk. No one talked. There was only the slight sound of feet slipping on the rock.

Finally we emerged. It was very dark outside: no stars, no buildings. Only brush, rocks, and an occasional tree. We seemed to be climbing. At one point, in a dark cove, someone met us with litters, and Merope and I were carried; Lyca trailed along beside. No one made a sound. In the darkness, I could barely make out their forms. My litter bearers walked swiftly yet carried me so smoothly I could sometimes hardly believe we were moving. When once I started to whisper, one of them put his hand on my lips so tenderly I wanted to cry.

The reek of Androgeos' body stayed in my throat. And Tauros' eyes, upside down as Minos held him, were with me constantly. And the thud of his body against the tile. And my mother's breathing. I looked into the black, still sky and wondered how the Great Mother could hold all this horror within her.

Then, although I was afraid to close my eyes, I must indeed have slept. When I woke we were in a tunnel and the litter bearers were being changed. There was a small lamp and I could see their faces. They exchanged a few whispers, though I could not hear what they said. They did not pause long. The new bearers set off at a fast pace. Merope's litter was just behind, but I could not see Lyca anywhere. We seemed still to be climbing, as if we were crawling up inside the body of the mountain.

Everywhere I felt the presence of the Great Mother. The beat of my heart in my ears seemed to echo a beat in the rock. I felt as though the Goddess were pulling me to a place within Herself that was also within me, and where I would look straight into Her eyes. I knew it had to be so, had known from childhood. But though I had thought about it from time to time, it had always seemed a long way off, on the other side of a screen. Now the taste of death was in my mouth. My eyes held its color and my nostrils its stench. And the screen was gone.

I lay on the litter as on a boat moving upstream to the source of the river. There was still no sound at all except sandals upon rock and the voices of the mountain itself. I understood then that the silence was not for stealth as it had been before, but for awe of the Goddess. This was the journey Merope had promised.

When we came out again into the open, light was just beginning to touch the sky. The litter bearers did not pause. The path they took up the cliffside was so steep that I felt sometimes as if I would slide off. I suppose my clenched fingers told them my feeling, because they would immediately raise the litter so that I was lying straight again. Once I glanced to the side and the sheer drop down into darkness shook my stomach. I gasped. The litter bearer at my foot bent forward toward me and smiled. He still wore a hood, but I could just see his face. He was one of Merope's night visitors, the one who had followed me the day I escaped from Lyca's guard in the palace when Merope had gone home to her village. His was a kind face, not young. When he smiled, the wrinkles at his eyes and mouth seemed also to smile. I felt safer than I had for months—for longer than that. It was like those days when I played with Icarus, and when Merope would hold me as she told me stories, and when my mother, when she came near, would smile.

Finally we reached a level spot around which the cliffs seemed to lean together and touch. We went inward from the ledge and came to a stream trickling from the face of the mountain into a pool. Ringed around the pool were many hooded figures, standing silent in the attitude of prayer. Merope's litter was let down first and someone brought her a basin of water. The litter bearers averted their faces as she washed her hands and feet. Then she came over to me. At once my bearers placed me on the ground and knelt. All of them, all the men who had carried us, knelt as I stood and averted their faces. Merope said something to them, and they rose silently and went away. Those who remained were all women. They pushed back their hoods and knelt as Merope led me to the pool and removed my clothing. She held my hands and looked up as we prayed. The sky was getting lighter. From our high position we could see far off the foothills of the mountain toward the east, but the sun had not yet appeared. At Merope's word (there was no other sound) I let myself into the cold water. I sank down and down. There seemed to be no bottom. Just as I thought fear would come into me, my hands reached out against the water like separate beings and pushed me upward. It was as if the Goddess had moved them. When I reached the surface, Merope caught and held me. Voices roared in my ears and I gasped at the cold air. At that moment, through the water on my eyelashes, I saw the sun come out full over the hills.

Merope helped me out of the water and dried me. They gave her a rich white robe and golden sandals that she helped me put on. She led me over the rock to an opening under the waterfall and motioned for me to enter the cave. When I could see in the dimness, I made out the figure of a woman in the distance, sitting behind a tiny lamp. It was the Sibyl! As in Merope's tales. I took off my sandals and went over to her and knelt. She was so old she was like the rock itself. She spoke to me for a long time. As I listened, death and life became one flow through the veins of the earth. The stench of Androgeos was absorbed into the sweet clay, and my mother's agony became a part of the constantly returning agony of the deep rock. It seemed to me that I too was part of the rock, part of the body of the earth, and that nothing would ever be separate again, that everything would go on and on forever.

The old seeress blessed me and extinguished the lamp. I knelt in darkness for a time, then stumbled toward the opening. All the women, Merope at their head, turned to me and chanted a prayer. They addressed me as queen, and I understood that my mother was really dying. Each word pounded a heaviness into my heart. For the first time, as I blessed them, I felt the weight of their dependence upon me. But I did not know that I would never again be free of it.

Then I rested in an underground chamber near the sanctuary. It was richly furnished, though nothing like the palace, of course. The women came and went but asked nothing more of me. Merope said that it was time now for me to rest and heal. If I slept well, it would be a sign that the Goddess was pleased with me. It was the first time I had not been afraid for a very long time. I felt as though the earth held me in her arms.

# 5

MY SLEEP THAT NIGHT WAS DEEP. No dreams. Perhaps the *rhyton* had contained a drug. Perhaps it was merely the great sense of peace at being among only those who communed with the Great Mother without doubt.

But I woke to nightmare. It did not seem so at first. At first it seemed heavenly—the fresh scent of alyssum, the sun slanting across the open doorway, a bird singing somewhere close. My limbs felt heavy and full. There was a vague ache in my back and a flicker of pain across my loins, but all gentle, almost pleasant, nothing fearful. A continuance of the feeling that the old Sibyl's words had given me, the touch of rock within, heavy, not without pain, but steady, enduring. The cushioned rock bench on which I lay seemed the best bed in all the world, and I felt as though I had melted into it. Presently I became aware of a stickiness between my thighs. I remember wondering whether I were really melting. What a child I was not to have guessed at once what was happening. When finally I did examine myself, I felt transformed. This was the real confirmation of the Goddess' presence, her blood within me, flowing through me, joining us forever. I was exhilarated. "Merope!" I called. "Quickly!" I could not wait to tell her, to see her joy. But there was no answer; only the bird. I called again and again until the bird stopped. The silence surrounding my call seemed as enormous as the sky. It smothered my voice. I moved toward the door as if pulled. The peace of the cave was suddenly all gone.

The morning light shone full in my eyes. I saw green and blue rays, felt warmth, felt golden clarity as if I had stepped into another realm, so bright that whatever had been solid was washed away into a single radiance. When my eyes adjusted to this light, the shadow of a tree appeared and solidified, black bark and drooping green limbs, and hanging from one limb, drooping and black, was Merope's body. She dangled like a puppet with limbs of clay. A rope was around her neck; her face was black and silently shrieking.

I made no sound. Silence hung around me like a shroud. Then I started running, back into the cave and out again, and back, and out, past Merope's body away anywhere, the rocks tearing my feet. But whichever path I took led to another body dangling, another black agonized face. All of them, all the women were hanging like Daedalus' dolls.

I fled back to Merope and tried to take her down from the tree, but I had nothing with which to cut the rope. I climbed the tree and tried to untie it, but the rope was too strong. From the ground I could reach only her legs. They were cold, and when I let them go, they swung back and bumped my head awkwardly. I wept for Merope's helplessness. I lay upon the ground beneath her for a long time before I began her dance. It was the holiest ceremony I knew. I turned and turned beneath the sycamore. I felt my hair streaming across my eyes as I whirled. I felt tears drying on my face. And I felt the sun overwhelming everything. But I also felt the blood between my thighs, testifying to the Goddess' presence.

Suddenly I heard the sound of bronze. I ran back to the cave and lay upon the stone bench, trembling. Almost at once, the sunlight at the door was blotted out. It was Minos himself. Perhaps his men would not have invaded the sanctuary without him. He pulled me into the sunlight and knelt at my feet. Three men who stood near the pool knelt also. Merope and the other women still hung from the trees. I looked at them now in a different way, as if the presence of Minos and his men had altered my vision. The place showed little sign of struggle. They must have been taken by surprise. Merope's men had evidently counted on the sanctity of the place to protect us. For those unafraid of the Mother, it had been an easy victory, so quietly effected that in my heavy sleep I had heard nothing.

I felt hollow. There are reeds like that, dry, without center. The wind blows through them and they moan.

Minos rose and waved to the men to go. Then he talked to me, his rough voice muted as if in reverence. Merope and her women had betrayed me, he said, and had hanged themselves in contrition. Perhaps they had been well intentioned, had sought to save me from the violence and intrigue that had swept the palace while he was gone, had wanted to protect me from the agony of my mother and the shame of that other one whose name he would never mention again, but they had been misguided in their zeal. They had done wrong to deprive a country of its queen. "For the queen, your mother, is dead, and you are now in her place, Ariadne." The words, though almost a whisper, clanged like cymbals. I had known, of course, that Pasiphae was dying, but it seemed a process that would go on and on until some remote time when I would be ready for it.

I sat down on a rock. It was still early morning, the dew not yet dry on the buckthorn in the shadow of the cliff. Where the sun fell upon the rocks at the edge of the pool, two bees descended into a tiny forest of alyssum, then rose and descended again. I had been weeping for Merope for hours. Now I felt barren. The words of the old Sibyl hummed beneath my thoughts. I believed that my mother was dead, but I did not believe the rest of Minos' words. Merope and her women would never have hanged themselves thinking that they had done wrong. Minos had had them killed. I knew it as surely as if the Goddess Herself had spoken. Minos stood beneath me only a few feet away, silent now, looking out across the foothills in the direction of the palace. It was too far away. Only hills could be seen, and sky and sun and the cliffs behind us, the rocks under our feet, the prickly shrubs and little flowers around the pool. The waterfall still trickled. The sparse trees waved their terrifying fruit. Minos was small in all this, but he was large enough to have ordered these deaths and my own as well if he wished. The strength shone in his dark face, in his eyes that looked straight through, in his stance which was that of one who would not be turned aside. I thought of how he had done all this in the darkness and then waited, hidden, until I awakened and found Merope, ran in fear from one side of the sanctuary to the other, finding at each trail the dangling body of a woman; waited until I had returned to Merope and danced for her soul, grieving until I had no more tears—letting all that happen before he had appeared.

I no longer felt like a child, but I knew I was no match for Minos, not yet. Furthermore, I was alone and his men must be hidden everywhere. The moisture between my legs reminded me that the Goddess had touched me indeed. To this day, I don't know whether Merope had made it happen or not. "Go down the trail and wait while I pray," I said.

Minos looked sharply at me for a moment and left. I suppose he thought I might trick him in some way, leap from the cliff, or drown myself in the pool. That would have been the only escape, for all my people were dead. But something in my face must have reassured him.

The moment he was out of sight, I went into my chamber and bathed and hid my stained clothing in a corner. I wrapped myself like a woman and put on a clean white robe that Merope had shown me the night before. No one was in sight when I came out again into the open. I dipped my hands and feet in the pool. Then I went behind the waterfall and entered the cave. There was no light at all. I removed my sandals and waited for my vision to adjust to the darkness, but even after a long while I could still see nothing. Had the old Sibyl also been killed? I began to shake. Even remembering all the words that the old woman had breathed to me the first morning, the words that had made me feel strong as rock, did not help. I started to pray. After a moment, a whisper from the blackness joined me.

When we were through, I told her what had happened. There was a long silence. When I could stand it no longer, I asked her what I should do. Again a silence. Then a long sigh. "Go back to the palace," she said. "Rule well."

Again I felt the will of others clamp about me. Perhaps I had hoped she would find a way for me to escape, even to die. Instead I would have to rule, though with how little power even I did not dream.

"How will you live?" I whispered. "Shall I have offerings sent for you?

"No." Her voice was sharp suddenly like a hiss.

I waited a while uncertainly, but there was no other sound. As I started to go, I heard another whisper, but I could not tell what she said.

I came out into the open, thinking, at least they have not desecrated this holiest of homes. Perhaps they did not know it was there. Then in dismay I realized that I had now shown it to the watchers. They were not in sight. Only Merope and her women regarded me with blind eyes. I ran down to the cliff's edge and clapped my hands loudly. Minos appeared. "Let these women be buried with honor," I said. And Minos called his men to carry them, and me, back to the palace.

There was little honor in the return. The litters bearing Merope and the women were sent on before mine, and we never caught up with them. Minos' orders must have gone ahead also. There were signs everywhere along the trail of hasty tidying, remnants of a struggle, but no bodies except once, as we rounded a sharp curve, when I got a glimpse of the chasm wall strewn with corpses from which carrion crows rose at the sound of voices. It was too quick a glance and too far away to see who had been thrown there, but I understood the honor intended for all my supporters.

Minos had gone on ahead, also. I still believed the Goddess would strike him down. At every bend I expected to find a chasm into which he had fallen. Or rocks crushing his body. The breathing of the Great Mother sounded constantly in my ears. Perhaps the sea would rise; Poseidon, however much adored by Minos, would not tolerate the slaughter of priestesses. Surely even Zeus would not condone this assault upon the Goddess. Perhaps the men carrying me felt this too, for there was no sound among them as we crept down the mountain. The sun rose to the highest point of his journey. We covered our heads. My white robe and golden sandals glistened as though the eye of Zeus held them. But even on the litter I could feel the trembling of the Goddess.

Halfway down the mountain I demanded to be set down. They assented, these strangers who were Minos' minions, but they stood close. I removed my sandals and stood in the hot dust of the trail. I knelt with my hands flat against the rock. The earth was shaking far down. I could tell that the men felt it also. Their faces showed fear. When I prayed, they put their hands to their foreheads. When I waved my hand, they bowed. At that moment I could have willed them all to retreat to the cave or to leap from the cliff. I could feel the blood of the Goddess pounding in me. A rock tumbled down the cliff above, crashed on the path before the litter, and spun off over the side. We waited for the Goddess' anger. But the sounds died away and the air was still. As we stood breathless, a snake emerged from the rock, crept down upon the path, and regarded us with steady eyes. I sat upon the ground and the snake came toward me.

Suddenly a shadow fell over me and the snake scuttled away. It was Minos. He said nothing, but from then until late that night when we reached the palace, he walked at my side.

It seemed that the palace servants had all been changed except for Chione, who turned down her eyes as I came in. They took me to my mother's room. It was empty but blazing with the light of many lamps. On the bed were her robes, choked with jewels and moving as if they were alive. I saw them rise and form into her shape. They approached and hung before me, wreathing air. I listened for the Goddess' voice to issue from them, but it was still. And the robes and the jewels went back to recline on the bed.

When the women bathed me and discovered the blood, they all fell back and bowed, even Chione. Then one of them ran away, perhaps to tell Minos. I stood in the lustrum, listening. Above me the high ceiling writhed with dolphins. As I looked up they descended swimming about my head, almost touching their smooth wet bodies to my hair, their eyes burrowing into me, filmed with water. I listened and listened for the Goddess' voice to wash from them into my mind. But they returned to the ceiling, silent.

Chione dressed me in my mother's things, binding them to me with gold thongs. How had she escaped, I wondered. Had she been Minos' spy all along? We knelt in the horns of consecration on the south balcony. In the dim light, a solitary bee appeared and settled in my hair ornaments. A dove stirred and rose as if at a command but alighted again. Then Chione took me down to the spring. The owl of the shrine opened his eyes wide when she left me alone there, and I waited for the Goddess to show Herself, but She was nowhere. Only at the pillar shrine did I feel Her incessant trembling, but She did not speak. I wondered whether it was because Chione was with me.

They brought me to the Great East Hall just as the sun struck the bronze double axes ranging along the wall, and I saw the *larnax* holding my mother's body. It stood on the dais, glowing with the colors of roses and lilies. Strange priestesses began a chant of mourning as I entered; the lyre was struck; seven young *kouretes*, new to their priestly duties, began a slow dance, beating their bare chests with thistles. There were no familiar faces among the celebrants. Minos met me and bowed, and all the people did likewise. Then the priestesses formed a wall around us so that no one else could see, and as Chione blew a conch shell they turned their backs. Minos reached forward and raised the lid of the larnax and pushed my face down toward the face of my mother. Her eyes were hidden by a thin strip of embossed gold, but beneath that, her teeth gnashed out of a twisted black mouth. Her belly was flat under the gold dress. I wondered what had happened to the child.

I think I was supposed to cry out the mourning prayer, but I could not make my voice come. Minos shook me and bumped the *larnax*. My mother's face fell to the side, leaving the mask with its embossed eyes staring straight up from the side of her head.

Abruptly he closed the lid and began the prayer of lamentation. The priestesses took it up at once so loudly that no one could have told whether or not I was chanting too. Minos' hand clenched my arm like a chain. I moved through the dancers as if a string were pulling a Daedalus doll. I was another Merope dangling on a tree. The ceremony went on around me, and by the time I had to ascend the altar alone, I found that my arms and legs worked of themselves in the familiar movements. At the moment when the High Priestess alone is heard, I was amazed to discover that some string had found the secret of my throat, and I heard my voice go on and on in the chant as if I were listening to a distant singer. But it was not the Goddess' voice.

I became a doll. Chione or her women raised my hands and dressed me, bathed me, fed me, steered me into the Great Hall for ceremonies, pushed their voices under mine when it failed in the chant, carried me like a great puppet to the bull ring, lifted my arms to pour the libations, and stretched them skyward in the old gesture of offering when one of the young Athenians hooked his chest on the bull's horn and rode about the arena like a pheasant on a spear.

Though the same people moved me about every day, I did not know any of them, except Chione and Minos. I recognized their features, but they seemed to me to have no depth, as though they were shadows on papyrus. I was told later that when they left me, I sat motionless and silent until they returned and moved me again. I have no memory of this. It was as though a great light had grown in my eyes, increasing in intensity and size until it filled all the sky and the earth, the palace, the sea, everything. As if I had been drawn into the sun, hot and white, a constant noon absorbed my sight, and in my ears was the incessant buzzing of all the world's bees, not so much speaking to me as covering up a sound that I kept trying to hear.

I was never alone. Even during the night there were always two women in my mother's room, which was now mine. While one slept, the other watched. I never spoke to them. I never spoke at all. My throat was hot and dry even as they poured water into my mouth. The only sound that came through it was the strange cracked chant in the ceremony.

One day they brought Phaedra and I cried. For though she was so small, not even to my waist, she looked exactly like my mother, the enormous eyes and full lips and black ringlets hanging in front of her ears. They had even painted her face and adorned her with jewels not appropriate for a child. But when I noticed that her breasts were full, I knew they had worked some kind of spell upon her, and I grabbed her hands and ran down the corridor with her until they stopped me and carried me back, screaming.

Minos had disappeared again. I was in the hands of Chione and the strange women. After the visit of Phaedra I screamed often. I heard myself doing it, but I could not stop, nor did I want to. The scream made a thickness in my throat, almost as if it were a substance, a gush of blood, perhaps even a snake. It terrified me, but it made me feel connected. For a moment, the hot light would disappear. There would be a glimpse of deep cool shade, though it would fade as I approached. It was my only sensation of the Goddess, though an evil one. Her blessing, my flow of fertile blood, did not return with the new moon. Nor with the next or the next. I was dry and barren, caught in a steady dream of noon on hot sand.

Suddenly Minos was there again. Where I had thought there was only white light, his form took shape. I felt him at my arm once more, a chain drawn so tight that my arm seemed to separate from my body. The black hairs on his forearms curled and matted. I saw them close against my face. The women had disappeared. Walls rose up around us, and darkness. I think he must have been carrying me, for I had no sensation of walking. There was no sound, none. This seemed to go on for years, as though we walked through all the caverns of the earth.

Finally he stopped. We were at the bars of a large chamber lit by tapers. He sat me down (I felt the dampness of the rock) and opened the gate. Then he took a taper and pulled me over to a huge *pithos* standing on a dais. He knocked the cover to the ground and shoved my face to the opening. "Look," he shouted, but I could see nothing. He flung me down again and reached into the jar and brought up something. I could not make it out at first. An animal, a bird? It was dripping with some thick substance. He held it toward me, shouting so that I could not understand, and as some of the substance dripped against my face, I tasted honey. When he brought the taper up against the thing, I saw that it was a dead infant, a monstrous infant with a head like a beast. I heard him shouting that this was the child of Tauros and my mother.

Then I saw Tauros, alive, in that dark room, chained to a pillar, humped over as if he were broken. His eyes shone in the flicker of the taper and he looked at me and howled, a hoarse guttural howl like an animal or like a man whose tongue has been pulled out.

# II

*Black is his robe from top to toe,*
*His flesh is white and warm below,*
*All through his silent veins flow free*
*Hunger and thirst and venery,*
*But in his eyes a still small flame*
*Like the first cell from which he came*
*Burns round and luminous, as he rides*
*Singing my song of deicides.*

J. B. S. HALDANE, Daedalus

# 1

DAEDALUS:
*Knossos, the first day:*

WE HAD BEEN ROCKING in the blue-black waves for days, huddled out of the reach of rowers and spray, the boy squeezed against my side, his mother hiding her head under a shawl, all of us stinking of fish and salt, with gulls swooping past like nudging spirits, and at last there it was, straight ahead. A cleft peak—Iyttos. Naucrate peeked out of her shawl and confirmed it. "Womb of the Mother," my grandfather had called it, mumbling in a steady sound out of his black corner. The noisy life of an Attic house had hummed on about us, I remember, but only I, a child, had seemed to hear his voice. It was thin and wheezing like air through a cave and it slipped back now and then into the old Cretan tongue. "Take care," he had whispered in my ear. "Follow the ritual. The Mothers watch our hands. The stone will not take all shapes without breaking."

Indeed, it is a return. I have become my grandfather, retracing his steps out of the motherland, back to my origins, to my grandfather's childhood, to the days of the first Minos. "There were goddesses everywhere in those days," comes the old man's voice in my head, and I marvel at how no sound is ever lost. "The Mothers loomed overhead, moved underfoot, moaned in sea and cave. Warnings were all about, but within—the stillness of a peaceful heart. And the queen moving in splendor . . . " I shall lose my head utterly if I go on like this. How the past hangs on to us.

Long before the boat docked, I saw figures on the shore. Brown men with cinched waists—you can tell a Cretan from far off. They were gathered at the dock, watching us. Suddenly they scattered. Slowly moving down the rock steps appeared a litter made of some precious metal that flashed under the moving clouds. I could not see, inside, the figure of the fabulous queen, but I knew it must be she from the attitude of the men. Curious as they had been to see us, they stood still now, turned toward the litter. We were closer. I saw an arm reach through the curtains and casually wave. The men moved away at once and busied themselves with ropes and moorings to fasten our ship to the dock. Then I saw another litter descending. It was open and in it was a young girl gorgeously dressed. Now there seemed to be women everywhere. The men made way for them as if they were all of noble birth.

Not until they were seated, every one of them, in chattering groups on the rocks, did I notice the man standing at the top, regarding me. His waist, too, was cinched but with a golden belt. And on his head was a helmet with brilliantly colored plumes. It had to be Minos. I heard him speak and there was a general turning in his direction, as when a leader commands. But just as my feet touched the pier, a strange thing happened. A Cretan happening. Nowhere else would it be so, not now.

The curtains of the queen's litter were pulled back and a fantastic woman leaned out, laughing. I have seen rulers flaunting their power but never quite like this. Enormous painted eyes, full naked breasts adorned with gold, black curls full of jewels—she is as beautiful as birth and riches can make a woman, but the power she wields is something more than that. All the men, even Minos, dropped their swords and stood with hands on foreheads, eyes lowered, in an archaic gesture of adoration. What a thing they make of this queen worship even today! No wonder my grandfather remembered.

I knelt on the warm rock before her and made my obeisance, Attic fashion. I gave her a gold cup I had made according to an old Cretan design, all spirals and rosettes. It cost me a fortune and I hated to part with it, but these monarchs must have recognition, there's no getting around that. Besides, I hope to make plenty here to justify the investment. And she had given me a royal welcome. It's good to know you're valued, but you have to pay for it.

Minos greeted me rather formally, and we all followed the queen and her daughter back to the palace. The road along which we traveled is not remarkable, nor is the first view of the palace itself. There are no walls, no large gates or enormous foreboding figures as in Egypt. Only a building rising gently out of a hill as if continuous with it. But once inside—the mind gapes at the luxury. Corridor upon corridor painted with flowers and portraits. Jewels heaped in *pithoi*. Gold and silver plates, lamps, cups. (My gift seemed suddenly diminished.) It's a palace bulging with wealth and people. Too crowded, but rich, rich.

I am treated with deference by the rulers. My quarters are comfortable, even luxurious. My Cretan wife is happy to be home. My son is jumping with curiosity. This first day in the homeland of my grandfather bodes well.

*Pallas, revered friend,*

*I send you greetings from Knossos, beautiful eternal city. For me it has been a glorious refuge and a chance to get a new start. The offer came at just the right time. As you must have heard, the blasts of the tribunal were still ringing in my ears over that Talos affair. Never take your relatives into the business. Old truth, but I ignored it, to my sorrow. He was my nephew, you know. Upstart boy, without morals. Talented, no question of that, but all those underhanded dealings designed to discredit me and take over all my work—I had to get rid of him. Well, enough of that.*

*As I said, the messenger came at the right time and loaded with gifts. I was in a shaky position to refuse, had I felt so inclined. But far from that. The prospect was enticing. Unlimited budget, a free hand, an ancient gorgeous treasure hoard to house. Angles and vectors intersected my dreams from the first night the rich envoy opened his chest and displayed the enticements. Who wouldn't have jumped at the chance? Besides, my grandfather was Cretan, my wife too, as you know, and she was dying to get back to see her family. Oh, I suppose there will be some problems, but the work will be most gratifying, I'm sure—a magnificent old structure that I have been given freedom to reconstruct in part, to enlarge, and to embellish. The wealth here is unimaginable. The local artisans are supremely skilled and materials of the most exotic kinds are shipped in daily. There's an astonishing array of goods on the docks. Copper from Cyprus, gold from Nubia, obsidian from Melos . . . the harbor bristles with ships. You wouldn't believe how many.*

*There are certain restrictions on building, of course. The palace has been constructed on a low hill in an enclosed valley. On an axis with the palace to the south is another hill, gently moulded. A higher, double-peaked mountain lies just beyond. That's Iyttos. One can stand on the porch of the palace or above on the highest balcony and look past the hill rising below the cleft of the mountain. From that angle the hill seems to separate the peaks. This is of ancient religious significance, and the view must not be altered under any circumstances. I've been told I must keep this in mind. It's of supreme importance, the priestesses remind me repeatedly.*

*There are priestesses everywhere. The old religion is rampant here, as one might expect. The ceremonies are exotic and interminable. The Goddess still reigns supreme in the view of the commoners, though the sophisticates of the royalty show Attic tendencies. Minos, in particular, is eager to learn Athenian ways, though he puts on the trappings of Mother worship, to keep his power, I suppose. But he's been in office long past the old deadline and plans to pass the throne to his sons, as far as I can see.*

*The queen is magnificent, more beautiful even than the rumors we heard over there. She hardly shows her age, is unbelievably licentiate (all in the name of the old religion, of course), and is addicted to pleasures of every kind. Fortunately for me, she has an insatiable lust for jewelry—rings, bracelets, hair ornaments—and also for golden cups, bronze daggers, new frescoes, and any and all representations of the sacred cattle that she seems to favor far beyond the similarly sacred dove and snake. For me it is a glorious artistic adventure. I'm given immense freedom. Any materials I suggest are at once sent for—precious jewels, rare stones. The designs are mainly mine, though I also encourage the vastly talented local artisans who execute their work to perfection. However, they're rather pedantic. Their creative powers are curiously weak in comparison with their skill. It is as though some major element had disappeared. Where is the genius that conceived the marvelously lifelike frescoes of the old corridors?*

*The king is a strong man, small and dark by Athenian standards, but tall here. He's traveled enough to see how things go elsewhere in the world and is determined to stop the succession of women and go as we go, from father to son. Oh, he doesn't say so outright, but anyone can tell he's grooming his sons for power. The older son is much like him. The second is a fop—sensual like his mother. But they're no trouble to Minos, the boys. He wants them to have power—after he's through with it. No, his main problem seems to be his daughters, particularly the elder, Ariadne, who is (by custom) heiress to the throne, is doted upon by the people, and is an astonishingly clever child. More of that later. I have just constructed a dancing floor for her in a mosaic of semiprecious stones. The pattern is in part traditional, since it is to be used for religious dance. But I have taken some liberties, with the queen's enthusiastic consent, and the result is most gratifying to me—one of the best things I have yet done. I only hope that Ariadne will like it. It's hard to believe how much power the women still have here. The other day a toy I had made for Ariadne (at Minos' request, no less) was thrown out, I'm not sure why. It was considered blasphemous, I believe. Naucrate gives me some insights on these things, though she was evasive in this instance. Slightly fearful. I shall have to do some research. There must be a significance that escapes me. A doll on a swing? What could it mean?*

*My son is very happy here. He takes his lessons in the royal classroom and romps with the princesses through the palace. I'm glad I made the move for his sake, if for no other reason . . .*

*Notes on Avoidance* (according to Naucrate):
    Images of bees
    Double axes
    Images of goddesses, queens, *any women*

In the middle of the night she whispers the list into my ear. She is frightened and tearful, and the minute she has breathed this litany, she runs out of my room into the darkness, probably to a shrine. She is afraid for me because in my ignorance I have blundered into construction of objects that must not even be seen or touched by nonbelievers, much less constructed. She has warned me because she is afraid the Goddess will destroy me. And now I suppose she is terrified that by doing this, she has herself betrayed the Goddess.

So that is why my dolls were destroyed by the old priestess. Yet the queen knew what I was making and she said nothing. I walk on shaky ground.

*The Second Year:*

Well, then it is not a perfect refuge after all. Something is going on—I can't tell just what. The priestesses mutter, the queen laughs. Minos says nothing—to me, at any rate. All he wants from me are ships and weapons. He's delighted with my new sword, though the queen turns up her nose because it is not sufficiently decorated. I am also working on the design for a new sail that should catch the wind more efficiently.

But there's something brewing that disturbs me, disturbs Naucrate even more though she won't talk about it—just rushes in and out with a cloudy face, clutches Icarus fiercely, then pushes him away. She's not the same woman she was in Athens, seems to be ashamed of me, wants to get away, is gone most of the time, at night too. She is forever busy with palace business—priestess business, I should say. The old religion is reclaiming her, I guess, though there's something more in it than she'll admit.

The boy's not happy here anymore, that's clear. Something's occurred—though he won't talk about it either. But I've decided. I'm sending Icarus back to Attica. There's a ship leaving in the morning. The captain's a friend of mine, he'll bring the boy to Sounion to my old friend, Pallas. He'll learn my trade, he's old enough; you never can begin too young. Naucrate weeps, but she'll get over it. Besides, she doesn't really oppose his going. That's part of the mystery. Anyway, he'll be safe. The captain's a solid man. Besides, I've promised him first chance at the new sail when I've perfected it.

I'll be sorry to see the lad go, though, just when he's getting old enough to talk to. Still, it's for the best. Things are going on here that—well, best not write about it.

*Dear Lycus,*

*I am deeply indebted to you for your extending such gracious hospitality to my son for all these weeks since the death of my old friend, Pallas. As you*

[ 60 ]

have probably heard, these are troubled times in Crete, hard enough for even an old acrobat like me who has learned to land on his feet in more than one country. But Icarus is a gentle, affectionate boy and suffered greatly here because of his monstrous Athenian father.

You're partly right about Minos. He does rule the seas with an unsheathed sword. But he wants trade. Crete would collapse without it. There's very little here of the materials he needs for his enterprise. Everything is imported—copper, tin, basalt. Crete produces only olives, grapes, magnificent cattle, gorgeous art, and beautiful women. Can you build an empire out of that?

As for the trouble here—there is much angry talk and the nights are full of intrigue, but I think nothing will come of it. Minos is an Athenian in spirit. He'll take care of it when he returns. He has much more power than I thought at first—arms his men and pays them well. And in spite of my first impression, the old religion seems to be dying out of itself. The queen doesn't care, is too engrossed in her passions, of which Minos seems unaware or pretends to be. It's true there are rumors of rebellion brewing. It's because of the hunger in the villages, I suspect. Crops do not flourish because of the drought. Grain is scarce. The trees are dying . . .

My dear friend, Lycus,

Such ghastly things have happened—I cannot explain it now. Naucrate —my son's mother—is dead. I will tell you more sometime. But now, as you love me, tell everyone that she met with an accident in the mountains. I suppose you must tell Icarus. You had better give him the same story. No. Say that she fell ill while traveling to the home of her ancestors in the east. And if he wants to honor her shrine . . . no, tell him that she met with an accident while on the journey, that the news came to you by the same messenger who first brought it to me, that she was buried by devout villagers—no, just say villagers, in the mountains, that I know the place and will make a pilgrimage there sometime. But not now; above all, do not let the boy leave now. Keep him safe and out of sight. I will explain this to you at a later . . .

# 2

ARIADNE:

S UNS AND MOONS RACED through the sky, one after the other.
Toward what, I wondered. A black twisted mouth falling away
from permanent gold eyes?

I seemed to be wandering through endless tunnels, shining my
blind light against walls that yielded sometimes to my touch and
engulfed me. Or turned hard and shiny as polished bronze so that I
saw my face repeated and repeated in them. Sometimes the walls
were alive, pulsating like throats. The floor moved underneath me
then, and leaves sprouted up through the tiles. A high wall of water
filled the passageway behind me, standing upright and churning, as
if held back by an invisible barrier. When I moved, it followed
along behind me like a dog. When I stopped, it stopped. I could
not see what restrained it. I expected in each moment that it would
break over me and I would drown.

DAEDALUS:

The ceremonies go according to the ritual, but she moves as if in
a trance even when they end. Mostly she sits and looks as if without
seeing. She will not speak.

The people believe she is communing with the Goddess. Minos is
of two minds, I think. He is glad she does not oppose him. Even I
can tell that he has introduced some changes in the ceremony,
elevating his own part. (As Aegeus did in Athens some years back.)
I think it is Minos' plan to increase the changes until Zeus shines
equally with the Goddess. That's the trend all over. Ariadne does
not seem to notice, though I have heard some murmurs among the
craftsmen.

ARIADNE:

Then I seemed to be at the mountain shrine, but the mountain now was made of bronze. I knew that Daedalus had changed it. Three priestesses in white robes walked slowly around the pool, following a man in a feathered ceremonial helmet. On the great flat rock lay a bull, bound by red ropes. Blood ran from his throat into a vat. Merope was at the altar, a *rhyton* in her hands. As she began to pour the libation over the offering, Minos ran in and picked up the vat of blood and spilled it over his own head. Then he tore the flesh from the bull and ate it. The bronze mountain did not move.

DAEDALUS:

The drought is worse. The well at the south portal has gone dry. Some of the mountain streams are reduced to a trickle. People have to carry water for miles. There are murmurings everywhere. The crops are not growing properly. No grains are forming on the barley. The grapevines have withered. The animals are affected too. Many sheep are sick. The wool is thin and lank. Pigs are often born dead. Cows dry up before the calves are weaned. Bulls are losing their horns. Bees are leaving the hives.

ARIADNE:

I was riding in a chariot drawn by griffins. Shells of sea crabs and cuttle fish crunched under the wheels. Partridges were lying in the path and the wheels sliced them into fragments. In the steady wind, beating to stay afloat, danced all the butterflies of the dead.

DAEDALUS:

It is not just that there has been no rain for so long. There is a pestilence in the air that affects one's breathing. The oldest Cretans have never known anything like it. The newborn and the aged suffer most. I am trying to discover whether it might be caused by some change in the wind's direction. Minos is impatient with this study. "Give me ships," he says. "The Athenians will provide our grain." I am supposed to laugh at this, as at any jibe at Athens. But I suspect the wind may be drying the Attic fields as well.

ARIADNE:

I saw a dove drop from the sky. A serpent arose out of the rock and swallowed it. Swallowed the sky and the sea and the earth. Swallowed itself.

DAEDALUS:

Minos is worried about the young queen, at last. Not about her health so much, though I think he should be. This trance has gone on too long. She doesn't eat, either. She's too young for this sort of thing. If it goes on much longer, she'll fade away. But what bothers Minos most is the power she seems to hold over the minds of the populace even in her dreaming state. They follow her about, worshipful, waiting for the words of the Goddess to tumble from her mouth. Thus he cannot use her as freely as he would like. Also, he cannot be sure that she hears him or agrees to his suggestions. At any moment she might interrupt the ceremony and speak, in ecstasy, words that would condemn him. He has ordered me to cure her. "Talk to her. Wake her from the trance. Aren't you a learned man?" No one can sneer so well as a ruler.

ARIADNE:

Dove eggs dropped from the sky into pockets abandoned by snakes. They fell in such great numbers that they overcast the blue. I thought that they might dredge rain from the underside of the moon, from between the ridges of teeth of the angry Goddess. But they spoiled and their shells burst.

DAEDALUS:

At last I am in a position to examine the real thing! I have made a very exciting discovery. One of Minos' sailors—an ignorant man, but grateful (I'd helped him cure his boils)—just this night has brought me a manuscript that he said he had found in the innermost temple of the Mother somewhere on an island, he won't

[ 64 ]

say where. It's written on lime bark, and much damaged. There's evidence that someone had tried to destroy it, very likely this sailor himself before he realized what he might gain from it. Still, it is partially legible, though it's in the old script. And the man knew its value even if he can't read, for he wanted a large price in spite of his gratitude for the boil cure. Fortunately, Minos has been generous.

ARIADNE:

My dress stood out stiffly from my body. I knew I must be shrinking. It was not a bull that Minos had sacrificed. It was a woman.

DAEDALUS:

The old text is clear. When the vegetation dies, the high priestess must go over the water in a ship holding the sacred tree. Her consort guides her. The masts of the ship are pillars topped by horns of consecration. At the prow is a dog's head, at the stern a fish's tail. She goes over the water to a fertile island, plants the sacred tree, and offers herself to the Goddess. But if the high priestess is not fertile, the sacred tree will die. All the trees will die.

As I thought, they believe it is the barrenness of a queen that causes the forest to wither. That explains the distress of the people. Ariadne's menstrual flow has not returned. Only the initial showing at the time of Pasiphae's death, and never again. Of course, she's so young, I think it's not unusual, but they won't talk about that.

Minos speaks now of sending for an Egyptian physician. I think he hoped I would feel insulted. Instead, I told him I welcome it. "It will give me more time to build ships," I said.

The people still clamor for the Sibyl, but she will not come to the palace. They say she feels it has been defiled.

ARIADNE:

The women took me to the shrine at the sea's edge and I saw charcoal on a low round tripod table painted red, white, and black. I saw conch shells. Clay figures of women and animals, fragmented.

Hanks of hair in gold cases nailed to the wall. Jugs with handles and spouts. A *rhyton*. The skull of a bull.

I heard bells and the blowing of a conch. A lyre struck. Flutes. The shaking of a sistrum. The dance took me. I saw the earth swirl under my feet. Dead branches encircled me.

The Goddess was absent.

DAEDALUS:

News today. One of our ships sighted a wreck, picked up one survivor. My heart fell when I heard it, I was so sure it was the ship Icarus is coming on. But no. It hailed from Egypt, carrying the physician Minos had sent for. The physician is drowned. The survivor is his slave. A knowledgeable slave, an apprentice, one might say. He values his training, too. He was found clutching part of the wrecked hull with one hand and a tin box with the other. He refused to yield the box to anyone but me. He kept saying my name, the only word our men could understand.

And so they've brought him here with his box; but he is in bad shape. Drifts in and out of dreams. His face is baked and swollen from the long exposure, and on one foot several toes are missing. A shark perhaps. Why it would not have eaten him entirely, I don't know. Perhaps our crew interrupted. I don't know whether I can save him.

I am studying the contents of the box, waterlogged as they are. Various herbs I do not recognize. Spells. Several instruments that fascinate me—a finely cut knife, a drill. A manuscript called "The Code of Imhotep."

The Egyptian's name is Ahmosi or Amasis, I cannot tell which. Perhaps one is a diminutive. His fever rages and he tosses from one side to another as if in pain. He has moments of clarity, but he speaks rapidly and my knowledge of the language is imperfect.

I had bathed his foot and applied herbs, but suddenly he woke and asked me to apply one of the drugs in the tin box. It was not clear which one he wanted so I brought them all, and he pointed and whispered something that I could scarcely hear. The directions

[ 66 ]

for its use, I believe, but he drifted off again before I could question him. I do not know this drug. I hope I have used it properly.

Ariadne continues the same. I have tried all the remedies I know.

ARIADNE:

I went down into the chasm, past the offerings of rotting fruit, past the fumes rising from the cleft in the rock, past the underground water. I looked into the darkness and waited. "Your eyes are knives," said the shadows. "They have peeled paint from clay and gold leaf from ivory. Only a vision will heal them." But I saw in the depths of the cave, only the depths of the cave.

Then there was a long blank time in which I stared and saw nothing.

DAEDALUS:

I have been turned into a physician. These sick ones take too much of my time, though they fascinate me too. I want to talk to the Egyptian, who seems to be an educated man. Perhaps he can tell me something of the construction of those tombs rising out of the sand as if they were mountains. How I wish I could go there and examine them. Minos wants to question him, too. About the royal succession, I suspect. Whether Queen Hatshepsut continues in strength or the young king has replaced her. Minos is much interested in matters of succession.

The mountain people are worrying him now, though. They came in a crowd this morning to demand that he have Ariadne brought to the Sibyl. But Minos will not yield on that, even though he can surely tell that they're turning against him. I see why he can't do it. He's got to have a cure without the old seeress, very important in his plan. The pressure is upon me. I would welcome the help of this unfortunate Egyptian. I pore over his documents but can make little sense of them. The water has washed away many of the words.

Ariadne sits silent and immobile. Her eyes are always open, but she seems not to see us. The people stand in the courtyard under her balcony, praying for her to return. They say the Raging Ones have taken Ariadne's soul and unless it is returned, the land will die.

There is unquestionably an upsurge of the old religion, as is usual in time of distress. I can't help but hear of it, though my sources are more remote now that my wife is gone. Minos hears it too, from inside as well as out, I suspect. He falters sometimes as if an inner voice interrupts. He is only half-emerged from the old net, which is why he thunders so fiercely at times. If he were less troubled he would handle things more smoothly, as he did with the squelching of the Tauros rebellion. That was neatly done. Of course, the queen's death was unlucky. And now Ariadne's illness. It seems he cannot attack the women without penalty, and even when they are ill, the people say he has caused it. Well, maybe he has.

The Egyptian is dead. No more help there, though I have his boxes. Minos sent men to explore the wreckage and they have salvaged a number of treasures, among them another box apparently belonging to the physician, sealed with wax, miraculously sheltered from the sea water, stuffed with dry papyrus. Minos called me and presented it in great excitement, and I have been exploring. How I wish I had the language perfectly. There are many mysteries that will be cleared up by this box, I feel, though it seems to me that none of the records is medical.

I am now left alone with the sick queen. Minos will not yield on the Sibyl. My days are spent translating. I hope I can find a clue to Ariadne's illness. I believe my life depends upon it.

ARIADNE:

One day, as if after a long sleep, I awoke suddenly. I was in Daedalus' room. It was filled with shadows. Daedalus was picking up objects and naming them. And as he named each one, it formed itself cleanly apart from the others. Object by object, he removed the shadows from the room. It became filled with things whole, equal, fully seen. They were there to the eyes and the hands. They remained behind me as I moved my head. I could turn back and find them exactly where they had been, and when I touched them, they were firm.

A plastered bench. An ebony footstool inlaid with ivory lions, a palm tree, an octopus. A stone table. A gold cup. An ivory chest with lilies and ivy leaves in gold. A rug woven of fine white wool. A heavy shawl. I do not know how many days or months Daedalus had been naming things to me. It seemed to me that years went by before he noticed that I was listening to him. Perhaps they were only moments. But I remember his actions clearly as if they were being painted upon a wall.

He seems tired. He covers his eyes with one hand and sighs. Then he pushes himself away from the table and begins to pace about the room. The sun intercepts his head as he limps back and forth into shadow, sun, shadow, sun. He is talking about anything now—the grains of Crete, the minerals of the Hittites, the ancient languages, the temples of Egypt and Babylon, ships on the dark seas lashed by the great northern winds, the deserts of the east, mountains to the north higher than Iyttos, higher than the clouds, probing into the abode of the immortals. "If one could climb there, one could prove everything," he says. He leans against the door and looks out across the balcony. "To the south is Egypt," he murmurs. "Some day I will travel up the great river to the source. And then back again to the temples, the tombs, the amulets, and the sacred scarabs." Now his voice is sharp again. "The Egyptians say we are beetles," he says, "pushing our great dung heap, the earth, laying our eggs in dung and springing forth from it. Our palaces are dung. Even the soaring tombs and temples of Egypt are dung."

His head is enormous, riding like a great ball of dung on wooden poles that bend and creak as he limps back and forth into sun, shadow, sun. "The world is dung," he says, "but the mind—." He splits the air with his sharp hands. "It is the *mind* that transmutes that dung to jewels, and embossed gold, and bull *rhytons*, and palaces, and monstrous goddesses . . . "

"Yes," I say.

He whirls to look at me.

"Yes," I say again. "Yes."

# 3

DAEDALUS THE SPIDER, spinning out of his mind a glistening web that touched all points of the dung heap and connected them in intricate patterns. Daily he pulled me with him across fine threads so transparent that I wondered whether they were really there. Sometimes the thread would not catch. He would spin and throw at something beyond even his own reach and it would stop a moment on air and then drift reluctantly dungward.

I could not spin at all at first without dropping into emptiness. A void lay behind each object. I had to name things to keep them from fading into it. Daedalus took me through the palace naming. Twenty-five *pithoi* filled with olive oil in the west corridor. Forty cists of grain, twenty-eight barley, twelve flax. Fifty baskets of gourds, peas, and beans. Thirty-one jars of honey. Figs, grapes, dried herbs. "And look, Ariadne, barley bread and goat cheese." I was an eager spider, learning the craft of thought webbing. But only in sunlight, and only regarding things I could touch.

The world had become flat, outlined in black so that stone separated from stone, white gull from blue sky. I ordered new frescoes on the walls of my chambers to cover the dolphins and dancers—lilies, angular, elongated, and flat like the designs in the Egyptian box. But at the last moment I canceled the order.

I had scarcely missed a morning ceremony, in spite of my illness, though I have little memory of them. Apparently I went on like a doll with a voice, but I was a creation of Daedalus, not of the Mother. I was also Daedalus' creation in the classroom, but a different sort. There even he could not wholly control my seeing. I was in his classroom every day for hours. I learned how to build stone-lined cists, drains, sewers. Pillars that would not fall when the earth shook. Ships that would skim water like gulls. On Daedalus' lips were the constant questions: What is in the world?

Where is it found? How can it be used? The earth was a tool for him, clay in his hands as in the old tales of creation. My days seethed with the tools of this world.

But my nights shook with demons. Pasiphae carrying the monstrous child. Merope hanging. Around corners I would come upon them. Or they would follow me, faces gray, no eyes, snakes coming from their mouths. I would wake and light all the lamps and sit until daylight watching the sleeping women. But I no longer screamed.

Chione seemed to be with me now all night. Daytimes too she would follow me around, but I would not let her come into the classroom. I had never liked her; I did not trust her. How had she escaped Minos' slaughter of the priestesses? Had she informed him of the journey to the sanctuary? I was certain that she had been his bedmate even while my mother was alive. Had she hoped to be queen? That would have meant my death and Phaedra's. I did not think Minos felt strong enough to go so far. Besides, he did not seem to care much for her now. He kept a Syrian slave boy with him most of the time, even when he went on voyages, a beautiful boy scarcely older than I. Chione's thin, lined face seemed ancient in comparison.

The people were overjoyed at my recovery, so much so that Minos had to order an elaborate ceremony of celebration. On the morning of the festivities it rained, and the people danced and prayed, taking this for a sign of the Goddess' return to her daughter. My menstrual flow had not begun again, but when we came back to my room after the morning ceremony, Chione sent the other women away and whispered to me fiercely. Then she showed me cloths on which she had dropped the blood of a weasel. We were to pretend that the flow had returned so that all would be in accordance with expectations, and the people would be reassured that the Goddess had indeed come back to me.

She trembled as she spoke and her eyes moved constantly from me to the doors to make sure none of the women would come in and hear what she was saying. I could tell that she half-expected that I would call guards to kill her. Or that the Goddess would reach out and engulf her. "It will be a sign to the Goddess, a promise. It was practiced in ancient times," she whispered, her eyes darting.

I said nothing. The dancing ladies on my mother's walls seemed to smile. Had it always been like this? The ceremonies based not upon the evidence of the Goddess, but rather upon evidence created some way, any way to justify the ceremony? As if one danced a story against the substance of events and believed what one invented. Designs to hide the void, like the objects Daedalus had named. Barley bread, goat cheese, and look, Ariadne, the blood of the Goddess. Yet it *had* rained. The Goddess had shown a sign.

No doubt Chione took my silence for assent, for she took the cloth and dashed out onto the balcony overlooking the central court, where many of the people were still assembled, waiting for the afternoon ceremonies. I could hear her crying, "Look, look! The Goddess has returned to her daughter!" There were cries of joy and prayer.

I lay on my mother's bed and listened again for the Goddess' anger. It did not come.

From that moment for many weeks, Chione never left me. She sent all the other women away and all alone tended to my needs, as well as keeping up the deception of the blood-stained cloths. How she managed it I did not even ask. It mattered as little to me as the journey of a fly around a honey pot. When we were alone, she chattered on and on about my power over the people and how if I lifted my hand at the right moment, I could get their support on anything I wanted. She was vague. She did not mention Minos, but I recognized Merope's tone, and I expected every nightfall to find hooded visitors invading my rooms. None appeared. However, Minos' cold eyes watched us even as he shouted prayers. Often when we returned to my quarters, we would find some of the other women there, cleaning or repairing, they would say. Chione thought they were spies.

One morning I woke to find her gone, and the women told me that she had become ill during the night and had crept out, not wanting to disturb me. Before dawn, they said, she had asked to be taken back to her village, to the sacred spring. I never saw her again. About ten days later, word came that she had died. No one spoke of the nature of her illness.

I was sure that her deceit about the blood of the Goddess had been discovered, but I found no proof. Her death did not move me, though I could see the value of what she had done in the increased reverence of the people toward me. I had become for them a real queen. Minos saw this too. For the first time, I was able to select my own chief attendant. I chose a slave girl, fresh from some distant island. She was quite young and very beautiful, but mute. Her tongue had been cut out when she was captured. I chose her publicly the morning that I was told of Chione's death. Minos was silent. The slave girl's name was Korkyne.

I had no idea how I would manage the menstrual deception. However, they would not be likely to ask me to show more proof, at least for a while, and Korkyne was mute and did not understand our language. But before another moon had passed, the blood of the Goddess really did return to me and in such volume that all the palace priestesses were called in to take my linen and wash it in the sacred spring of the dove shrine.

Minos' face was hard to read. I think he must have known of Chione's deception. I was sure he had had her killed, though I did not know how to confirm this. Now it seemed to me that he was shaken, as though he felt the Goddess' judgment. His voice in the ceremony shook with emotion. It woke me from the half-sleep in which I had been moving through the ritual, thinking of something else. Suddenly I noticed a change, the introduction of a long address to Zeus, who had been there before only in a minor action, as guardian of the sacred king who must die so that the world can continue. Now there was a long interlude in which Minos alone prayed to Zeus, and in such a way that he seemed to be almost as powerful as the Goddess. How had I not noticed this before? I tried to remember hearing it, but I could not. Had he introduced it just now?

There were other changes. Small ones. Four more *kouretes* had been added to the processional, and a larger role had been given them. Their dance had been lengthened, and they now brought offerings not only to the Goddess but also to Zeus. I pretended not to notice, but at the next ceremony, as if absentmindedly, I made a cut in the service that excluded the address to Zeus. Minos' face grew red with rage, but he said nothing. The next time, he interrupted my last words with his Zeus prayer. I cut into his words then also and managed to eliminate at least a few minutes. Next time he tried to do that with my prayers, but the people were more familiar with those, because they were traditional, and there was considerable murmuring about it in the courtyard that must have come to his ears, because he did not attempt it again but only vied with me for the complete insertion of his own paean to Zeus. Never once did we discuss this.

For me it was a game, though a deadly one. I knew quite well that Minos was trying to make me powerless, though he seemed a little fearful of his own daring, which must have been why he prayed so fervently. I seemed to have gone beyond fear. I watched the ceremony, even watched myself moving in it, as though it were simply an old tale someone long ago had invented to keep herself amused or to keep from being afraid in the darkness, or even just because people wanted such tales, perhaps needed them in order to live. In the Egyptian manuscripts, there were similar stories. And Daedalus had told me others from Athens and Anatolia, and from the far northern islands.

Even at night when the figures of the Raging Ones flew at me constantly, there was a peculiar coldness in my heart that kept me wakeful but not afraid. It was as though I had already had my life's share of fear. Or perhaps it was that the emptiness that I saw behind the world's objects was also inside me, in all the space where I had once felt the Goddess. What could I name to fill myself?

It was Korkyne who first awakened my feelings again. She was all softness and quiet. Very gentle. Timid. The sudden sound of clanging metal made her drop her head between her shoulders as if expecting a blow. I learned to move slowly near her so that she would not tremble, and to speak almost in a whisper. Though it was said she did not know our language, she seemed to understand well enough the few things I needed to say to her. I talked very little outside Daedalus' classroom at that time.

At first I was only grateful for Korkyne's silence and her understanding of what would make me comfortable even when I did not ask. Baths, a soft robe, the brazier lit in my chambers on a chill day, lamps enough so that I could read the old manuscripts Daedalus gave me. And at night when I woke, stiff with the coldness inside and out, she would be there without a call, bringing a lamp, a warm drink.

One night after she had been with me for several months she dared to touch me. I had been sitting upright in my bed looking into the lamp, trying to stare down the image of Merope, twisting and blackened on the tree, that had come out of my dream into the room. Korkyne brought me warm milk and honey and extra lamps, and even a sheaf of Egyptian papyrus that Daedalus had given me to test my learning of the language, but none of it could take away that dangling presence. I don't know how long I had been sitting in that fashion, but suddenly I became aware of her hand on my arm. I turned to look at her. I said nothing of my dream. I had never mentioned Merope to her. But her eyes were so compassionate, it seemed as though she had been with me down the dark corridors. For the first time since the mountaintop, I began to weep. She wept with me, both of us silently weeping through the long night.

Daedalus knew nothing of my nights and little of Korkyne. I never took her with me into the classroom, nor did I take my dreams. I left them at the threshold, like dusty robes, so that I could plunge naked and new into Mind.

As he translated the contents of the Egyptian box, Daedalus taught me what he knew of the language. Sometimes we would come upon a sign that he had never seen before and we would try to guess at its meaning. He was pleased with my conjectures, said often that my mind was beginning to rival his own. He would look strange as he said that, remembering his nephew perhaps, or thinking that I might.

He knew, of course, what had happened to my mother and

Merope, perhaps even what had happened to Tauros. I suppose that if I had asked him whether Tauros really were alive somewhere in the palace, mutilated and chained, he might have been able to tell me whether or not that was a dream. But I never asked. Tauros' name was never mentioned by anyone in the palace.

Sometimes, though, Daedalus would ask a question about the ritual, cautiously. "The invocation to Zeus, when was that introduced into the ceremony? I do not find it in the oldest texts." Or, "The earliest records of offerings to the Goddess list only grains and fruit. When was the slaughter of animals added?" Formal questions, having to do with history more than with belief. Questions that, it seemed, he could answer as well as I. We did not trust each other in those days.

When did trust begin? It is hard for me to remember how it happened. Daedalus' old journals and undelivered letters give some evidence that there was struggle within him as well as within me, but the moment of the joining of our minds, that opening between souls that allows the deepest thoughts to pour through—that moment seemed to happen without noting. No doubt it occurred while we were on some mind's journey among the islands, or to Athens, or up the Nile, or through the desert to the great tombs, or north to the mammoth stone temples of the sun. Daedalus had traveled everywhere. Architects were homeless, wandering men, he said, selling their skills to any purchaser. Only in his old age had he come to dwell in one place. But for me, it was a journey of the mind alone and could be no other. Bitterest of all edicts from the Goddess was the rule that no Cretan queen could leave her land without forfeiting the throne. Only at the going-over-water to the shrine at Dia, when the time came for my virgin child or for my taking a consort, would I be able to travel upon the sea, and then only to the shrine. And while I was gone, the people would tremble in prayer as in the dark of the moon, fearing destruction and death until at last I returned, fertile, promising life, and they breathed again. It was a tradition that could not be broken.

Thus, it was that I followed Daedalus' tales eagerly, as if they were happening to me. I made him draw pictures, name temples, list queens—and kings. There were more of the latter, he said. The kings had risen, the queens had given way. In the old stories it was different, but everywhere he had gone, the men had taken power, the goddesses were dying, except here in Crete, he said smiling, and in Egypt, with its great queen, Hatshepsut.

Coldness would spread inside me as he talked. But I needed to know the world and I would demand that he tell me more, that he bring manuscripts from far lands, and tablets, and teach me, teach me. I was desperate to learn it all. I could not bear to think of how much there was in the world that I would never see. I read quickly and questioned and demanded more.

Sometimes I would feel Daedalus studying me as I read. I remember once—perhaps that was the moment I began to trust him—I had been reading an Egyptian paper silently, but Daedalus knew what was in it. It was an account of the creation of the world, an ancient poem:

> *Lo, there was the chaos of primordial waters,*
> *And Ptah looked upon the waters and in his mind*
> *Saw rising from them the hills of Memphis,*
> *An earthen mound, and a word formed upon his tongue,*
> *And he spoke and commanded the earth to be.*

I looked up to find Daedalus' eyes upon me. He pointed to the papyrus. "This is your death, Ariadne," he said.

I could not breathe.

His voice was hardly audible. "An earth goddess should not follow this path, should think with her womb."

"Why did you teach me then?" I said. "Did you want to destroy me?"

I had always known his eyes were knives. He cut straight to the truth. "Have you forgotten that you begged me for knowledge?"

I flung the papyrus upon the floor. "The poem is a lie," I said.

"The poem is the outer sign of thought," said Daedalus. "It

leaves emotion behind. It will go on of itself, that thought—long caravans of reasoning purified from love and hate will traverse time, coldly erecting and demolishing without tremor."

But I felt the tremor inside me. "It could not happen without you," I said. "You are making it happen."

His hands were shaking. "It is happening to me also. It will go on whether I wish or not."

I crushed the poem. "I will stop it."

"Too late," he said. "It is inside you."

# 4

DAEDALUS:

SHE DEVOURS THE MANUSCRIPTS as if after a long famine. And yet she continues in the ceremony as if untouched by thought.

A battle rages between her and Minos for control of the worship. He has inserted a prayer and expanded it, and he is having scribes record on tablets the story of his receiving the laws from Zeus on the mountaintop. It is remarkably like a Babylonian tale I once heard. Only there the king's name was Hammurabi.

Now I am made schoolmaster and shipbuilder when I would rather work on palaces. Though there is some talk of a new building just to the west. A "little palace" for his dwelling is what Minos is after. Ariadne wants a temple. She has been reading. She is a woman now, and very willful. Her long illness seems to have strengthened her, and her mind is crystalline. How can this rise out of the bloody shadows of the old religion that strangled her childhood?

Only a small part of the Egyptian box is concerned with medicine. The physician—or his apprentice—was a scholar and a traveler. In ancient Babylonia, he notes, a surgeon who opens an eye sore with a bronze instrument and who saves the man's eye is rewarded handsomely, but if the eye is destroyed, they cut off the surgeon's hand. I do not believe it is necessary to show Minos all the documents.

*Notes on the Climate:*
Rainfall: mainly between autumn and early spring. Usually heavy enough to nourish crops and grazing lands. The drought of some years back has been relieved. But not enough, I think.

In Knossos—plenty of wells. Only a few are dry.

In the mountains—numerous springs.

In fields at middle level—trouble. This is where the water will run out before the crops are grown.

Minos uninterested. Counts on imports, conquests.

*Revered friend,*

*I am in need of your library again. My queen is interested in the stories of Babylon, particularly those concerning the goddess Inanna. Also, do you still have the sketches you once made of the circular temple in Cornwall? If you would induce an artisan to copy them and send them to me, I would be most indebted to you.*

*The messenger will bring you two seal rings as you requested. They are among the finest in craftsmanship that I have seen here. My queen sends them to you in gratitude for your . . .*

*My dear son,*

*How joyful I am that you will at last come, after all the failed promises. Ariadne asks that you bring for her drawings of the Temple of Isis in Egypt. Go to my friend, Actaeon, for advice. He has built many temples and traveled far.*

ARIADNE:

*Notes on Egypt:*

Hathor, goddess of love and childbirth, wore the horns of consecration. Osiris married the queen (Isis) and died and was ruler of the underworld. And his son, Horus, married the queen and died, and every king is Horus.

Maat is order, truth, justice, and righteousness, is the harmony of the world, unchangeable, eternal. (Where is the Great Mother?)

The sketch of the temple wall shows weeping women, their arms upraised in prayer, tears falling from their eyes. Why does Daedalus say they are widows? Clearly, they are captured priestesses. Or goddesses dying.

Queen Hatshepsut is strong, but not warlike. She wishes to trade with Crete. She employs many architects (all Egyptian) to construct great monuments, statues of basalt, limestone, and granite, and enormous temples and tombs. Thutmose is her son and her consort.

(Why are the goddesses dying?)

DAEDALUS:

"Tell me how the mind works," she says, and I search for words. It is easier to work for Minos. His demands are simple. "Design a ship that will outdistance all those known." Or, "What weapons do the Hittites use?" (Though that is not so simple. Minos' men captured a Hittite spear harder than bronze. I cannot discover what metal this is.)

Do I dare to question her about the women's mysteries? I've been told that the most important secrets were never written down. But of course many things were. The sailor's manuscript proves that. Too bad he died before he could bring me more.

Perhaps Ariadne would tell me about the rites. I'll have to be careful how I phrase the question, though. In spite of all her curiosity, she's a woman. A priestess, too, sworn to secrecy.

I cannot contain my excitement! We were examining a papyrus—damaged—from the Egyptian box, something about Ptah, a poem, perhaps a prayer. And suddenly she says, "When is it, then, that thought begins? With a name?"

I was transported back into my childhood. I replied, speaking in my old teacher's voice, "We are always already in the middle of an action before we become aware of its cause, its nature, and its consequence." I was swept away into thinking of her as a new issue of my young self. And then she broke the spell completely.

"I woke in the middle of the dance," she said. "My hands were raised and I was whirling, inviting the Goddess to descend into me. The snakes were coiled, the doves were in their places. There was even a rumbling in the earth as if it were speaking to my feet as they touched in the intricate pattern of the dance worship. But instead of the vision, I saw pieces—each thing separate and apart. And I stopped. I knew it was all surfaces. One thing does not connect with another. It is all lies."

It's a confession! A confidence. The closest I have got to the old mysteries. She has rejected them!

Perhaps now I can get her to show me the ancient manuscripts, the ones that the priestesses keep secret. Minos would give anything to see them.

ARIADNE:

Now he questions me. I was wrong to trust him. For all the brilliance of his mind, he's just Minos' tool. His wisdom is of the skin and the sword. He sells to Minos whatever skill is demanded.

I think I prefer Minos. At least he is strong. He bends everyone to his will, even those who are far holier or far more brilliant than he. Those like Daedalus, whose mind carves magic, but who is weak. He can scarcely carry that enormous head about. And he is old too, much older than his years, unless he has lied about them. Perhaps it is because he is Athenian? No, I think it is his mind that has made him old. Yet Minos handles him as if he were a hatchet.

He shall not handle me.

How my mother used to hang on him. When I was a child he loved me. His arms were very strong and brown. And when he laughed his teeth shone. Did he always have these deep lines in his cheeks? But he is much younger than Daedalus. He still loves Phaedra. He plays with her. But of course, she is a child. I hate him.

Soon I shall take a consort. Minos will not live forever.

DAEDALUS:

A strange question from her: "Can the Wind be my father?" As if she were a child again. As if she had not read, had not argued. Is she testing me? I did not smile but, as if it were a reasonable question, explained that the ancients had not known about paternity, which accounts for the legends. But she must know this. Else why the need for a consort in the old religion?

Perhaps she knows and does not know. For all her sharpness she is still immersed in the old magic, tales and chants and incantations, for hours every day. Even if it is only surface, as her abrupt confession suggests, it must have a hold on her, after that childhood in the hands of the old priestess, Merope. And what they made her do when the queen was dying! What darkness. Like my grandfather's days, or worse.

ARIADNE:

Only Korkyne does not use me. She is not afraid of me now, even though she must know I could destroy her at any moment. Why is she not afraid? Does she already feel destroyed? Minos says he purchased her in a group of women slaves from a Cypriot sea captain who had taken them from pirates in a battle north of Oeta. The other women are dispersed about the ports; a few of them were brought all the way back to Knossos, but none except Korkyne is here now. I don't know whether or not to believe this story. I was told she did not know our language, yet she seems to have no trouble understanding me. It's true that she does not read or write, or at any rate, I have never seen her do it. There is much about Korkyne that is mystery.

She comes to the ceremony, stands way in the back in a corner, closes her eyes, hands holding her robes, does not move. Perhaps she is praying, but there is no sound or movement in it. She does the same thing at night in my room after she has prepared my bed, until I tell her to go. Then she puts out all but one small lamp and lies down on her palette in my antechamber. There is never any brusqueness in her movements; even when she moves quickly, it is smooth as if her body were all of a piece, inhabited fully. (Unlike me. I go too fast, always too fast.) There is no difference between her life and her ceremony. It is as if she worships in every act.

But I cannot bear to stay with her during the daylight hours. All that sweet quiet turns into a dreary haze that stifles me, as if the incense of the sacrifice wove through my head and heavy images pulled me down. When the sun grows bright, I send her away. I never let her come into the classroom or wherever else I go with Daedalus—to the ports to inspect new shipments of cedar and gold, or to the artisans' shops to see how the work is progressing on the bronze bowls for export. Ships, arms, buildings, artifacts of fine construction, these are the pride of Knossos and its wealth. What does it matter that the grain is not as plentiful as it was? Our ships can bring it in from the Cyclades. Or wherever. If we cannot grow enough barley, we'll take it from others, that's all. Our people must not be hungry. We cannot allow it.

A ruler must know such things, not leave it to someone else. That was my mother's mistake. I shall understand it all. And control it. I will not need Minos forever.

My days seethe with business. I spend less time reading and thinking and more time out in the world, seeing to the welfare of my city. But at night, when the Raging Ones rise and come at me like dead leaves, I reach for Korkyne.

# III

*The hills danced with them;*
*And the wild beasts; was nothing stood unmoved.*

EURIPEDES, The Bacchanals

# 1

The spring that I was sixteen Icarus came back. I saw him first in a courtyard at the end of a long corridor, laughing with Daedalus, his bright hair shining in the sun. I ran toward him like a child. But then I stopped. He had grown to look like the first consort on the wall in the west gallery. No, he was more beautiful than that. He was like waves tumbling, like a barley field, like young roebucks leaping over rocks. I stopped, mute as Korkyne.

When he saw me, his lips moved as if he spoke, but I could not hear for the dove songs in my ears. When he came toward me, lilies lifted up on tall stems and gracefully uncurled, and anemones burst, their petals falling like rain. I don't remember a word of what we said, only the gleaming dust motes above us and the dancers on the walls of the courtyard who seemed to twirl out of the plaster.

Then he did a thing that seemed very strange, because we had been children together. He raised his hand to his forehead in the old gesture of worship and spoke those words that only a *kourete* knows. I looked around. We were alone. Daedalus was far off down the corridor, walking away. So I spoke the words also. He bowed and I kissed his hair, as the ritual requires.

We walked for hours that afternoon through the shimmering palace. The old red corridors closed down around us like arms. In the galleries the bull dancers leaped in joy and the cup bearers moved so solemnly that I cried. The birds and monkeys had grown bright and curious. The cat stalking a pheasant quivered with life.

Icarus kept saying, "Yes, there it is! And there! How I've missed it all, missed you all!" We ran through the halls like children to Phaedra's quarters. Icarus tossed her in the air. "She is like you were, Ariadne!" Phaedra laughed and shouted with us. I felt such love for her then. I kissed her and tried to hold her, but she ran from me to Icarus. He scolded and told her to kiss me too and she did, but reluctantly. I could see that my long neglect of her would not easily be forgotten. But Icarus made all sadness disappear, even Phaedra's tears when we left her, whispering that he had a present for her that he would bring when the boats were unloaded.

He wanted to see everything. He was greedy to find the absent years, he said, all the things that had happened while he was gone. That brought down the old gloom, and in the darkness of the west corridor, among the huge *pithoi* of grain and oil and honey, we wept for Merope and my mother and for Icarus' mother too, whom I had hardly known and had never thought of in all these years, though it hurt me to see how he had suffered for her. I started to tell him about Tauros and the infant, but just then one of the potters came by carrying a spouted jar with palm leaves and tulips in red and black, very thin and finely made. Icarus asked to hold it and curved his palms about it with tenderness. "It is all so much better here. Here people still know the old true ways of doing." I agreed with everything he said as if I had never thought of anything else.

In the shops the silver cups and golden bowls delighted him, and most of all, an ivory bull leaper being carved by an old man with trembling hands, who spoke to him in a guarded way about his mother. "This is a thing I can do well," said Icarus, rubbing his fingers along the smooth figure. "I will show you, Ariadne. I will make something for you." I laughed and laughed. Everything looked beautiful to me, cups, bull leapers, olives, beans, pigs.

We walked all afternoon, into the market, down to the docks where the ships were coming in loaded with logs and gold, through the orchards and the vineyards, past fields of pigs and cattle, past the arena of the bull dance, into the hills where the olive trees closed above us as if to protect and the bees' song was a steady whisper from the Goddess.

I must have smiled the whole time. When I got back to my quarters, my face felt stiff. I rubbed it and smiled some more as I told Korkyne about Icarus. I had never talked to her so much. She nodded and smiled in reply, helped me bathe, rubbed soft unguents on my skin. The drink she brought was as sweet and fresh as an offering.

Now I was amazed at what a pleasant life was led in the palace. The corridors and great halls seemed suddenly populated with charming people hurrying to banquets, processions, celebrations. Great carved ebony tables were laid with silver platters heaped with fruits, cheese, grains, vegetables, crisp barley bread savory with herbs, sea food, olives, honey. From golden cups embossed with lovely scenes of priestesses whirling in worship and the boy god descending to them, we drank sweet mead and sometimes grape wine, though Icarus would have none of that.

The ladies of the court were magnificent in their tight embroidered bodices and skirts with flounces and pleats bordered with gold rosettes, their ropes of glass beads, earrings, and huge tiaras encrusted with amethysts and carnelian (how was it I had not noticed?), their hair waved and shining, descending to a point in the back, tight dancing curls just in front of each ear, their eyes painted delicately with kohl to seem larger and more luminous.

I was in a frenzy to think how I had neglected all this. I called in artisans of all kinds and ordered dresses and jewels. They were charming men, silversmiths and weavers with smooth, lithe bodies and strong hands. And the men of the court, how pleasant they were to look at in their tight cinched golden belts and colorful loincloths, brown thighs and arms shining with bracelets.

But none of them was half so beautiful as Icarus. Every morning we met in the fragrant gardens of the main courtyard or at the West Porch under the old frescoes of the bull dancers or in the corridor of the Procession of Youths and Maidens bringing offerings to the Goddess. Whatever place we met gleamed with love, even the classroom where I went less and less frequently and where Daedalus' cold eyes followed us about and looked through us sometimes as though we were only a mirage. Always when we met, if we were alone, Icarus would greet me with the gesture of worship and speak the sacred words, so that I began again to feel the presence of the Goddess.

For Phaedra he had brought bracelets and pendants and a signet ring showing a mischievous little demon, with a grin and curved horns, his hands raised in surprise. My presents were more solemn. A votive double axe of solid gold and a serpentine *rhyton* in the form of a bull's head, with horns of gilded wood, rock crystal eyes, and a muzzle of shell. But the best present was still unfinished, he said. It was the one he worked on when he disappeared for hours in the afternoons, was probably of ivory, he hinted, like the bull dancer we had seen the old man carving. But it was much better than that. Not that the carving was finer, but it was more—he could not find words.

I found them, I thought, in an old poem from Sumer:

> *Lion, let me fondle you,*
> *My embrace is sweeter than mead;*
> *In my bed-chamber, flower-filled,*
> *Let me enjoy your manly beauty.*
> *Consort, let me caress you.*

It was an Egyptian translation of the ancient language. I found words for it in our own and brought them to Daedalus for correction. His face was clay. Only his eyes darted about, checking the manuscript, then my translation. He made a few changes, then got up heavily as though the Awesome Ones dragged him downward. He walked to the door and looked out silently into the courtyard. Against the bright background I could see only his monstrous silhouette. He spoke softly, but with great distinctness, quoting a phrase from the same leaflet of papyrus, another page, another mood: "Flatter a young man, he'll give you anything. Throw a scrap to a dog, he'll wag his tail."

It was as though he had spat into a sacred libation. I snatched my papers and ran from the room.

I did not give the poem to Icarus at once. We walked past the orchards. In the air was the scent of blooming. Here and there among the sparse leaves were blossoms. A few grain sprouts jutted upward out of the dry ground. "A sign that the Awesome Ones have been appeased," said Icarus. He questioned me about the purification rites of the last Anthesteria. My tongue stumbled as I replied. His faith was so deep, I could not tell him how I had spun through the ritual on the edges of my mind, while thinking of something else.

He had brought his lyre. When we entered the olive grove, we stopped. I lay down on the warm ground and looked up through the twisted branches to the blue sky. He sat at my side and played. Then he sang. The wind breathed through him, all the dead souls crying, and his voice turned them sweet as honey and seeds in the purest offering. He put down the lyre and lay beside me. I whispered him the poem then, sun all around and covering us, kissed his eyes and his hair, he mine, and our hands met and our tongues. Like waves on the shore, our pulse, slapping and breaking on the shore. I wondered why he cried, lying there beside me, upon me, as if his soul were pouring out upon the ground. I felt free, though I seemed also to be dying, something sweeping me along, sending messages to me or ahead of me that I could not understand.

We prayed. I think it was a prayer, though whether it came to us or from us, I could not tell. I wanted to drink his tears.

# 2

DAEDALUS:

I HAD THOUGHT HE would be safe by now, a grown man with some knowledge of women, rulers. He's traveled and studied, but what for? She plays with him as with a pet fawn, and he runs leaping about her feet. There's no talking to him. He looks at me with those soft eyes, as if forgiving me my blasphemy. Damn all deities! I sent my only son away to save him from the stench of the old religion and he's come back a bigger believer than any here. I've spawned a fool.

Yet he's not entirely an idiot. If only I could talk to him, but he doesn't trust me, that's clear. I came on too heavily with my ideas, I suppose. I've seen it happen over and over. You turn the young away from you that way, but I thought I'd controlled it. I did control it, damn it. No emotion in my letters, no strong blood push, just cold reason to appeal to the best, highest qualities of the mind. I know how to use my head. I can teach if I can do anything—lead the way through the intricate argument, enlighten, tear through the old fog to the sharp skeleton of form—I've done it time and again. Talos was an apt pupil, one of the best until—and Ariadne, there's my masterpiece. They'd almost destroyed her, sent her whirling back into ancient chaos, and I retrieved her better than any hawk, made her mind work like a skilled craftsman. Damn her, what's in her mind now, what plan, why does she pick my son to use? Minos' daughter, after all—some malice against me must move her; she'll destroy the boy if she can to get at me, but why? I'd thought we'd come together in an understanding. For years there's been no sign of that child-hate the old woman taught her. For years now she's been all clear and eager, fine-tuned, rising like an obelisk out of a swamp—where's it all gone to? I loved the girl

like my finest ivories, and she turns on me and hits my weakest
. . . or is she all mindless now, sunk again in the old hog wallow?
There's no talking to her; she avoids me, not even a look; twines
around him like a vine, like a viper, rather, making some soft
sound like a low wind around the angle of a wall, and he's
entranced, possessed like a *kourete*. Next thing he'll be in the
worship, in the procession; is that what she has in mind for him?
She must have a thought in mind—you don't go backwards into the
darkness once you've learned how to reason, measure, build. I'll
make her talk to me, damn her . . .

And Minos watches, does nothing to interfere. It suits some plan
of his, no doubt, but he'll not talk to me of it, arrogant brute . . .

ARIADNE:

Every morning we walk through the spring, every morning we
come together like the sky and the earth blending, every night he
comes to my quarters and Korkyne lets him in and goes out to pray
in the antechamber.

There is a humming in the air now always as if thousands of bees
are speaking. Not just outside in the apiary, but all over, wherever
I go. Right now here in my room, I feel the humming. I had a
dream once that I told my mother. How did it go? There were bees
and I told her they spoke to me. That was not true, I made that up,
but now they are speaking. I will tell Icarus. He understands
everything, even Korkyne.

We have discovered that she can write a language that he knows.
Last night, before she left us, he used a word he had learned from an
old slave in Arcadia, and Korkyne began to make moaning sounds
and became very excited. Dashed to my chest and got lime bark and
brush and began to write. A strange script I couldn't make out at
all, but Icarus could! He stumbled through it and she nodded,
laughing with tears streaming from her eyes. It was just a simple
question, Icarus said. "Do you understand this language?" Something like that. And he shouted, "Yes!" or whatever the equivalent
is, and she cried some more. Then she grabbed the bark again and
wrote, but he could not make it out, so she wrote in slow large

strokes, "I will write it more carefully," took the bark and left. I think she knew we wanted each other more than we wanted to learn her story. She sees that we cannot stay apart long. It feels as though the earth had broken into parts when he leaves, but then he comes and we heal it. All night we lie close and move with the mother's pulse. He is strong and solemn. Always he greets me with the sign of reverence. Sometimes he weeps. I do too. I did not know there would be pain in love.

DAEDALUS:

I'm tired of it. Seems a man should have a chance to work on what he can do best without this constant demand for services. Ships are all he has on mind. Cease work on Ariadne's temple. Cease work even on the plans for his little palace, and build ships that can endure the waves of the outer seas that skirt the ends of the earth. Minos is mad for sea journeys. Poseidon's son, they call him. But it's gold he's after. He's heard of new mines open for the taking, far to the west somewhere, must have them, will try at all costs. The men shy at it, I hear. And with good reason, in my judgment, though it's monsters they fear. But Minos prevails, and so I'm shipbuilding again while in my head stand pillars instead of masts. Minos will go with them on this new journey, he says, to give courage and direction. A foolish move, I think. The country's still disturbed by drought. Hunger in the mountain villages, much murmuring.

If I had power, I could handle it better, it seems to me. Hungry people are dangerous. Anyone might kill for food. Unless you want to starve them outright, you've got to provide it or the night raids start. Aegeus taught me that. And it's the king himself who has to dicker with the complainers, mollify them, send in a caravan or two of supplies. Console. Promise.

But Minos has turned it all over to this lieutenant, Pandareos; thinks he can handle it, which he will, no doubt, like a brute, all sword and club, and there'll be trouble in the mountains again. I said as much or tried to when Minos came with the order for ships, but there's something about kingship that dizzies the mind. He laughed at my fears; said there were supplies for years in the city and the mountain folk would wait patiently enough, knew what would happen to them if they didn't, and would cheer his return with prayers and ceremonies befitting Zeus himself. Gold was what the land needs, and slaves; he'd bring them. Meanwhile Pandareos would keep things in hand here at home. Minos was never wise, but when he was younger he had judgment in office. It's slipping, has slipped into tyranny. He needs a counsellor at hand, not a butcher.

Well, at least he didn't mention my foolish son; cares nothing for that, or seems not to, though he certainly knows about it; there's no secrecy in the young fools. Maybe he thinks it will lessen Ariadne in the eyes of the people, giving herself to a half-Athenian. It's a distraction, that's certain. She's forgotten that Minos exists, or the people, or anyone in the world beside that idiot, my son. And he's as bad. Damn, but it makes me writhe. All that youth and energy tossed down the old ditch. Blind, blind. And the only thing good in it—the temple she thought she wanted, got Icarus to study, used months of my life and eyes to plan—now, in the middle of it, she abandons it, too, cares nothing for Minos' order to shift to ships, stares as if sunk again into a trance, fondles Icarus, looks with calf eyes, smiles. He, too. Stares, smiles, fondles. She's grown beautiful suddenly, I'll say that. Her mother all over. Love! Well, it's a trance I can't really begrudge them, but it won't last. And it's dangerous to dandle a queen, especially here. What will happen to Icarus when her trance lifts? If only I can get him away again.

ARIADNE:

In the old ceremonies, there is no wine and no flesh. These are not clean; the Goddess is against them. Korkyne writes it, and Icarus says, yes, this is what he has learned, too. It has changed here, and even more elsewhere. That is why the Goddess is angry and withholds the fruit and grain. Korkyne is writing out the ritual for the festival of first fruits, the Thargelia. They are both distressed that a man should see this, but only Icarus can understand her script. So Korkyne says it will be all right, since he is a *kourete* (his father doesn't know this), but she makes him burn the lime bark after I have memorized the lines. She doesn't seem to know that I am writing them down again to make sure of them.

First fasting for purification. Then the carrying of the olive branches, twined with the wool of an ewe lamb, to every door. (But that is the same as we do.) Then, in the grove at dawn, the pouring of the libations. No wine. Only spring water and honey. Then the offering of seeds. No, I have it mixed up. I shall have to ask her again. She is so earnest, and Icarus says, yes, it must be that way. So I shall do it. Perhaps the Goddess will really be with me again.

DAEDALUS:

Weapons are what he wants now. Get that metal the Hittites use. Quickly, more spears, daggers. Forget the decoration, just make them work. It's Pandareos' influence. He's fresh from Thrace. Has been charging up and down the coast, ravaging and laying waste, according to his own boast, as if it were a thing good in itself. What's Minos want with so blatant a pirate? He's taken to him as if he were his own son. Maybe he is. Minos has planted many seeds. But this one is no prize. He's aping the Athenians, the worst element. No regard for beauty in construction. All battle axe. But that's the way Minos is tending more and more. He'll end up being enslaved by his slaves, no doubt. It's happened before. And where will I go then? It may be time to think of that. Pandareos looks at me oddly sometimes. He's heard something in Athens, I suppose, that he thinks he can use to control me. That's his way. Well, I've leveled with Minos and he knows my worth, which is beyond the comprehension of his lieutenant. But who's ruling whom? And if Minos leaves, putting this bronze man in charge. . . . Protect the shores against invasion at all costs, he says. Well, there's some need to worry about that. Minos has been lording it so long. Hostages, slaves, loot. People get angry. Why doesn't he concentrate on the riches Crete has over all the western lands—the craft, the beauty. Oh, we could teach the world art. But it's all a waste. The old absorbed in killing, lording. And the young, the ones I'd counted on, floating backward into mindless darkness. Damn, if I didn't know it would end soon, I couldn't bear it.

ARIADNE:

He brought two presents this morning: an ivory image of the Goddess, so beautiful I have never seen the like. Not even Daedalus could do this. Icarus says it looks like me, but it is only his eyes that would see that. I shall keep it close for my most secret offerings.

The second present is a seal ring that I shall wear until I die. It is gold, and on it in the greatest detail are a young man and woman being led past the tree of eternal life to the Goddess. Above their heads are the butterflies of their souls. On each side are sacred lions attended by little priestesses. Ivy sprouts from the dead trunk of the tree to show that they will live forever. He has made one also for himself. We shall wear them always.

Icarus says love is stronger than death, is the way to the Goddess, is how the earth will flourish and only beauty shine, is how the Raging Ones will be laid to rest so that spirit and body blend in peace. I told him an old poem Merope taught me long ago:

> *The orchards are bright with fruit,*
> *The lion does not kill,*
> *The lamb is not snatched away by wolves,*
> *All rest together in the Mother's arms.*

That was the way it was here before the Goddess was forgotten, as in the oldest frescoes—no hunger, no suffering. We are preparing the ceremony in the ancient fashion. The souls must be resting. I no longer dream.

But in fact we dreamed constantly through the days and nights, with no vision of how the world went. Before long I knew that I was with child. Then, truly, I did feel the Goddess within me. When I told Icarus, he pulled me from our bed and we went together through the night to the Mound. Amidst the sound of little animals rustling away in the grass, we dedicated our child to the Goddess.

Minos was gone again, but I had no fear of his learning of my pregnancy. Every queen has a right to have a Virgin Child even without a sea journey to Dia. They would all know it was Icarus', but it would be called a Child of the Virgin, a God's Child, a son or daughter of Melichios or of the Wind, as I myself was called. It would not be Icarus' unless he were my consort, but I did not want that for him, now. I was back in the belief of the old religion. It was as if my talks with Daedalus had never happened. Even Pandareos and the other warriors moved like shadows behind the curtain of my faith.

We make our worlds. My world at that time was the Garden of the First Mother. Its only inhabitants were full of love. How simply one arrived there, I thought. All one had to do was to follow the oldest movements, with serenity in the mind and the hum of the harp sounding the chord of creation. And the Great Mother's touch would become a caress, the rain would come, the ground would stir. Love would be manifest in dew, web, and wing. The wind would breathe through death, the fire of the altar would be steady, and all would bow to the revealed, the simple truth.

I was swept into the faith like a leaf in a mountain torrent, feeling the Goddess in my fingers, in my womb. Minos' soldiers and all the rich, thoughtless people of the court did meaningless dances on the edge of nothingness. I watched them, when I remembered, in silence, sure of their certain end. Icarus had no doubt of it, and Korkyne with him. I agreed, I agreed. If there was any doubt in me, any remnant of the skepticism of just a few months before, I brushed it away as smoothly as one brushes the ashes from an altar. I had too much to do to think about it. The ceremonies had to be purified, the old ritual taught to all the participants. And when the child within me began to stir, the God's child, connecting me with the First Mother, I had no will not to believe. But I did not go near Daedalus.

The first harvest festival came and we fasted for three days as in the ancient time. When all had been purified, I made the offerings of honey and oil. No animals were sacrificed. Some of the people remembered that this was the way it had been done of old, but others complained about the changes. Icarus spoke to them at length and they seemed to be persuaded.

When the Thesmophoria came, the autumn festival of sowing, they were readier to accept the old ways. When, after the planting of the seeds, I went into the Great Hall and declared all prisoners released and all law courts closed, they applauded. I spoke the words of the Thrice Plougher: honor thy mother, rejoice the Goddess with the fruits of the earth, do not injure animals. The people sighed and nodded. Pandareos stood with sullen face but said nothing. On the final day, I went to the Mound and emptied one vessel toward the east and one toward the west. I cried to the sky, "Rain," and to the earth, "Be fruitful." There was dancing in the fields, and in the arena even the bull leapers shouted and laughed. Only Pandareos and the metal men he kept near him were silent. Daedalus was nowhere to be seen.

In the winter, on a cold bright day, I gave birth to my child. It was an easy birth. Korkyne attended, showing me how to move to allow the child to come and setting up a shield of prayer, love, and comfort that almost blotted out the shrieks of Pasiphae. The touch of the baby's sticky skin against my breast and the tiny, tiny hands healed all. I called him Deucalion, my Virgin Child. When I showed him on the balcony, all the people cried out. Even Pandareos moved his lips.

# 3

WHAT WAS THE FIRST SIGN of a tear in the shield? The stench of pitch on my doorway smeared there by Korkyne to catch the Evil Ones? Icarus' indrawn face as he translated Korkyne's script? Or was it those lines I read as the infant tugged at my nipple? "The consort reigns for a day each year and dies at its close, his blood sprinkled for fructification of fields and crops." At that, the child seemed to fall apart even as the milk flowed from my body into his. I looked through tiny fingers into bare bone. I have never forgotten that moment. I pushed the lime bark script away from me with such force that it fell to the tile and they both turned on me their soft fatuous eyes, doglike and worshipping. I felt cold as stone. Had it not been for the nursing infant, I would have run outside. I did stand and start to go, but the child cried for more milk, Icarus bent to pick up the script, Korkyne moved my chair to another spot (warmer, I knew she was thinking, out of the breath of the Raging One), and the moment passed. A cold draft shook the buckthorn over the arch. I pulled a white woolen shawl over the baby and quieted him with milk.

Preparations were being made for the spring festival, the Anthesteria. Korkyne was writing out the ritual, the ancient pure rites she had learned in her own country before her capture. We knew her story now. She had been a queen and a priestess. Her sanctuary had been invaded, her women ravaged, enslaved, she herself bound and raped on her own altar. They had chained her naked in the market place, and when she had broken the shamed silence crying for the Goddess to appear, her people rose with stones and fists against the spears. Then had come the knife at her tongue, the blood rushing backward into her throat, and blows against her ears so that she had sunk into a long silence, hearing nothing, only watching, bound and mute, as the dead were heaped in mounds and left unburied; chained to the mast of a ship as the seamen raped her priestesses again and again until they died and were thrown to sharks; as they brought in other women who stared at her with wild frightened looks and were raped over and over in her presence, yes in front of her eyes, for if she closed them, the knife came to her lids and the writhing mouths spat at her.

At last she was tossed into a dark box for a long while. All blackness stood about her then, full of the whispers of the Awesome Ones. She had thought it was death and was glad. But they dragged her out again to be shackled to the mast while they brought in new captives, little girls this time, tiny hands beating against the bronze blades until they were severed. Back to the darkness. Dragged again to the mast. Over and over, the darkness creeping into her eyes, she welcoming it, hearing the solace of the Benevolent Ones. But they would not let her die, forced a thick liquid into her wounded mouth, held her nostrils until she fainted and must have swallowed. After that a long darkness and then a change. Two eunuchs pulled her from the box, bathed her, dressed her in a long white garment, chained her arms with gold, and brought her to a rich room covered with furs, where other men appeared with black hair and cinched waists (Cretans? we wondered) and looked long at her, talked between them (she still could hear nothing), took gold seals from a pouch, and gave them to the eunuchs, who left. Then, covering the doorway with a heavy fur and putting out the lamp as if afraid of being seen, they had chained her to the floor and raped her again and again until the darkness had come for her once more.

She woke in another ship among many other women. She saw them whispering to each other when the men were gone, but she could hear nothing. One was heavy with child, her great belly lined with blue veins. They kept her naked, refusing even the light cloth they had given the rest as shelter from the cold wind. When the men came to take a woman, they would stop to look at the gleaming belly, prick at it lightly with their daggers, or squeeze it until the woman's face sagged out of grimace into faint. When at last she went into labor, no one could help, all hands chained to the floor. The men came with cooked grain, poured it into unwilling mouths, and stopped a while to watch her twist and shudder. At last it was night, and one of them came back, a young man with a deep red scar slashing his chest. He crawled in silently, dagger drawn, freed one of the other women and directed her to help the birth, threw down his cloak for covering, but held his dagger at the point and kept looking about in the almost-darkness to see whether someone else was coming.

The baby came first, still born, the cord wrapped tightly about its neck. The mother looked and turned away. The woman who had helped her chewed the cord in two with her teeth, then suddenly snatched the child and threw herself and the infant into the sea. That brought down other men with torches and swords swinging. They killed the scarred man first, slicing his throat and throwing him among the women. Then they pronged the mother, but she was already dead. One woman's hand was torn off when they dragged her away without first freeing her from her chains. Her mouth was moving as if she were shouting at them. They took a long spear and married her to it, the tip of it showing through her back.

At this point, Korkyne broke off her writing and would give us no more of her story, asked for her scripts back, and destroyed them. But Icarus had already translated them for me and they were burned into my memory. We guessed at the rest of her story, the coming of Minos, the bringing of her with other slaves to Crete for sale and gift, and my choosing her. What more had she suffered? When had she regained her hearing? Had she given birth to a living child and killed it, as the rumor went? We were afraid to ask. There were rumors also that all the men who had raped her had died and that she had become an object of horror to the others, even Minos staying away from her, though her beauty made her shine out of the group of women like a rightful queen. They said she was full of sickness, that demons dwelt in her womb. I had not heard this when I chose her, but Minos must have known it all. Why had he allowed me to have her? Had he hoped she might make me ill?

"Tell her she's safe here," I said to Icarus (pushing away the shadows that dangled across my eyes).

Korkyne as I knew her was gentle and whole. The infant and I flourished under her care. Icarus spoke of her with reverence, said she was wise beyond his dreaming, that she knew truths I would need to know. I must learn them at once as he translated, in case the scripts were destroyed and he were not here to help her. He spoke as if he were going away. I refused to listen. I pulled his hair and ran to hide. But he was in a solemn mood and would not play. He was transcribing the ritual for me. I peeped over his shoulder. "Two baskets, one containing evil, one good; one containing nothing, and one containing *sacra,* which is life . . ." Suddenly he covered the words with his hand.

"I should not be knowing this," he said.

I was annoyed. "No one else can understand Korkyne."

"You will, soon." He stared out into the courtyard.

It was true. I was studying Korkyne's script and she mine. Already we could get along without Icarus much of the time. I knew I should reassure him, but I was impatient. The day was cold and bright. I felt like running over the rocks, lithe as a child again. "Let's go down to the sea and watch the ships unloading," I said.

He turned suddenly and bowed, hand to his forehead in the ancient manner, and spoke the words of worship, the *kourete* words. I felt a flash of anger. It was the old pull downward, Merope, Lyca, all that soft rapt devotion hanging upon me like stones. I left him bowing and went out to the balcony. The sun blazed through the cold air, struck snow on Iyttos, and shone like a lamp, but the brown humps in the foreground were parched and dull.

When I returned to my room, he was gone. I looked for him in Korkyne's chamber where she played with the baby, but when I asked her about him, she only looked at me in a sad mysterious way that made me feel guilty. I was angry with her for that. I wanted to snatch away the child and take him out into the sunlight, but there was something about her face that stopped me: not a scar—the skin was flawless, not even the slight indentation of her cheek falling inward to the empty mouth—something not\physical, yet tangible as rock, the mask of the victim. I fled outside.

All Knossos seethed before me, colors flashing, voices sharp, full of life. I called for a litter and ordered the bearers to take me down to the ships. I could not stand the slowness of their pace; shouted until they ran and stumbled; jumped out and ran ahead of them, feeling the rocks sharp against my sandals; grew impatient with their humble, eager attempts to stay at my side; and sent them home, taking first from the shortest one a cloak that covered me down to the ground, head and all like a slave, hiding my dress and jewels. I pushed back my hair and wiped the kohl from my eyes. A woman noticed and retreated into a doorway. The litter bearers hesitated to leave, but I waved them away in fury and ran quickly around corners so that they would not be able to follow.

I walked more slowly then, keeping the rhythm of the crowd. Men carrying huge baskets of wool. Women driving asses heavily loaded with pots. A silversmith I knew well from his work on my bracelets. I pulled a corner of my cloak over my face as he strode quickly by, oblivious to my presence. The game began to fascinate me. I forgot about Icarus, Korkyne, even my baby. I blended myself into the people, became just one moving part of many, and felt a surge of relief as though nothing more depended upon me. Soon I noticed that occasionally someone passing by would stare at my feet and then look upward, questioning. My sandals jutted out from under the cloak as I walked, and the jewels caught fire in the sunlight. It was difficult to keep the cloak folded over the gold leaf on my skirt. I stopped and leaned against the wall of a house. There seemed to be someone staring at my back. I turned and looked through a window straight into the face of a woman. She pulled hastily away into the dark interior.

I found the door and knocked. No answer at first. Frightened, perhaps. Maybe she had seen my dress. I knocked again, and this time she opened the door a crack and peered out. I pushed in against her half-hearted resistance. The room was tiny and dark, the only light from that one small window. It was almost bare, with only a ragged pallet on the floor and lying on it a tumble of dirty children, frozen in the midst of play, their eyes enormous in the dim light. The woman trembled visibly. I asked her whether I could buy a skirt and some shoes. Alas, she had only what she was wearing. "Let's trade then," I said, and threw the cloak down in a heap. At the sight of my dress, she fell down and bowed her head to the floor. Irritably, I took off my clothes and threw them to the children, but the woman was half-dead with fright. I pulled her to her feet and started unfastening her skirt. Then she came alive, as if catching on to the game, and quickly disrobed. I put on her clothing, grabbed the cloak, and left while she was still bowing. The children were leaping about and crying as they fingered the embroidery of my skirt. As I went out the door, I saw the sharpness of their thin faces.

Back in the street, I felt safe from discovery in the dirty skirt and heavy shoes. The woman would be too busy prying jewels from their settings to notice which way I had gone, and she had no reason, in any case, to pursue. I could smell the sea. A long ship was at anchor and men were unloading cedar logs. The fragrance of the wood surrounded me. I leaned against a mooring, feeling the movement in the pile as it creaked back and forth in the thrust of the waves. No one looked at me, except for one sailor, sweat running down his naked chest as he climbed back to the ship. His eyes ran appraisingly across my face, stopped just a breath, and moved on. It made me think of Icarus, and a pain settled into me like heavy anchors settling into the sea. I started back to the palace. Suddenly, as I passed the log pile, another man grabbed my cloak. I ripped it away, but not before he had brushed his hands roughly across my breast. I heard him laughing as I ran.

Now it seemed to me that the crowd in the street had been transformed. They had heavy threatening faces, twisted backs, gnarled hands. They all seemed to be cripples and beggars, their dark filthy clothes rubbing against me as I fled.

At the palace, the guards looked at me strangely as I hurried down corridors and through halls. I could not find Icarus. Korkyne gasped at my clothes and would not let me come near the child until I had bathed and changed. Icarus did not come even when I sent servants to find him. Finally a note arrived. He was leaving for the mountains to visit the shrine of his mother. Would I bless him and let him go at once? I ran all the way back with the messenger. He was with his father, but I embraced him as if we were alone. And then he bowed, in front of Daedalus! I whispered him the words and kissed his hair. I walked with him to the edge of the city, talking little, holding his arm against me. His face was strange, as though he had decided some secret sad thing. But he kissed me and turned back waving again and again until he was out of sight.

Icarus had promised to return in two days. On the fourth day he was still gone. I went to Daedalus. He was examining a gold seal pendant, engraved with a flat-headed minotaur eating its own hand. When he saw me, he started to chatter about it as if that were what I had come to hear, as if I were a visitor to Crete, knowing nothing:

"The craftsmanship is exquisite, in the glorious tradition of the Cretans, envied by all of us late-comers. Note the delicacy of this engraving. It's certainly from the finest period. A masterpiece. Too bad the name of the master is lost to us. The creator lost in the blind past, as well as the blind present. But no doubt it was a woman. Right, Ariadne? A priestess, continuing the work of the Divine Mother. Blindly creating, as we all blindly create, tools in the hand of a Great Engraver, fashioning not what we will, but what is willed through us."

"Why isn't Icarus back?" I said.

He motioned for me to come with him into the sunlight at the doorway. "Note the perfection of the circle," he said. "It's not meant to be a ring, though, unless for an infant queen. It's too small even for your finger. But you know better than I. Wasn't it meant for dangling on a golden chain, as puppets dangle on the chains of the Great Puppeteer, thinking that the dance is of their own making? Twirling and bowing in an ecstasy of the spirit that in reality may be only the absentminded twitch of a finger, a careless gesture, without thought or meaning?"

He pulled me out onto his balcony. "Tell me, my queen," he said. It was not the voice of my old tutor. It was unctuous, bitter. "Instruct an ignorant suppliant concerning the nature of the minotaur. He's a lesser creature, I know that. A mere consort. Your old nurse would not have crushed him had he come from my hands. Or would she?"

I tried to go, but he held me.

"Why is he half-bull? Is it the prank of a Jester? Does the Mother amuse Herself? That's it, isn't it? Why else fashion a man who cannot escape the beast?" He laughed loudly, but there was no joy in it. Once again I watched as he limped into the shadows of his room and out again.

Suddenly he held the seal up close before my eyes. "Look at the horns," he whispered. "The queen has given him power!" He looked at me until I thought he would never stop looking. "The horns are a queen's birthright, Ariadne. This man has forgotten that. Shouldn't she have killed him? Or is that what is happening now?"

He turned away and leaned upon the bannister, looking out toward the mountain. But presently he was back again, waving the pendant in front of my eyes, talking, talking. "This bull man is enchanted, Ariadne. He dreams of a new state, of honor, of all the trappings of majesty. He tries on the horns of power you have given him, and they fit, he thinks. They must be his natural attributes. But oh, how can he keep them? Poor fellow, he can't. Hasn't the right to inherit nor the brains to maneuver. See that flat head? Sliced straight across the top. That's lack of intellect. *Mind*, Ariadne! Transmuting dung to golden seals to empires. For all his muscles, this fellow's power is nothing, is dissipated, washing back to the old wallow, all dung. Remember, Ptah looked upon the primeval waters and *in his mind*, he saw the earth and formed it with a Word. But this fellow lost it, couldn't use it. Slid into the dungheap, washed away. Suffers. See how he eats his hand? No use. Brains aren't there. Let him go." He threw the pendant on a table.

"Ptah's world leaves out love," I said.

Daedalus' eyes were like his carving tools. "There is a quality in dung that makes one particle cling to another for the sake of producing more dung. When that is accomplished, the quality vanishes."

"Did you send him away?"

"I?" He laughed sharply. "The Mother has taken him."

"Which shrine did he go to? Where is it?"

"Beyond reach."

"Didn't he tell you when he would come back?"

"Oh, if he did not tell *you* . . ."

"Will he come back?" I asked.

Daedalus was silent, looking closely again at the little seal.

# 4

A WHISPERING WOKE ME in the dead of night. The lamp in the antechamber threw huge trembling shadows on the wall. It was cold. I pulled a robe around me and crept out. Icarus was back, talking to Korkyne in her language, faster than I could follow, punctuating his words with harsh, rapid movements. His clothes were torn and filthy, his face and hands scored with fresh wounds. He bowed when he saw me. They both bowed and tears came running down their cheeks. When I tried to embrace him, he moved away. We must not touch each other, he said, we must purify ourselves so that at the Anthesteria . . .

But before that there was something I must know. His face was haggard in the flickering light, lined as if he had aged twenty years instead of twenty days. My hands went to touch him almost without my knowing, but he moved away. And then the ghastly tale came shaking from his lips. The shrine at the tomb of his mother had been desecrated, all the priestesses killed or carried off. Even the Sibyl, the ancient mystic crone (was it the same one I had seen?), had been murdered. And through the mountains ran bands of women—priestesses, matrons, even young girls—driven mad by some new potion, some substance, brought from far away, from Thrace, perhaps (but Korkyne shook her head). It was hard to learn how it had started, but some said (he looked in the corridor to see that no one was near) Pandareos! And he had found such a band of women, or, rather, they had found him, as he lay sleeping, had recognized him as a *kourete* from the gypsum daubed on his face when he went to pray at his mother's shrine, had allowed him to come with them—no, had made him come, carried daggers with which they cut him and themselves, licking the blood afterwards in some distorted ritual. When he refused wine, they had given him what he had thought was pure water but what must have contained this drug. It sent him down into nightmare, trees exploding, the mountainside opening up like a wound and demons emerging, dead souls raging. He thought he saw his mother, frenzied, uncouth, babbling, and he crawled toward her like a worm until the sky came down and took him up so that he was flying, a transformation of worm to winged man flying upward against the sun, the heat blinding and burning until, charred and lifeless, he plummeted straight downward into the sea and was no more. Nothingness stood round him like a ring of faceless ghosts for what must have been days.

When he woke at last to sunlight, he was lying on a bed of leaves, and an old woman was nursing him furtively, creeping out of the bushes to wipe his wounds and to bring him milk and honey, looking about her as if pursued, darting away, and then creeping back, all without a word, though he questioned her. But at last when he was able to stand, she led him down a steep path to a small hut where a group of mountain people had gathered, women and men, pious people who knew who he was, who wished to send through him a prayer to the Great Mother; yes, that's you, Ariadne. Purify the worship. Bring back the old faith. Give to the Great Goddess that which she has always demanded so that the rains will come and the barren earth will yield fruit and grain. Give to the Great Goddess that which she has always demanded so that the Evil Ones will be placated, so that the souls of the dead will no longer rise to madden the living. For there is famine and madness and death in the mountains, and in the parched forests the trees are dying, and the valleys are dust. Come out of the evil corruption of the court and walk among the people. And give to the Great Goddess that which she has always demanded so that the people may live.

They were both bowing. I alone stood cold as a pillar, the breaths of the dead rising through me, as though I were impaled upon their will.

We completed the preparations for the spring ceremony. Icarus appeared only in Korkyne's presence. He would not touch me, nor the child. We talked gravely without caresses as though there had never been anything more between us. I wanted him more than ever, would have tumbled him into bed at any hour, forgetting the rules of abstinence, but his manner reminded me—a certain delicacy in his walk as if he were conscious of the powers under the earth, the thinness of his face (he was fasting), the unbearable sweetness of his voice as he sang with the lyre. He seemed so vulnerable, I wanted to spread my arms over him. Still, he was full of energy and busy every moment, teaching the ritual to the other *kouretes* as I was teaching the women. Some of them welcomed the changes, remembering the old customs as their grandmothers had described them. But others murmured. I don't know whether Icarus noticed, he was so absorbed. They changed in front of him, also. His intense faith quieted them. His voice in song and prayer seemed to enchant them. All the same, when they were away from him, I heard protests.

A week before the holy day, he came for the last time. He must go with the other *kouretes* for the last purification, he said. They would go to a shrine and wait until the ceremonies began. Only one word. Here he moved with me to the balcony and spoke softly so that no one else could hear. "The Anthesteria is the holiest of days." I nodded, wondering why he needed to say that. He was looking at me intently. "This time," he said, "this year, in the ceremony, after the torches and the wheel of fire, at the moment of the Great Mother's entering into you, you must choose your consort." I shook my head. There was no way of delaying it, he insisted. I had had my Virgin Child and now I must choose a king from those who presented themselves. I was alarmed. Why had he not said this before? I had thought the choosing of the consort could be delayed for years. I protested loudly, but he stilled me with his glance as the others looked out at us. "It must be according to the old ritual," he whispered. I stood uncertainly. I wanted to scream the words that were whirling in me. Then he touched me just for a moment and left.

Anger raced through me. So even Icarus pulled strings and I must dance. This needed discussion. He hadn't mentioned it before, probably because he had known I would protest. I decided not to do it. Or if I did . . . I felt myself being pushed by multiple hands reaching out of the crowd. "Give to the Great Goddess that which she has always demanded." Well, if I did, I would not choose Icarus. My heart lightened at this thought. I would choose some foolish boy who was mad for martyrdom and treat him gently for a year, though I would not sleep with him; it would be a ritual marriage only. Icarus would be my real lover. And then, after the year was up, the poor lad could go to his chosen doom, and the people would be satisfied. But what if no one but Icarus came forth? I put the notion out of my mind and went in to nurse the child. Yet the thought kept coming back, and each time a colder shell grew around me.

I asked Korkyne about the ancient custom. I could read her language now, with difficulty, and she had learned much of our script. "Yes," came the answer. Her eyes avoided mine. She must have known that Icarus had already told me the rule. I gave her the child and left.

The dress and shoes I had taken from the poor woman on my journey in disguise were still in my chest. I had insisted upon keeping them, though Korkyne had been equally insistent about having them cleaned. I put them on and sent for the litter bearer whose cloak I had borrowed before. He was a short man, but strong. I decided to keep him walking at my side. I put several gold seal rings in a pouch and tied it to my belt.

The streets were more crowded than ever before. People seemed to have come from all over for the ceremonies. Perhaps they had heard of the changes. Perhaps they all knew of Icarus' visit to the shrine and the mad women. I searched faces and listened hard as I mingled with the crowd, but I heard little of interest. There was much wine in evidence, though, and I saw several groups of men lurching drunkenly. Suddenly I heard, clear as a bird's note,". . . now that Minos is back." It came from a group of sailors. There was a roar of laughter. I couldn't see which one had said it. I moved closer and waited. They were drinking from a leather flask, passing it from one to another and laughing heartily.

They were large brown men, with the full beards of those who had been on a long voyage. Their clothes smelled of tar and salt spray. I could not understand much of their slurred chatter. Suddenly one of them stood apart from the others, raised the flask high, and shouted something about "slave bitches," and there was a great bustle of shoves and laughter as they caromed into walls down the street. My servant was watching me.

"When did he return?" I asked.

"This morning."

"Is he at the palace?"

The man looked as though he wanted to run away. I gave him a small seal. He looked guilty. I could see that someone had sworn him to secrecy. But he took the seal. "He is purifying himself," he mumbled.

"Minos!" I was astonished. Did he mean to join the *kouretes?* Never before had he found it necessary to go through the long traditional rites of purification preceding the spring festival. All Crete, then, was joining us! Well, not all, I thought, as I studied the dangerous balance of the sailors in the distance. But a lively dance of ideas was starting up in my head and I felt much gayer than I had for weeks. Daedalus, master lore-monger, speaking of Sumer, had said, "Some kings dared to marry their own daughters when title to the throne needed renewal." It was the end of another Great Year. One hundred times the moon had come and gone, and Minos' term was expiring. Was he planning to ape the kings of Sumer?

I could no longer keep my attention on the people, my thoughts were spinning so. If Minos offered himself, I could choose him and carry out the ancient custom, which meant that he would die after one year. Or I could choose a boy and slight Minos publicly, decreasing his power in the eyes of the people. Or I could choose Icarus over him and follow Minos' own custom of ignoring the need for the king's death. He could not attack that, since he himself had instituted it and the people would probably accept it; they had had it so long. I twinged here. There was a fallacy in the reasoning, Daedalus would say. But again I brushed it aside.

I did not go out into the streets again. I was not fasting, because of the child, but I did follow the custom of seclusion and prayer, although my prayers were interrupted by plans. If Minos did this, then I would do that. I dreamed endless alternatives, felt a joy in doing it. It was like the old battle of the service when we fought to cut down each other's role. But every once in a while the thought of Icarus would stab into my exhilaration.

When the first evening of the Anthesteria arrived, I was in a solemn mood. I bathed in sacred water, put on my ceremonial dress of gold and jewels, covered it with a flowing white robe, and began the processional, carrying my lily scepter. From the steps of the palace all the way to the Sacred Mound, the path of the Great Mother was lined with people dressed in the clean white robes of purification, their hands raised in the gesture of prayer, their eyes turned toward me. House doors were hung with olive branches wrapped in white fleece to purge the souls of those within. A pink tinge gleamed on all the white as if the sun were giving his blessing. The only sound was a drum in the distance, near the Mound, and a soft occasional dove call. The sky flamed. Shadows deepened. I felt sharply aware of everything, not only of surfaces but of essence. Around the handle of the lily scepter the carved serpents seemed to coil in my hand, coil into each other, consuming each other, as the eyes of the people were consuming me.

It was the toenail that broke my trance—an enormously swollen black nail that jutted out onto the path like a demon and wrenched my eyes from the gaze of the Mother. A nail so ugly it seemed to lord itself in spite over its dirty fellows. Suddenly I saw down the long path hundreds of knobbed toes curling back out of the dust. Bony ankles disappeared hazily into folds of white, and out of those pure graceful columns rose flaccid necks, slack mouths, and blinking vacant eyes. I stumbled over a pebble. A hand reached out to catch me; I did not fall, but in that instant a great cold space opened up inside me. I saw myself stumbling, saw as from the outside the whole long ritual ahead, mumbled chants, missed cues, sweaty dancers, spilled grain in mud trenches, masks slipping, faces caked with gypsum and dirt. It was just a moment and the hole closed. The sun came down around us, the earth waited, the drum called, and I was part of the whole again, shaking blessings on left and right.

The ceremony had begun at sunset, when the mind begins to turn inward on the journey toward that spot within where each one feels the presence of all and where all opposites are reconciled, woman and man, timelessness and time. Gradually, the sun fell back into the earth from which it had come. We watched them blend in marriage, a magic act repeated and repeated so that the world of appearances would continue to show the hidden world to the opening soul, the infinitely joyous world ever present in the bosom of the Goddess Mother in whose being are death and life together without fear.

I stood in the center of the Mound and raised the double axe Icarus had made for me. The harp sounded the summoning song of the moon bull, lord of rhythm in the universe. Then as if in answer came the soft beat of drums and the short thin cries of a reed flute. Out of the darkness appeared a file of veiled *kouretes*, daubed with white, leading a black bull. They brought him before me on the Sacred Mound. I held the double axe above him and chanted the prayer for replenishment of the earth. And then the moon rose out of its old skin like a snake, lord of the tides, lord of the life-renewing dew, measure of the rhythms of the womb, of birth and death, of time and no time.

When I sent the bull away without killing him, a soft sound ran through the worshippers, of surprise or protest perhaps, or of gratification. I could not tell which, but it broke me from the trance again, and I thought, they have forgotten too much. I wondered whether the mountain villagers were here. I wondered, also, which of the veiled *kouretes* was Minos.

Then the priestesses surrounded me. One brought grain roasted with salt and one brought spring water. I washed my hands three times, turned around, and took the grains into my mouth. With eyes closed I spat them away and said, "These I send forth, with these grains I redeem myself and mine." Nine times nine I did this, turning to every point of the world. Then I opened my eyes and said, "Shades of the Mothers, depart." Now milk and honey were brought and seeds. I offered milk on a rock altar to the Benevolent Ones above and the wind dried it. I offered seeds on a hearth, took a torch from a priestess, and burned them for the Earth Mother. I poured honey and water into a trench and buried them for the Awesome Ones below. Again there was a sound among the people, and I thought, many of them miss the blood sacrifice, do not believe that the oldest custom forbids it. The hole inside me opened once more and I saw myself making jerky gestures like a puppet with too few strings. But as before, it was covered up a moment later in the movement of the processional, the torches carried by the *kouretes,* the cists holding *sacra* carried by the priestesses.

We moved into the sacred olive grove where Icarus and I had first lain together. Deep in its interior was a circular enclosure built round a spring. Two snakes were there, wrapped about each other as if in love. They coiled closer as we came near and one raised his head. The *kouretes* surrounded the enclosure on the outside, held their torches high, and turned their backs. The priestesses circled around the inside. From the darkness appeared a little priestess naked, approaching hesitantly. (It was Phaedra.) She came into the enclosure, carrying honey cakes. It is the old belief that if the snakes are gentle, take the food kindly from a virgin, and curl back to the spring, this is a sign that the Mother looks kindly upon the year ahead, that she will leash the Evil Ones. But if they frighten her . . . we watched Phaedra move slowly in the moonlight, stepping as though the touch of grass hurt her feet. Then she bent down, extending her hands. Suddenly there was a scream and a movement across the grass. She was running, crying, a dart of white in the torch flicker, until she disappeared into a dark cloak.

There was a soft moan down the circle of priestesses. I felt a slight irritation. When it had been my job to feed the snakes I had never screamed, believing it to be my duty to reassure the people that all would be well. Still, perhaps the snakes had really threatened her, even bitten. I would have to wait until much later to know. The sign was bad, and this time the murmur from the people was audible to all, before it was lost again in the jingle of sistrum and the start of the dance of the wheel of fire.

Now the images began to blur in my mind, the solemn processional of the fire wheel in the meadow, beginning slowly like the movement of stars, interweaving, interchanging, but keeping always to the circle, like the cycle of life upon life, all souls caught in the endless revolution. For the first time that night a grave peacefulness settled into me as if my bones knew their oneness with the soil and my breath's with the air. I could not tell which of the *kouretes* was Icarus, but I felt his presence everywhere. It was his will that had returned the rites to purity. The Goddess would accept them and bless us. The rhythm of the drums became faster, stopped, speeded up, stopped, started again. The flute cried wildly as if in terror. A *kourete* and a priestess leaped inside the circle, mimicking demons. Their faces were hidden under huge masks, their distorted grimaces and fiery eyes gleaming in the torchlight. They rushed in and out of the procession, shrieking like hawks, breaking through the inner lines of priestesses and *kouretes* into the rows of people moving in the outer circles. And everywhere they dashed there was chaos and shrieking, but only for a moment, and never stopping the slow steady march, for the Mother-of-All is mother of harmony as well as of discord, of good as well as of evil.

Finally the demons were absorbed back into the circle and the pace became slower and slower and stopped. There was no sound in all that mass of people as I emerged from the inmost circle of priestesses and began the slow sacramental dance toward the *omphalos,* the center of the circle of life, the navel of existence. Now only priestesses held torches. In silence they brought the materials of the sacrament. Again I made the offerings to the deities above and below and to the Great Mother. Again I heard the murmur in the crowd, as though here, at least, in this most somber of ceremonies, they needed a blood offering.

Suddenly there was a sharp choked scream, and a veiled *kourete* broke through the line of priestesses and came running to the altar. He was carrying a suckling pig, squealing and wriggling in his grasp. In his other hand he held a dagger. Before anyone could stop him, he dashed to the altar, held the pig above it, and sliced its throat, letting the blood drip down to mingle with the milk. The priestesses stood as if frozen. Then I screamed. The sound frightened me as I heard it tearing through my throat, even though I had made it deliberately to break the spell, to move the priestesses to action, and to regain the eyes of the people. The sound was huge and raw, as if my throat were being torn. It frightened the *kourete* too. He stumbled backward, dropping the pig and the knife, and the priestesses surrounded him and carried him away. I took up the pig and placed it in the trench. Then I washed the knife, placed it in the trench as well, and threw handfuls of earth upon them, chanting the prayers to the Ones Below. I scrubbed the altar with milk and repeated the incantation to the Ones Above. It was all a show to keep the crowd quiet. That scream had opened the hole inside me again. I saw myself acting. I was separate, watching myself.

The feeling persisted as I began the dance of the Mother. Whirling slowly at first, torches blurring around me, the drum beating, the moon dancing in a circle above, I thought it would pass, that I would regain the sense of oneness, but it did not come. I saw myself spinning in a circle of people in a field at night under an impassive sky, with a soulless earth beneath. I saw Minos' face under its veil, somewhere in the line of white daubed men, smiling perhaps at the disturbance, for I was sure it had been his doing, sending the man with the pig. Or perhaps the *kourete* had been Minos himself. The thought almost made me stop. Had I been sure it was he, I would have killed him in front of all the people. But it was too late; the moment was over. Daedalus would hear of it and be amused at the bloody desperate game we played, with intricate rules and heavy penalties.

I did not think of Icarus throughout that whole dance. His game was of a different kind, played with his soul. My soul had departed. As I whirled in the precise pattern, my body trained from childhood to know its moves, my mind laid plans to outwit Minos.

Even at the moment of the Entrance of the Mother into Her Vessel, the Goddess-on-Earth, when I felt the words coming from my mouth, it was as though I were hearing someone else:

> *I am She that is Mother of all things,*
> *The waters and the earth, the sky and the wind,*
> *The power of life and the power of death;*
> *The fires of heaven and earth, the sun, the moon*
> *And all the stars are My progeny,*
> *Women and men, cattle, eagles, serpents,*
> *Wrathful lion and gentle dove. At My will*
> *All things grow and fill the universe,*
> *Die and are renewed. Within My bounds*
> *All beings arise and die, are good and evil,*
> *Merciful and wrathful. All are within My womb.*

I took two baskets and placed them upon the ground. One contained nothing, which is evil, and one contained the *sacra* of life, which is good. I took from one and placed into the other, took from the other and placed into the first. But it was as though nothing passed through my hands.

Then began the tortuous ritual of birth, of the earth from the Goddess, of the sky and the waters from the Earth, and the long descent of the Mothers, in pain. The cymbal clanged, the sistrum rattled, and as I cried and moved there were cries and movement from those encircling me as though they were all helping. But the task was mine alone and all eyes were upon me, I knew. My own eyes as well. I was everywhere but within myself. I inhabited the moon and the wind and the grass underneath, the trees in the distance, the stars above. From everywhere I turned my eyes upon myself and saw merely a woman wriggling and moaning, very small and transient upon the skin of the earth.

At last I threw off my white robe and stood calm, reborn into identity. The jewels on my breasts shone forth the living-in-me of the Goddess. The circle of priestesses tightened. There was absolute silence. And into that, as I had known would happen, broke a voice shatteringly sweet. The priestesses parted and let him through, a veiled *kourete*, looking like all the others, but I knew this was Icarus. Only he had come through the line. He bowed to me and said the sacred words. Suddenly I believed again. Then he threw off his veil and sang the ancient chant that had not been heard in our land for generations. It was not only the words, it was the sound of his voice and of the harp he played that tuned our souls. Everything seemed to listen: all the rows of people, priestly and common, the trees filled with awakened birds, the beasts clustered in flocks in the pastures and those peering around the dark foliage of the forest, fishes in the sea, crawling things under the ground, rocks, stars, moon. It was all joy, all beauty. The birth out of chaos in pain, the dying son transformed by love, self-loving, self-perpetuating, himself the universe revealed in its own image (I gave him the mirror), manifest in tree, rock, and star, all one, all returning, born of the Mother and returning to Her. Being of all Beings. The Serpent Father. I believed, I believed. I took the pure spring water and blessed it. Then I drank and offered it to Icarus, and we came together. Time halted. Death slept.

I swam through the universe giving suck to stars from each of my hundred breasts. In my hand was a double axe, its sharp blades glinting. Pomegranates opened and closed, reddening the skies. Out of the earth sprang a giant narcissus with a thousand blooms. Heaven, earth, and sea laughed, but when I reached for the flower, the axe dropped and sliced its root. Then all my priestesses flung themselves against trees and rocks in uncontrollable rage. Wolves, bears, wild boars gnashed at them. A giant black bull tore the grass. I reached out my hand to quiet him, but my fingers were knives. Ten thousand wounds opened in his sides and blood poured from them. I followed the blood down into the earth. All about me were coiling things, roots, worms, serpents, tunnels, wandering waters. I went down and down as the blood dropped until I lay at the bottom of a deep pool. I understood the language of blood. Swimming things whispered to me. Seeds dropped past and settled into the soil on which I lay. Some swelled and burst. Some decayed. From them arose a powerful smell as of stars burning. After that, I remember nothing more.

Until they came, who knows how much later, in bleak sunlight, with the news. Icarus had been found at the foot of a cliff. Dead.

# IV

*"Peace," as the term is commonly employed, is nothing more than a name, the truth being that every State is, by a law of nature, engaged perpetually in an informal war with every other State.*

PLATO, LAWS

# 1

THEY COULD BRING ME NOTHING to prove it was not a dream. A tumble of bone, a torn bit of cloth. No proof. The birds and the waves had taken the rest, they said; someone had taken the rest. There was no proof that it was Icarus. Not for me. I did not believe them. In the mountains there had been a long blackness and he had awakened on leaves, the old woman nourishing him. I waited for his awakening.

Now I saw how ugly Korkyne was, sniveling in with the child, her eyes vague and shifting, her black mouth moaning no sound I wished to hear. I would not read her scribblings. Only once did I read them, that first morning when the hot sun broke through the scanty leaves and I awoke in dirt, encircled by women in stained rags, their eyes averted, silent until one of them whispered it (Macris, that old hag, whispered it), and I struck her so that she fell into brambles. And I ran without attendants to the cliff, to the shore, to the palace where I grabbed Korkyne and shook her, her horrible empty mouth falling open and her eyes like crystal. ". . . for a day each year and dies at its close . . ." she wrote. "At the close of a day? Or of a year?" I shouted at her, but she would write no more. Nothing. Only prayed silently and bowed to me constantly until I sent her away, would not see her, had someone else bring her the baby, then took the baby from her too, and gave orders that she be kept far from me in the women's quarters.

But I did not believe in his death until the diver brought me the ring that he had found in the sea below the cliff. On it the boy god passed the great tree of eternal life to the Goddess. Above his head was the butterfly of his soul. It was the match to my own, made by Icarus himself.

I took the two rings and placed them in a gold casket, sent the baby away to a nurse, and talked to no one. Days broke over me like waves. I did not stir. All my doubts descended like carrion birds, snatching away what wretched rags of belief still flapped in my mind. I sat still while they stripped me bare, yielding totally to Daedalus' world of dung.

Around me surged the life of the palace. I drove away whom I could, but the priestesses and *kouretes* to whom we had taught the new-old ritual swarmed about me like bees. I felt them watching to see whether I would suffer in public, as though this would please them. They seemed to care nothing for Icarus—or me—only for the thrill of getting close to death and being able to walk away. I brought Korkyne back to me, and Deucalion too, because of the staring and conjecturing. Now we sat, another trio, in silence. No writing or reading. Korkyne was cut off. Even when she tried to write, I would not read.

I felt used more than ever. I saw that I would have to do this again and again. I picked up each separate moment I had had with Icarus and held it, examining on all sides its perfections as one examines an ivory figure, each finely carved movement, each word sung into the harmony of the moment, but in the next instant, shattered.

Should I give Deucalion to this? A new thought burst into my mind. Perhaps my mother had loved Minos once and did not want him dead. Or perhaps she simply did not want him dead.

Minos came, but I would not look at him and he went away. Someone brought Phaedra and I saw that she had not been harmed by the snake, but I would not speak to her. Then one day I was summoned to the Great Hall. When I refused to go, two of Minos' men invaded my quarters, brushed aside Korkyne and the chattering priestesses in the antechamber, and carried me there. Minos sat like a judge on the dais, ringed by Pandareos and his warriors. Before him, on the floor, writhing and babbling, were a number of women.

"Heretics," he said, "blaspheming the Mother, roaming in frenzy through the countryside, carrying off infants whom they tear limb from limb and eat." The women were mad, eyes rolling, drooling at the lip. One of them, I realized with shock, was Lyca. I had not seen her since the night Merope had taken me to the Sibyl. She had disappeared somewhere on the journey, had never arrived at the shrine. Now she looked incredibly feeble. Her hands waved limply in front of her face. Her eyes passed over me without any sign of recognition. I kept thinking, did I look like that at the ceremony? When Minos sentenced her to death, I remained quiet.

I was trapped in a cast of quiet, though I seethed there like molten bronze, seeking out the intricate contours of a new form. For months I was obsessed with one question: how did Icarus die? Did he throw himself from the cliff? Was he killed by Minos? Was he sacrificed in the ritual by my own priestesses, perhaps even by me? The questions raged in my mind. Why did I *not* know? Had we both been drugged?

Yet I did not question others—I feared their answers. What I did not want to hear was what I must have known from the start. The script was clear. The action would have gone the same in any case. ". . . Reigns as consort for a day each year and dies at its close." What did it matter, the length of the reign or the manner of its close?

I do not know how much time went by, but one morning I took the gold casket with the rings, went to the fateful cliff alone in a brilliant dawn, and, when the sun rose, threw it into the sea.

Dreams shrink into ideas, rocks into pattern. I ordered Daedalus to complete the temple, following the designs Icarus had brought, and at its center I had a fresco painted in his likeness. Almost at once a rumor started that the figure was really Zeus. That was Minos' doing. I countered by having Icarus' name inscribed at its base and a prayer to him included in the ritual. Minos' reply was a repetition of his journey to Iyttos to receive the divine laws of the Sky God. A great occasion he made of it, his men armed and lining the road, drums pounding, people fawning about him as if they had never raised their hands to the Mother.

And so I wrote a new ritual, the story of the life and sacrifice of the boy god. I taught it to all my followers—priestesses, *kouretes,* artisans, children. They wept voluminously as they performed it, but in the next hour, they cheered Minos' celebration of the laws of Zeus.

The coldness I had felt at the Anthesteria was with me always. Monsters were merely designs in wax. Sacred mounds could be sliced away into building blocks. Even love was only an image. I kept Korkyne close at hand, but I would not be alone with her if I could help it. The sight of that empty mouth aroused a rage in me that I was afraid to let go. But I did not want Minos to get at her. It was the same with my child. I saw him daily, but I did not touch him. My breasts dried and I grew thin. I spent much time in courts with stewards, suppliants, visiting princes, merchants, artisans, judges. With Minos, too, and even Daedalus, though we rarely spoke to each other and never privately. At night I bedded alone, reading through the dark hours.

Word had come from Egypt of Queen Hatshepsut's death. Almost before the ceremonies were over, the defacing of her cartouches had begun. Sometimes there was even an attempt to destroy her monuments. And that raging boy, Tuthmosis, whom she had held leashed, now whipped his armies against Syria and Mitanni. Everywhere the spears were out. Cretan ships were attacked, not only by pirates on the seas, but even in port, by the warriors of Tuthmosis. Minos added more arms, demanded ships for speed and strike, not cargo, and sent out fleets to find and capture the new metal of the Hittites that kills more surely. Trade waned. All was given over to war.

The earth continued to die. The forests were retreating up the mountains. Wild roses and lilies were all gone. Many springs dried up. Orchards withered, and barley fields. Two-thirds of the land became stony waste. Hungry people lined the streets. Whole families begged along the Royal Way. Whenever they saw me, they began a low chant, over and over, a weak kind of gasp, muttered so that one could not understand the words, and their hands waved in the prayer gesture. But here and there it seemed to turn into something else. Fists raised in adoration changed almost to threat, and the voices were harsh with an undertone of anger. The promise of the ritual had expired in the dry furrows. The seed of Icarus was dust.

I wore a knot on my shoulder to keep back death, not for my own belief but for the people. They died all the same. In the palace there were guards now watching every entrance, because someone had been stealing food. Once as I returned from the beggar-lined streets, the hem of my skirt stretched and frayed from the clutching of skinny, clawlike hands, the stench and ugliness of their misery hanging inside me like a demon, I announced that all who were in need would receive grain. As the cry streaked out from throat to throat, I had servants bring fifty *pithoi* of barley to the north porch. I stood there as the people came with cups and bowls, hundreds of them fighting to push forth their receptacles for the food. First they were given bowlfuls, but when we saw it would not go far we changed to cups (there was resentment at that) and then later on to spoons. Still, we ran out completely before the line was gone. I think some of them went back to the end of the line and came round again; I saw an old woman with a strangely woven scarf who came twice, I know. But when the *pithoi* were empty, there were many still waiting who had never come by at all. I sent down for more grain, but the servant did not return. When I left, there were angry cries. After that, there were heavy guards about the food in the palace. Our own meals were as lavish as ever, but I had no taste for them. Once I took a basket of cakes to the north balcony and threw them down to the row of beggars groveling there. They fought for them viciously, trampling the cripples and the children. But when the cakes were gone, still more people had gathered. They turned their faces up to me and waited silently.

More and more there were reports of wild women in the mountains, tearing infants apart and eating them. I did not know how much of it was true, but it sickened me.

Again in Minos' court a mob of writhing, frothing women, rags brown with blood stains, eyes darting back and forth. There is no one I recognize. I try to talk to them, but they do not hear, only whirl, leap about, crawl over each other like snakes. Others sit rigidly as if they are stone. Do I look like any of these at the ceremony?

There is a eunuch among them, wearing a shaggy skin, arms and face smeared with mud. In one hand he carries the rotted tail of a fox, in the other, a bull bladder. He shakes these in my face and laughs.

Again Pandareos and his men ring the court in their bronze helmets, and Minos hands down judgment. I am called in to witness. Again I say nothing, and they die.

I spend much time alone. I look into the mirror. Behind me often stand the Mothers, eyes empty and teeth stained. I stare Them away and light lamps. When I have just forgotten Them, They return, huddled again in the mirror. I see how much They look like me. But my eyes can cut Them away. A manuscript demolishes Them.

I study Egypt. They bring me papers, news gleaned from the latest ships, from the islands also, and from Attica. All recorded by some clerk when Minos' messengers arrive, flying to him without a stop at my chamber. When I enter the Great Hall, silence.

What friends do I have left? I am surrounded by women I scarcely know, all deferent, bowing. I taught many of them the new-old ritual and watched them that night moving with torch and *sacra,* but I do not talk to them about what happened. I trust no one. Though some of them have been near me for years, I can see only as far as their eyes.

Daedalus with cold face, hands busy with plans, does not look at me. He says not a word about Icarus, but I sense his hatred. Was he watching that night? Hidden in a mask, perhaps, a cold examiner of the frenzy? Did he see the killing of the pig? Hear my cry? The song of Icarus? And did he see the blades of the double axe, the red pomegranates, the giant flower, the priestesses' rage, the wolves, the wild boars, the bull? Did I kill it? Did I kill him?

Once I approached Daedalus to ask. I had wakened cold before dawn in a dream of blood, Icarus dying over and over in front of my eyes, and I ran down the empty corridors to Daedalus' room. He was already awake, on his balcony, looking out over the mountains with his old man's tired, sleepless eyes. He turned when he heard me, looked down (I was crawling to him, mortifying myself), said nothing, turned away.

# 2

EVERY MORNING I LISTENED for the rattle of the death carts over the stones, gathering up those who had died during the night and carrying them to the cave tombs where the common people were given back to the Great Mother. There was always someone wailing. As the carts passed near the north balcony where I hid, the wails were louder. It must have been well known that I crouched there every dawn, waiting for the carts to pass, wearing the knot on my shoulder but hiding my face. Perhaps the people thought that a real queen, one whom the Goddess loved, would have shown herself, would have come down among them and gone along to the tombs, weeping.

I could not make myself go down. I tried to keep my thoughts and feelings as secret as the movements of the men who were sent out by Minos night after night to steal grain from the people and bring it into the palace. But we were both watched, the thieves and I. Now and then there were protests from the dark fields; sometimes a thief would be killed. And from the mountains, increasingly, there came rumors of rebellion against the rule of the consort.

Now Minos made a sudden strange proclamation. He had gone to the Sibyl for counsel, he said. He had begged to know why the land was dying. And the old seeress had replied, "There is one among you who is evil." I was baffled. Was I to be called the evil one? And how did Minos dare to speak of the old seeress as alive? The mountain people would know his lie. Icarus had been very clear in his description of her murder. But perhaps it was not the same one. Perhaps there was another Sibyl. Even I could not be sure. I began to see how this confusion could be used.

"Pray to the Mother!" Minos cried to me in the midst of the ceremony. "Find out this evil one that the land may be cleansed!"

He knelt before the dais, and I saw how thin his hair had grown. His mouth trembled, too, and under his eyes was the shadow of illness. For the first time, I believed that Minos was afraid. Perhaps his victims were visiting his dreams. I wondered whether the Awesome Ones brought them back to him in the night. Did he think getting rid of me would send them away?

But presently there were whisperers again, and with a different message. In the courtyard a woman paused beside me as if for the briefest greeting. Her words came hastily, her eyes on guard. "Kill Pandareos!" She was gone before I could question or reply. On the way to the Great Hall the next morning, at the bend in the stairs, another woman stumbled against me, brushed close against my ear, the words so clear in the rustle of moving people that I looked around startled to see who might have overheard, but there was no sign of anyone noticing. It was a priestess this time, Thera, who had brought the spring water at the Anthesteria. The words were the same, but I could read her eyes no more than those of the stranger. The next time, it was a blind suppliant, an old man, his sightless eyes bent whitely inward, mouthing the words as he trembled at my feet.

Then Minos pleaded again at the ceremony. "There is one among you who is evil." Suddenly he groveled at my feet. "Pray, pray." His voice was pious, his hands unsteady. More whisperers continued the same theme, as if I were being primed to follow Minos' plea, as if I were the one who had to be persuaded of Pandareos' guilt.

I watched them all and said nothing. I took no drink at the ceremonies for fear of being drugged. The trance was easy to assume, and my mind remained cold. The response Minos wanted was clear, but I did not know the reason. Why would he want Pandareos damned? The man was his hatchet.

I studied him closely. A bronze giant who spoke only with blows, a bringer of drugs and madness, a curse upon the lips of women, but all in Minos' service. A wine drinker, but never drunk. A wagerer on bulls and athletes, but not often a loser. A wrestler, but not a brawler. Some stolid strength held him still but at the ready. "A fine tool," Daedalus had once called him. There was no sign of his disloyalty to his master. Why would Minos turn against him? Was Minos mad?

I watched them together. Down among the ships Minos seemed younger than in the palace, but not so young and strong as Pandareos. Only the gold and the robe marked clearly who had power. Jealousy, then? But it would not explain why he did not simply have him killed. He had never hesitated before. Why did he want the order to come from me?

Word came again from the mountains. A brown youth appeared before me one day in the courtyard with an offering of fragrant thyme. He was named Pharos, he said. He had come from Dhikti. I thought at first he was one of the whisperers sent by Minos, but his words were different. The mountain people were with me, he said. They would do whatever I wished. His voice was raw with no manner of the court, and his eyes were naked as a deer's, but he knew secrecy and would talk only when there was no one else around. We did not mention Icarus. At the name of Minos, he stiffened.

I went out again into the streets in rags, this time with the young mountain messenger. Pharos was known to many of the common people. My disguise now was for the court. As I walked, potters and weavers brushed close and murmured. All adoration now. No sign of threat. I wondered what had happened to their anger and what I would need to do to keep it away.

We in the palace were still smothering in feasts, but the watch was close to keep the grains from the beggars. Minos continued at the ceremony with his recurring refrain, but he made no open accusation. He seemed not so keen as he had been. His eyes had lost their hardness. Some disease was eating him, I thought, or the blood of the priestesses had infected his dreams. He listened eagerly, expectantly to my chant, but I did not say the word he wished to hear.

He spoke to the people often at games and processions. "I have made you greatest among powers, on the seas, and in the markets, as destined by Zeus. I have put down your enemies, forced them to pay tribute, and Zeus has blessed me, has blessed you . . ." When the beggars wailed, he added, "But there is one among you who is evil." He did not mention the Goddess except in the ceremonies, and then it was as if he were afraid not to. Then he seemed to whisper, not for the people, not even for me, but for himself.

One night he came alone to my room and knelt. There was no one else around, yet he went through all the gestures of a suppliant. His arms seemed flaccid and his eyes feverish. The hair in his nostrils had become white. I had heard rumors that Daedalus was called every night for potions, and that they had sent again to Egypt for a physician, in spite of the threats of the young king. So it is Minos' turn to feel the anger of the Raging Ones, I thought. They wait for all of us behind the smiles of the dancers.

When he had finished the ritual, complete with the prayer to cleanse the land of the evil one, he did not leave but stood silently by the door as if waiting for my reply. But I too had learned the value of silence. Finally he spoke. He had a story from an old text, he said, for my ears alone. It told how in the ancient time, the daughter of the Goddess (who was also the daughter of Zeus, he said) was left by her Mother in a holy cave on Iyttos, guarded by two serpents while she spent her days weaving a mantle of fine wool on which was represented the unfathomable secret of the universe. The Mother told Zeus of their daughter's whereabouts, and he transformed himself into a serpent and went to the cave to watch her weaving, her hair falling down over her breasts, her eyes shining with wisdom, making their own light in the dark cave, her fingers working the subtle pattern in white wool upon white wool that only the eye already wise might discern. And Zeus was so struck by her beauty and grace that he appeared to her in his own glorious form and she loved him and took him as her consort forever.

His story was an outrage of distortion. I knew the ancient script. It was the son who visited the mother. Never, never would the Goddess have allowed a father to be his daughter's consort. I could hear Merope's wail of horror. Even my careless mother would have been stirred to anger. Yet, for the first time, I was almost persuaded that Minos believed his own words. Had someone deceived him? I remembered the story Daedalus had told of the kings of Sumer. My old tutor served his master well.

Now I began to see my way through the maze of Minos' mind. Death runs throughout the land. The king's arm is aging. Souls of the murdered claw at his sleep. He is afraid of what he has done and of what he would like to do. He must offer a *pharmakos,* a cleansing before the first fruits, and perhaps the Great Mother will bless him even as he violates Her.

I said nothing, and finally Minos left. Once again I sat through the night, staring into the shadows. Korkyne came with drinks and robes, but I sent her away. Before dawn, I knew what I must do.

Bewildered, flattered, Pandareos came hastily, stumbling over my threshold as though he were learning suddenly to walk with new legs. I was curious to see how this bronze man's veins would throb with dreams. I caressed his arms and his chest, admired the gold belt cinched at his waist and the brilliant loincloth, the strong thighs. I touched the fine brown hair of his legs. He was firmer than Minos. He roused easily, fairly trembled with passion but was afraid to approach, had not thought this would happen, grinned inanely, dreaming, dreaming. Yes, I felt desire, it had been so long, but then the thought of Icarus wiped me cold as stone. I touched Pandareos' snake and smiled, then walked abruptly away out of my chambers into a hidden niche where I stood listening. I could hear him pace in silence for a while, stutter at the question of an entering priestess, and finally stumble down the hall, looking about, wondering.

The next day Minos was walking with me in the courtyard. "How wise you have been," I told him, "to find a lieutenant of such noble proportions. Pandareos is a man like a god, built to father heroes."

The morning silence was split by shouts and a rush of footsteps in the corridor. Thera brought me the news. Pandareos had been killed! Minos himself had killed him. Why? Because it was he who had given drugs to drive women mad. All is now known. Minos has proclaimed it. The evil the old Sibyl has warned about has been found! Now, through Minos' hand, divine justice shines according to the promise of Zeus. End of proclamation.

So that is how it is done, I thought. One can kill without touching the knife. The drug-monger was gone. Minos' hatchet hand was empty. And I had forced him to empty it without his getting, through me, the blessing of the Mother.

As I started to laugh, I saw Thera's eyes. "Ariadne laughed," she would report. I flew at her then. I would have scratched away those eyes, I think, but she slipped from my grasp and ran out the door. Suddenly I wept. I called Korkyne and clung to her as when she had first come. She brought Deucalion—to cheer me, I suppose—but he made the tears come faster. I could see that he was frightened even when I held him close against my shoulder and moved round and round as if feeling my way in a new dance. Korkyne was distressed, but I think she was also pleased that the coldness in me had broken. She must have seen it as an acceptance of Icarus' offering, for she wrote to me eagerly, "His soul will be at rest now."

I buried my face in the infant's damp curls and felt sorrow wash through me in unending waves. It was the loss not only of Icarus, but of all my faith. A separating sorrow that left me apart from child, friend, even enemies. Like driftwood on thin sand covering dead rock, with no Mother waiting underneath to receive me. Long before, I had thought that She was dissolved in Daedalus' light, but She had lived somewhere in me and sprung to life at the breath of Icarus' faith. Even his death had not stopped Her, for there was renewal in it. No matter who had killed him, there was renewal in it. Now I had killed Pandareos, but it was the Mother who had died.

Like Queen Isis wandering in the Egyptian Underworld, I had been stripped of my selves, layer by layer, and I was down to bronze. Daedalus' art, that—the dismantling of visions and the forging of weapons.

A white rock on Iyttos glinted in the sun. The same sharp light outlined the horns on the balcony. A clean cut of rock, horn, and stone in the hot blue of midday, and a sharp silence around the shouts of the guards and the soft thuds of Pandareos' body being dragged down the stairs below. My hand on the stone ballustrade seemed to be melting.

There was a bronze flash. The palace guards streamed into the Royal Way. Even height, chosen for stature, they looked like a decoration on a vase. They were all high-born sons of Cretan priestesses, but many of them had Attic fathers. Though their faces were almost hidden under the feathered helmets, I could see that they showed no sign of sorrow. Pandareos had been hated by the guards.

But what of his followers? I studied the warriors as they assembled, row upon row. Theirs were variegated faces, brown, white, black—not a Cretan face among them. They were an assortment of islanders, Africans, Syrians. Adventurers, fugitives, they were exotic reminders of Minos' sea strength. How did he hold them? And would he hold them now with their leader gone? They stood in lines, swords crossed, faces impassive. The guards shouted. Slaves tumbled the body like a bag of rocks onto the path, tied it to an ass, and drove off scraping the face over the paving stones. The warriors stood still. Minos gave an order and they marched off in another direction.

# 3

WE WERE RIDING IN A closed carriage, but the dust crept through every opening and hung thickly so that it was hard to breathe. I peeked through the curtains. It was all dust. I could not tell where we were going. The hills had been left behind and the horses pulled now with no strain. When we stopped, a man rushed up and helped Minos from the carriage. I climbed out by myself, my cloak pulled up tightly across my mouth. There was a great whirling of dust as the horses moved away.

Minos' voice was in my ear. "This way." He led me to a stone seat. The sun burned through the dust without settling it. There was no wind. From here and there came sounds of scuffling and men's voices shouting. A form appeared close and Minos spoke to him in a muffled voice. Then a shout rang out loud and another farther off and still another. After that, silence. Gradually forms emerged. The sun glared behind them. As the dust cleared, I could see that they wore metal not only in their helmets, but also decorating their shields. At their sides were long spears. At first glance, I thought they had stolen all the double axes from the Great Hall, but the shape was different, a single blade tapering to a point. I had never seen so many. It seemed as if all the men in the world were in that field.

A cloak covered me except for my eyes. I was in disguise this time at Minos' command. The men were not looking at me, nor even at Minos. Someone else was approaching and their eyes followed him as if they were spellbound. He seemed to be covered in metal. It made his huge body seem broad as a bull. He walked heavily, yet with grace, as if accustomed to the weight. In his left hand was a spear, in his right a sword. A dagger was stuck in his belt. His face was expressionless, as if it, too, were covered with metal. He greeted Minos abruptly, dropping words like stones. Something about moving to another spot across the plain. He gave me not so much as a glance. We moved at once, Minos steering me roughly like a slave. Again we sat on stones, halfway up a mild incline.

We had moved onto damper ground. The dust was less. I could see the men more clearly. Pandareos' warriors were there, but there were others, too, all of them armed. They stood in a row now, just below us, fidgeting at the metal, adjusting clothing, rubbing their skin as if it had been chafed, muttering to each other. When the heavy man stepped out in front of them, they fell absolutely silent. Minos gave a brief laugh. "That's Asterios," he whispered.

Just then three carts rattled up, again raising large clouds of dust, which settled more quickly this time. There was a great clank of metal as they unloaded the carts. Hundreds of spears were struck into the ground or leaned against trees. Daedalus was directing it. I had not seen him before. Perhaps he had come in one of the carts.

When the spears had been arranged in clear order, each one separate from the others, the men formed into another line. Daedalus moved farther up the hill. He had not once looked in our direction. Again Asterios stepped out and the men fell silent. Beyond them, a strange procession appeared. At first it seemed like several horsemen driving sheep, but as they neared I saw that some of the driven ones were human. They clustered together and seemed to stumble as if they were tied. They were all naked. Most of them were women. They stopped at a distance. One of the horsemen was leading a goat. Suddenly, he rode across the field in front of the armed men, the goat running behind him. After the goat came the sheep. Spears flew from all the hands. Most of them fell short, but some hit the targets. An ewe staggered bleating across the whole field with two spears stuck in her side before she fell. One blade struck the eye of a lamb and it went down shaking without a sound. Another tore open an animal's side and blood spurted out, making the whole creature red. It ran dizzily toward the men, sprinkling its blood among them until someone brought a sword down sharply and severed its head. It came down not two yards from where I sat, its life soaking into the dry earth. Some of the sheep got through the line without being hit. The horseman lured them away with the goat. Slaves went into the field to drag away the dead. Men retrieved their spears.

A fire had been started in the distance. Swiftly slaves skinned the sheep, cleaned the carcasses and staked them over the flames to cook. Asterios was talking to the men. They were clustered around him. I could not hear what he was saying. Minos walked over and spoke to him but returned at once. Again the line was formed. The horseman leading the goat rode back across the field, the sheep following. Again the spears flew. Again some of the sheep were killed. The hides were piled into the carts. The smell of the cooking meat rose strong in the air. The horseman took the goat and the remaining sheep out of sight over the hill.

Once more the line was formed. Now from the group of naked slaves, one was released. A man. I could see him hesitate as if confused. Minos leaned toward me. "Last night, this man killed two palace guards at the east portal." I was sure he was lying. I had heard nothing of this. Still, it could have happened. But what had been the man's purpose? There was no time for talk. I saw one of the horsemen charge at the naked man, but he dodged and ran off away from us so fast I thought he would escape. The horseman went after him and knocked him down. Another horseman joined him. All was lost in dust for a while. Then both horsemen came racing directly toward us. The man seemed to be pursuing them, running so fast he appeared to fly. It was not until they swerved and started across the field in front of the line that I could see the rope around the man's neck and his hands straining at it to keep from choking. As they crossed the field the spears flew again. One of the first pierced the throat of a horse and it went down, its legs thrashing. The horseman was caught under its body. I could hear his voice in short harsh wails. The slave seemed to dance at the end of the rope as the spears fell around him. Suddenly one pierced his ear and emerged on the other side of his head. For a moment he stood as if suspended on it and then slowly his legs gave way and he sank down. He tilted and the blunt end touched the ground and held him again for an instant, half-upright before he fell.

A scream went up from the other slaves and they started running away from us, but the horsemen herded them back and chased them across the field. Few spears were hurled; the men were not ready. Asterios threw one; I saw that. It struck a woman. I could see no blood, but she went down at once. The other slaves dragged her along, stepping on her body, falling, until the horsemen stopped them, cut her away, and drove the others out of sight. The woman lay still at one end of the field. At the other, two warriors lifted the spear that had pierced the man's ears and carried him dangling from it toward the fire. Minos rose abruptly and spoke to Asterios. An order went down the line. The two soldiers dropped the man and tore the spear from his head. Then they tied his legs to a rope held by a horseman and dragged him away. As they passed the woman's body, they stopped and tied her legs to the same rope.

Around me the men were stirring, tearing off helmets, throwing down shields, retrieving and cleaning spears and piling them into the carts. Their faces were flushed, lips swollen. They shouted, clapped each other on shoulders and backs, laughed, leaped excitedly, threw down the clean spears with more-than-needed energy. They looked like dancers in the ceremony. Asterios alone was calm. He stood at the side, talking to Minos. Suddenly he reached for a spear and with one smooth powerful movement threw it at the distant fire and pierced neatly the carcass of a roasting sheep. The slave tending it jumped back with a scream. A roar of approval went up from the men. Minos looked at me and smiled.

Then I saw the horsemen returning with the slaves. One by one the men fell quiet, watching them approach, a strange quiet after the hilarity. Again they stared as if in a spell. One stood just behind me. I could hear his breathing. Suddenly, somewhere in the crowd, one of them gave a shout and ran down among the slaves, grabbed a woman and pushed her to the ground. They all moved then, and in the din and confusion, I could not see, did not let myself see what was happening. Minos' hand was a vise around my arm. His

[ 142 ]

breathing, too, was hoarse. He jerked me up suddenly and ran toward the slaves, then turned as if dazed and ran back the other way to the carriage. The driver was still there, but his eyes were fastened on the scene beyond. Minos threw me into the carriage and shouted at him to go, but he did not move until Minos struck him with the flat of his sword. Then he cried out and turned the horse toward the palace, but his eyes still went back again and again to the men and the slaves. Back there, only Asterios stood quiet now, watching.

Asterios, Bull of Minos. Women would learn to shudder as he passed. Not all would learn his nature so quickly as I had that day, but inevitably it would come. He was established at once and publicly as Minos' lieutenant. Master of Ships. Master of War. Slave Controller, Order Keeper, Enforcer of the Laws of Zeus, Catechizer. In the courtyard, in the arena, in open fields, he would assemble the warriors and drill them.

"What is the primary virtue?" he would cry.

"Courage," they chanted in reply.

"What is the primary use of the virtue, courage?"

"Valor in battle!" They shouted in one voice and joyfully, as if freed. Occasionally some man in the onlooking crowd would join them, an artisan, even a beggar. One could learn the answers quickly. They were always the same. The questions as well. No one dared to ask others, at least not aloud, though I thought of it, planned it.

"What of compassion?" one might ask.

"The primary virtue is valor." The answer would come as if one had not spoken.

"What of love?" Whisper it at least.

"Valor in battle," would come the chant.

"And what of the Great Mother?" Even I did not mouth the question. But if I had dared, the answer would have remained the same: "The primary virtue is courage in battle. Against the enemies of Zeus. Against the enemies of Minos. Against the enemies of Crete."

[ 143 ]

And then would come the lessons in killing. No one would argue that Asterios was not a master of his trade.

Minos did not insist on my observing him again, but I could hardly escape the sight. There were more warriors than ever and many of them now were Cretans, though few were mountain people. In the ceremonies, Minos repeatedly gave thanks to Zeus for taking away the evil that had afflicted the country. He seemed himself to have recovered health. "Zeus has redeemed the Mother," he said. "Zeus has preserved Crete." His logic was baffling, but no one seemed to question it.

There was, after all, no triumph for me, though I had abandoned innocence. Minos had needed a purge to show the people his abhorrence of the invasions of the old shrines, the murder of priestesses, the spread of drugs, and the corruption of women. He had wanted it done through me to show the blessing of the Mother upon his own pure desire to preserve the ancient faith, even while introducing another. I had avoided that, but it was a small victory. Minos had won the larger one. All the while, he had had Asterios at hand, ready to be brought out. Cleaner than his predecessor, unknown, but, as we all discovered, more deadly.

I thought I had climbed out of clay limbs up the strings into the hands that pulled them, but there were hands above those hands. Nevertheless, my apprenticeship had begun. A design as intricate as Daedalus' dancing floor began to spread out just under reach of my eye as though a fog hung over it that, if I sunned and winded it just right, would lift and reveal a maze with Minos at its heart waiting for the knife.

*For these three things I am greateful to fate: first that I was born a man and not a beast, second that I am a man and not a woman, and third that I am a Greek and not a barbarian.*

THALES

# 1

DAEDALUS:

ALL THIS INTRIGUE AND BUTCHERY—night whispers, stealth in the halls, knives at throats, it gets in the way of thought. A strong ruler's what I need, who isn't worried about the blood he's spilled. This one's sick, but in no way I can remedy, even with the help of the elegant Egyptian he bought for a shipload of Cretan craft and nursed through dangerous waters. They're all taking to the sea these days. Just when his wit is needed most, Minos sickens and comes begging for herbs. They won't help. If you ask me, nothing will help him now. He's washed too many altars in the blood of priestesses, yet he still can't get the old religion out of his system. Offering a scapegoat! He's an anachronism. Pandareos' death is of no consequence. He was a tool; the people see the hand behind it, and in that hand a worse tool now. Why Minos bothered, I don't know. Or was it Ariadne's doing?

That's a name makes my stomach fail, though I still don't know who's used and who's user. Just when I thought I had a son for my old age—but he was a fool, a fool. Rapt in dreams. No match for any of them. What did he think would come of it? The people's love? They're fickle, will take all bones flung and cry for more. No, Icarus believed in miracles, thought the Goddess Herself would open the Divine Larder and pour forth her fruits if he performed the old ghastly ritual. And here's the harvest. Famine creeping in like a marauder. People killing each other for crumbs. Where's the sanctity of the sacrifice? Even the pitiful likeness she had painted for him is defaced, renamed, lost. Yet Icarus wouldn't have had it different, I suppose, his mother's child always, afraid of the daylight, lost in the old winding paths down to who knows what foggy mysteries clouded in incense and dirt. I've yielded that. I've yielded him, hard though it has been. But now I'd like to leave. The fun's gone out of life. Too heavy, all these blood debts. And the land's dying. Some wind of death blows incessantly the wrong way. It's time to go.

Except for Ariadne. She's a fishbone stuck in my thoughts; I can't get rid of her. Yesterday morning she appeared suddenly on my balcony as if nothing had happened, as if it were the old classroom and Icarus were safe in Attica. What could I do? She's queen, whatever else. The power is back within her, too. She's crawled out of the muck again and has a strength now I haven't seen before. In she came without a knock and laid before me documents outlining the wealth (the poverty, rather) of the country—ships, sheep, olives, bronze cups, ivory images, daggers . . . she's done her homework. Must have set the stewards quite a task assembling the inventory. "Prepare a plan," she says. "Use your brains, get us out of trouble." Goddess-on-Earth begging the unbeliever to fix things up! But not a word about that, not a flicker in her eye, though she didn't look at me much. When she did, it was cold and bright as Iyttos' peak. And curiously without guilt. I'm certain she doesn't believe in all that rot. I don't even believe she wanted Icarus dead.

And so I plan. We plan. She's the driver now, lashing my brain like a fierce Syrian soldier at a tired horse. In Knossos alone: twenty thousand sheep, seven hundred pigs. Fifty bulls of the first excellence, for the bull dance. Wild goats, horses from Syria, fish, sponges, and octopi. Corn, oil, wine, flax, figs, date palms, quince, plums, chick peas. Blue and mauve anemones, white and dark pink ranunculus. (Though what commerce she expects from these, she did not say. What does it matter? The hot wind of the southeast kills everything.)

Ariadne says, trade, don't fight. Minos laughs. Bring water from the mountains to the dry plains, she says. Minos is impatient, scoffs. I will study it. It could be done—we've moved water to fit our plans before. (But I am tired. I do not dare to tell them how tired.)

Supply the craftsmen, she says. Bring them gold, silver, tin, and lead. Pay off the pirates or kill them, but bring the metal, so that the seals and bowls and vases, the gold cups and amphora, the bracelets and pendants cherished by the Cypriots and the Egyptians can flow as they used to from the shops of Knossos.

While she speaks, one could believe it will happen. But out of her presence, the will flags. A drunken scuffle among the guards. The careless gesture of an artisan. A ripple through the gaudy prison of the bull dancers. The dark glance of a rower chained to the galley. There is restlessness everywhere. Too many slaves in the palace and the shops, in the arena and the fleets. Too many fugitives among the warriors, from Africa, Mycenae. Too much tribute forced from the colonies, too many priestesses killed for treason. And the drug Pandareos brought spreads throughout the countryside. Minos condemns it, but all the same his new lieutenant, Asterios, unloads it openly on the docks, calls it "sacred nectar," and sends it out packed on slaves to all parts of Crete. The officials smirk in their hands and turn pious faces for public show. There's the sense of an ending here, though Ariadne won't have it, reads it otherwise. If I were younger . . . but then, revolution's not for me. I've had my fill of blood. Still, there's something in it that I'd welcome. She's got the brain, the pure demonic power of a leader, which is what Minos seems to be losing. Under her I could build again, if she could get the people behind her as one. The mountain folk are with her now, I see that. But the slaves, the fugitives, the hungry peasants, which way will they go? If I were younger . . . but she needs a general. That country boy, Pharos, is too innocent.

The problem of bringing water from the mountain springs to the plains is not insolvable. The rains still come, though scantily. If only we could save the water. A wall could be built to keep it from washing down the mountain and back into the sea. It could be stored, held behind gates, perhaps, and released in the dry times into ditches winding through the fields. Or if that should prove too costly, wells could be sunk in sufficient number and depth (twelve to fourteen meters?) and a constant relay of asses employed to bring the water to troughs that could be raised to tilt toward the immediate surrounding area. And where troughs could not be laid, or where no wells drew water, slaves could be employed to carry or to tend asses carrying the water to the dry outlands. Or perhaps the wind could be caught as in a sail and made to draw water from the earth.

But at every moment I am distracted from my work. The simplest command does not go through without strange delays, exchanges of glances that convey another language, even among the household servants. I cannot get a message through to Ariadne without a stir. Yesterday I walked to her quarters myself to discuss a problem, trivial but immediate, and there was a scurrying away down the corridor like insects at the approach of a lamp. Then Asterios appeared, blotting out the light in the passage with his bulk. Three warriors joined him at the stairwell, erupting suddenly out of the shadows as if from ambush. They were his men, one could see by the signals exchanged. They saluted me, but with a kind of disdain, and watched as I moved down the way Asterios had just come.

Ariadne was alone, musing at the courtyard door. When I entered, she whirled as if at bay. She was glad to see me, though, and chattered eagerly and with acuity about the problems of transporting the water. But something else was on her mind. She would pause in the midst of a phrase, for no discernible reason, and then rush on with the matter at hand as if closing a door over a seethe of unspoken thought. I am left out of it. Well, I can hardly expect to be her confidant after all that's happened, though occasionally there are signs that she trusts me. But not enough. And just as well. There are games being played here I'd rather not know about. We talk about designs for gold cups. The signs that the copper mines are giving out. The dying forests.

Underneath, something else is giving out. Dying.

I've been around rulers too long not to know with my spine when trouble's brewing. What it is exactly I don't know, but Ariadne's afraid, and Minos is half out of his mind. Every night now he sends for me. Herbs, he wants. Sleeping potions. The Thracian drug he'd like, too, but he is afraid and with good reason, in my judgment.

Dreams afflict him and he wakes staring, screaming for me. I am still his pet monkey, his tamed Athenian, performing at command. But it's not me he needs to kill the nightmares. Or maybe it is, but he doesn't know how to use me anymore. In the old days there was a strength in him that all the seas bowed to, but it's easy to see now that he's sliding backwards. How he rants in the ritual, expounding his everlasting tale of seeing Zeus on the mountaintop and coming back with his laws. "The laws of Zeus!" he shrieks and spells them out, the scribes scratching hastily. Has them read on every corner. Sends Asterios and his men burling down streets to find dissenters. There's a hanging every day. Women and mountain men, for the most part. Old believers. Those too foolish to dissemble.

There's a black whisper snaking about the court, too. Something to awe the ears, they say. An announcement to be revealed in the spring ceremonies. Who knows what malicious nonsense it will be. If it is anything at all.

Ariadne says nothing about it. Well, she would not confide in me. In any case, she is up to something that keeps her busy. Two days ago, without a word to anyone as far as I know, she disappeared into the mountains. Some slaves went with her.

# 2

ARIADNE:

THEIR EYES WERE CLOUDED with dream and pain, and they talked half in prayer, but the mountain people believed in me as they believed in the Mother, and without them I had no power at all. I went to the Sibyl because of them, crawled on the damp rock in the dark to feel for her bones, brushed past the filthy golden bowls of rotting grain they had pushed in to nourish her, year after year, keeping up the service in their blind way, no one daring enough, I suppose, to enter the innermost cave and see whether or not she still lived, waiting for me to come and do it, knowing I had to.

I went, believing nothing. Yet before I entered the cave, I bowed and prayed and bathed myself in the holy spring, and not altogether for my priestesses. There must have been some seed of faith in me, parched as the Messara plain, that yearned for the Mother's tears. I remember how the world stopped as I entered the darkness. I could hardly move. It was as though I were pushing against centuries. My foot brushed pebbles, a bowl clanked against another, seeds sprinkled over my ankles, something moved away. I went down on my knees as if I were pulled from below. The rock was damp under my hands, mossy, vibrating. I crawled, pushing away bowl after bowl, wrapped in webs. I closed my eyes and waited for cave sight, but when I opened them, I could still see almost nothing. The tiny entryway was covered with brush. No lamp shone as when I was a child. Still, one learns to see when the need is sufficient.

When I reached the inner chamber where the old seeress had sat, I saw the outline of her form. Bones and jewels among rags. She must have been dead for years. Icarus had known. She may have died just after Merope and all the others were hanged. Then as though the years were a funnel, the fear I had felt that day poured down upon me. I whimpered in the dirt like a child. But soundlessly, because of the listeners outside.

At last, exhausted, I leaned against the cold stone and stared at the dim opening. The walls of the cave surrounded me like a womb. What would happen if I simply stayed there, vying with insects and snakes for the grains of offering? Even Asterios might turn away, even Minos might go back to Knossos if I remained in the cave. No doubt they would post a guard outside to see that I did not emerge, or to catch the deluded faithful who would bring me seeds. Even if they caught them all, I would be able to live for years on the offerings already there if I were willing to take what the earth creatures had left, even longer if I were willing to eat the insects as well, like a true hermit. Perhaps I would become a seeress. The future would write itself on my eyelids.

The stillness of the mountain crept into me. It is like no other silence. You can listen inward to the heart of the earth, to the trembling and rushing that underlies the rock, that goes on and on as we live, as we die.

Suddenly the death stench reached me. Perhaps a breeze from the opening had lifted it. I looked around in horror at the rot and chaos that delivers one back to the Mother. I scrambled on scraped knees toward the opening, clawed past the futile bowls, scattering sacred seeds and treasures to the corners of the cave. I could hardly breathe, the cave was so full of death. I came gasping into the air. It was almost night and at a respectful distance stood the two priestesses who had accompanied me. Quickly they moved closer. "The Mother is dead," I said.

Their faces became distorted masks. A moan came from the younger and she fell on the ground. Suddenly I realized what word I had used. "I mean, the priestess is dead," I said, wondering whether that was what I meant. It relieved the women. They continued the mourning ritual, but not with the same sharp agony.

They prepared the ceremony for me and called the other priestesses to aid in the burial rites. I was impatient to get it over with so that I could meet with the mountain leaders before Asterios came. The rites were as short as I dared to make them. By the time they were finished, darkness was complete—no moon, no stars. I groped carefully down the path to where the men were waiting, fearing at any moment to topple off the narrow ledge into the ravine. The women guided me. They knew my eyes had been blinded to the mountain dark by the torches of the court.

A single lamp before the house shrine flickered shadows outward against the walls. The women sat on benches around the room. Behind them stood the men, uneasy that I had insisted on their coming in before the ceremony had ended. But it was interminable. I had prayed briefly and prepared to begin a meeting to plan Minos' death during the spring ceremony. I knew he would present himself as consort. It would be an ideal time to strike, but we had to order our actions carefully so that Asterios and the guards would be occupied elsewhere. There was very little time to decide. I had arranged to mislead the Bull of Minos when I left the palace, but he would have found the right trail by now and would be traveling loudly through the night toward the mountain shrine. There would be just enough time to set the plan, I thought, and then I had to get back to the cave of the Sibyl so that I could be found there, pious and ecstatic, to be passively returned to Knossos.

But Agriope, the head priestess, kept prolonging the ritual. More seeds to bless. More intonations. Another young priestess to kneel and hear the whispered wisdom. Another prayer. Until finally I had ended it all abruptly and sent out an acolyte to bring in the men. They came hesitantly and made themselves small and flat against the wall as Agriope glared. Her hair stuck in damp stiff strands over her eyes. Her enormous breasts hung over the tight belt squeezing her bulbous abdomen. I wondered whether she were pregnant, but she seemed too old. All the men appeared to be afraid of her. The women too. It was at least an hour longer that she stood behind the lamp in frozen ecstasy before she finally waved to the acolyte to place it again in front of my chair.

I spoke quickly then. About Minos' sacrilege: the elevation of

Zeus, the lies about his laws. The spread of the Thracian drug by Pandareos and Asterios, Minos' bulls of evil, sent to destroy the old religion. All this they knew. And the hunger and drought up and down the land was a sign of the Mother's anger. They nodded. But now, I said, there has appeared the greatest blasphemy of all— Minos' plan to be my consort. A gasp went up. Some of them had not heard the rumor or could not believe it. I waited for the shock to subside. "But now also is our chance to kill the blasphemer and restore all to the Mother." They seemed not to be breathing. "Pharos—yes, Pharos from your village—has agreed to leap the circle and kill the rival. But Minos' bronze men will be watching, will whip out swords and prevent him if he is alone. All through the circles there must be priestesses with daggers, *kouretes* with knives and clubs. Hidden in the trees there must be others who will close in upon the blasphemers and slay them. Can you see to it? Can you have it arranged by the time of the ceremony? Are you willing to kill for the Mother? Are you willing to die for Her?"

They swayed and murmured at my words, shocked and grim. Some of them were weeping. Agriope's face was stone. They seemed to be waiting for her to reply, but she kept silence for a long time after my speech had ended. Finally she rose. "If the Goddess-on-Earth has returned to the Mother, it will suffice. The Mother will destroy Minos. The earth will open."

"But we must lay plans," I argued. I was rational, pointing out the evidence of history. The blotting out of Mother worship in Egypt and Syria. The attacks on the temples and palaces of the great Queen Hatshepsut the moment she was dead, the effacing of her name from her monuments, the destruction of her priestesses. It was obvious that neither Agriope nor the others had ever heard of any of them. Agriope said the queen must have fallen away from the Mother or it would not have been allowed. I reminded her of Pandareos. And Asterios. Of Minos' usurpation of the ceremonies. His story of receiving laws from Zeus. As I talked, her face hardened. She waited again long after I was quiet. Finally, she said, "If the Goddess-on-Earth has returned to the Mother, it will suffice. The Mother will destroy the blasphemers." And she bowed to me in her arrogant way so that I felt she was really chastising me instead.

I looked desperately around at the others. There was not a leader in the group, all passive. One young man who stood guard at the door seemed restless. I spoke to him. Would he see to it that there were armed men in the circles? He brightened with pleasure, I thought, at my words, but his own were fumbling, and before I could understand his line of thought, Agriope silenced him with her strong stolid monotone. "If the Goddess-on-Earth has returned to the Mother, all will be taken care of." Her arms folded under her breasts and her eyes closed piously. I could have killed the woman, but I didn't dare show my anger. She ruled the whole assemblage like a goddess. Even the restless young man stood quietly now, eyes down, hand to his forehead in prayer.

There was no reaching them with reason. They feared it more than they feared Asterios, and they feared it in me most of all, for it seemed to them a rebellion against the Mother. All they would allow me was a sign of faith. It took all my strength to leash my fury at their ignorance. Always I felt Daedalus' sneering words creeping into my mouth as I tried reasoning without seeming to reason. But Agriope stood like stone and the others only watched her for a sign of what they should do. The Goddess-on-Earth, I saw, had power over them only on their own terms.

I was saved from an explosion into anger by a young priestess' rushing in to whisper that someone, many people, had been heard in the north canyon, fumbling along the old trail. "It must be Asterios," she said. "Mountain people would not take that route at night." I prayed with them gladly then that the path would crumble, feet slide. All the same, I broke up the meeting quickly, sent them all away to hide, and started for the mountain shrine. I parted solemnly with Agriope. She was stiffly formal in her obedience. The two priestesses again insisted on accompanying me, though I tried to get them to leave once they had brought me back to the cave. They would not. They bowed and were worshipful in their attitude, but they would not leave. I sat down on a rock near the sacred spring to wait. The older priestess stood some distance away in the posture of prayer. The younger one stayed close. Her hands were trembling and she took deep breaths, holding them a long time before they rushed out in heavy sighs. When I put my hand on hers, she began to cry. "Quick," I said. "Go behind the cave. They will not see you in the darkness."

My words turned her into a small Agriope. The little face closed into pious statuary. Now we sat side by side in silence waiting for the inevitable steps. Only once did she speak, in the faintest of trembling whispers. "The princess Phaedra—has she really given herself to Zeus?" She was shivering violently.

"No," I said quickly. "Phaedra is with the Mother." She continued to shiver. Perhaps it was only from the cold, I told myself. But one could already hear the clank of bronze somewhere in the night. I wondered about Phaedra. Guilt fell around me like a cloak. I had paid so little attention to her for so long. Perhaps it was true that she had abandoned the old religion. Perhaps Minos had seen to it. I wanted to ask this child what she had heard that made her remind me of my neglected duty, but she was withdrawn into her fear as into rock. I murmured a prayer, hoping it would reach her.

When Asterios came, his men took both priestesses away and they disappeared into the darkness without sound. The old woman moved slowly with dignity as if walking in a procession, but the little girl stumbled once and looked back at me, and I saw again that mask that falls across the faces of those who have been marked for sacrifice. Fury whipped through me like a bull roarer through the air. Had Asterios put his knife to my mouth, I could have shredded it with my teeth. But there was none of that. My mask was a different shape.

Another descent from the shrine in horror. The little priestess was barely nubile. There would be no Icarus for her. No infant. No moving in and out of another mind, another body with love, no primal giving and receiving, no yielding of everything to the womb child, flesh surrounding and protecting, even following after with cord and milk, armored by arms even after the inevitable severance.

None of it. Shadows moved by on both sides, but only now and then could I tell on which side dropped the chasm. The litter lurched as the men slipped, but I who was always afraid in the mountains was not afraid. The inevitable severance. Had it happened already for the little priestess? What was it like at last to feel the final closing down of darkness? She believed in the Mother, must have been ecstatic in her belief or she would not have volunteered for this. Again I felt a rage of fury. Why had Agriope allowed it? Why not two tired old women, if there had to be a sacrifice at all? Anger roared through me at the waste, the lack of love, the lack of mind. The journey was all for nothing, yet the child would die for it. No plan. No assurance of weapons in the hands of the festival dancers to support Pharos. And if they did not come armed, another futile sacrifice. I wept then in a way that Icarus would never have recognized. I was alone, upon the surface of the earth, balanced precariously above maggots, the child's last look hanging in my eyes like an abandoned flag in a desolate field.

# 3

DAEDALUS:

SHE'S BACK. Alone, without attendants (where did they go?) among the chesty brawn and the clanking swords, looking like something out of my grandmother's tales, some wayward daughter of the Mother, hunted down in the hills and brought back to perform some kind of dance with the sacred bulls to test her purity. There was a smudge of gypsum under her eyes, which shows she must have participated in an old ceremony while she was up there. I would not be surprised if she were recruiting rebels, as well. But that's all a lost cause. The force is on the other side.

They paraded her a bit, to let people know who's in charge, I guess. And then she disappeared into her quarters, from which has come no word, no sign. I wonder whether she knows how helpless she appeared.

Minos continues to rave at night. I pretend to help, though I have no cure for guilt. All night he fidgets. It is very tiring. I try to catch some sleep in the late morning, but it's not enough for a man my age. And it interferes with my research into the problems of transporting the water. I may be the only one who remembers that project.

If only I could get some peace. Minos screams all night, then puts on a show of strength in the daylight. He's relieved to get Ariadne back; fears her more than anything, it seems. But Asterios makes him feel like the old sea conqueror who gave me refuge, defying Attica. Minos has rewarded him with a sea journey to Athens to collect the hostages. (Has it really been only eight years since the last? Seems like a hundred to me.) I wonder whether I could arrange to go with him. I've got to leave this place.

ARIADNE:

"In the pillar shrine, as always," said the old servant when I asked about Phaedra. The shadow of an overhanging wall cut across her face so that her mouth was concealed. I could see only her eyes, wherein I read reproach, then irritably corrected the impression and read indifference, hatred, anger. But she was gone. I was reading images on my eyelids.

I tried to think, "Phaedra." Snakes scurried across the grass. "Phaedra." A flash of white engulfed by darkness. "Phaedra." A child's thin body on whom someone had bound bulbous breasts. "Phaedra." Merope whispering, "You must teach her."

The stairs wound down and down. I passed the hall of my mother and my grandmother, the hall of the Goddess with the spring bubbling in the light well, the hall where Minos dispensed his form of justice. Down, down through lightless passageways to the room which even now Minos would not enter, the room where petitioners huddled on the stone bench waiting for the Mother to speak, where, as I passed, several shadows raised hands to foreheads, moaning prayers. I blessed them automatically and entered the deeper darkness of the shrines, the first with lustral basins waiting to be used for the purification of the world. And then the second and the third shrines, where the stillness was of stone like the Sibyl's cave. As always the darkness closed round my mind with such force that for a time I forgot the frail movements above. I could see nothing. I heard breathing, but I could not be sure that it was not my own. As my eyes learned the darkness, the huge pillar emerged, and I saw a small arm encircling it, but the face was hidden. She was holding on as though a winter gale might tear her from it, but when I reached for her, she shrank away. I followed and found her, clenched to the pillar, cold as the stone. Her face was wet. I felt a sudden rush of love for her. We two alone were Pasiphae's daughters. No one else was so dangerous to Minos. No one else was in such danger. And she knew it, though she was still so young, knew as I had known when my mother died. We held each other and talked then for the first time as women. How much she knew without my teaching. How old she had become though she was still small as a child.

I told her everything about the journey to the mountain priestess, about the plan, about Agriope. Too much, I told her too much. Even about the little priestess left to be slaughtered. I spilled it all out to this tiny terrified woman as she shuddered in my arms, saying, "Yes, I see. Yes." What possessed me to chatter on and on to her about all the real and unreal horrors in my mind, my first confidences in all those years, whispered in blackness and snaked about with fear?

When finally we left, we discovered a priestess in the second shrine, praying. It was Thera. Had she been listening? Phaedra and I walked together, arms entwined as in the pictures of the two goddesses. I went with her all the way back to her quarters.

DAEDALUS:

It seems I'm a prisoner. One forgets the power of rulers while the winds are in the right direction. "No," says Minos. "You may not leave." And that's that. I had merely asked to go with Asterios to pick up the tribute. A diversion. A chance to study the movement of the ships with a view to making some changes in the design, speed them up, add weight. But Minos has not lost all his keenness. He knows the climate in Attica has changed. They'd take me back now, forget that ancient indiscretion. Who was Talos anyway? An apprentice, a dubious asset. Besides, the years have wiped out the pollution of all that. His mother's dead. And they could use my talents and my knowledge of Crete. King Aegeus is not entirely foolish. And there's talk he has a son hidden somewhere whom he intends to inherit the throne, though the Pallantid priestesses must oppose that. He's never subdued that clan. He could use me there. And would, indeed, whether I wished it or not. Always turmoil. I would like, just once in my life, to have a chance to build according to my own desire. Temples. Palaces. Fortifications, perhaps. Maybe I should try to go east.

ARIADNE:

As the spring ceremony approached, Pharos was hopeful. He had talked to Menor, his kinsman. There were many who knew what must be done, he said. Agriope did not speak for all. They would come. He himself had heard them say it. I spoke with a few of the priestesses, but there was no Merope among them. Their eyes were slow and they seemed to be moving in a dream. Or were they pretending? Minos' spies? I did not know. Korkyne sat shaking her head. But Pharos dreamed, and I did not stop him.

When the time came, he was left alone among the knives. I saw the swords all around, a closing in of thick-necked brutes who loved this hatchet work. They were holding me or I might have met the triton myself. I saw how they held Pharos, five, six of them perhaps, and I saw his eyes in the moment before the blades entered, for it was to me that he looked. What message he drew from me in that last gaze, I cannot tell.


DAEDALUS:

I am sick of these people and this place! I've given them more than I can spare. Almost a year since my son vanished, and no ceremony to mark the date except a barbarous bloody writhing in the dark.

When they started it, I went into my quarters and closed the door, as I had done the previous year. But while I sat reading, I could not help but hear the drum and the mumbled chants. Then, very faintly, a flute. One does not always know why one does things. I found myself moving down the corridor with the papyrus still in hand. I put it down, I don't know where, and stole out as if I were drawn by a slave cord.

For what? To find out who had killed my son? To find out why he had fallen back into the old superstition? To find my own infant fantasies? Even a man of reason slides into these things sometimes. I slunk along the walls, half-ashamed, wanting not to be seen. But there was no one there to notice. The halls and shops were emptied out into the night. No sign of guard or slave. The palace and all its riches (all its food!) had been abandoned, and that in the midst of poverty. As if no one really cared. I thought for an instant that this would be a time to leave Crete for good, but I had made no plans, had no ship, no crew, no strong alliances. Besides, there was something I needed to settle, something not wholly within me, something here on these dark grounds.

The wind struck my shoulders as I went out the portal. I had not brought a cloak. I remembered then that I had passed one lying on a bench in the corridor and I went back for it. It was a gaudy thing belonging to a courtier, no doubt, rich with gold and gems. Like the palace, abandoned. The thought chilled me more than the wind. What a prize was Knossos, a fat grape ripe for the picking and no real defenders to say no. It's a good thing one's thoughts are silent. I put on the cloak. It covered me completely. I would not be recognized, should any laggard worshipper notice an old man feeling his way in the darkness.

The streets were empty. Sounds came from the Mound. A flute again. Women's voices. Then a single cry. Was it Ariadne? The torches flickered in a line against the dark sky. I hurried toward them, still hiding in shadows—from whom, I was not sure. But before I reached the hill, the whole line of torches moved off toward the trees, swiftly, as if pursued. For a moment I thought the people were running from me, but then I saw the absurdity of that. No one had looked in my direction.

I followed, but they had got too far ahead for me to see what was happening. By the time they stopped again, they were in the grove, and trees and bushes concealed them much of the time. They seemed to be in a circle, many circles, row within row. It was hard to see. The torches appeared to be in only the inmost circle. But I was glad of the darkness. I saw that I had taken the wrong cloak. All the others were dressed in white. I decided to turn the cloak inside out, hiding the jewels and showing only the dull gray lining. They were moving in a kind of round dance, circle within circle, some of them masked, some of them with eyes closed or vacant as if in a trance. Abruptly the dance became wild, and in and out of the

[ 163 ]

line of dancers dashed ugly masked demonlike creatures, shrieking
and snatching at the others. They all became excited shriekers and
snatchers until just when I thought the noise would drive me back
to the palace, everything stopped. There was no sound at all in all
that crowd, no movement. I could not see through the line and I
was afraid to stir. Then something began somewhere inside the
circle. I could sense the straining in the crowd to look above or
through the inner line of torch bearers to see some spectacle. The
spirit of the thing caught me, I suppose. At that moment, I wanted
nothing more than to see what was going on there. But it was well
hidden. I cursed my lack of height, my lame leg that shrank me
even more. For all my Attic blood, I was smaller than a Cretan.

Behind me, some distance from the crowd, I saw a tree that had
branches low enough for climbing and thick enough to hide in,
unless the light struck it directly, but I could not move toward it
until the dance began again, and they were now all immobile as
stars. Even the moon moved more than they did. There was
nothing I could do but wait.

At last there was a stir as if the tension were too great. Or
perhaps it was in reaction to something within the circle. I took
advantage of the moment to reach the tree and hide in the upper
branches. I think no one saw me, for while I was still climbing, a
voice streamed out into the night, spearing their attention. It was
Ariadne's voice, but as I'd never heard it before. Hoarse. No, not
hoarse, deep. Impossible to describe. As if it rose from somewhere
beneath her.

Enough of that. One gets carried away. They drug the air,
perhaps, and the mind departs. I was awake, though—enough to
see that it was a tawdry affair to an undrugged eye, dirt and
writhing, drums. I left my tree soon enough. But not before I had
seen more than I wanted of the dark business. Ariadne grimacing,
eyes wild, fearful. It was Minos, you see, who had entered the ring,
just after the slaughter of the bull. The rumor had been true—
Minos was the consort! A gasp went through the mob. I suppose
they had not really believed that he would do it. A brazen violation

of an ancient taboo, father marrying daughter. Like one of the Egyptians whom the Cretans scorn—but imitate.

Now it became apparent where the palace guards had gone, and the warriors. Minos had stood in the circle scarcely a moment when another man leaped in upon him, dagger drawn. Minos turned, throwing him off, and suddenly there was a triton in his hands, pointed at the fool's face. I saw that face clearly. It was Pharos. Two soldiers reached out and held him down while Minos plunged the forks straight into his eyes. A groan of dismay ran through the line. Ariadne screamed. Then figures moved in, hands at the attack. It could easily have been the end of Minos, but suddenly his men were everywhere, swords up and slashing. I saw them slice arms in two as easily as soft fruit. And Ariadne continued to scream, eyes wild.

I left. Well, of course I was distressed, but I'm no hero. There was nothing I could do. I don't know what happened the rest of the night. I don't want to know.

# 4

ARIADNE:

WHAT FOLLOWED BUNCHES TOGETHER in my mind like the grotesque distortions on a seal. First, interminably, there is the scene of my toilette. A ritual bath, a ritual annointing, attended by many weeping priestesses. (Not Korkyne. She had turned her eyes inward and would respond to no one.) Then the adornment in one long scene after another—the selection and rejection of robes, perfume, jewelry, sandals again and again and again, with Minos hunching in a niche somewhere near or stomping about in the corridors amid the clank of bronze and the fierce grimaces of his assassins. Then the procession, slower than slow, with many stops for offerings and libations to Those Above and Those Below, to the winds and the ocean, to the spirits that dwell in the beasts of the forest, the grasses of the plain, the birds of the sky, the fish of the sea, the insects and all other crawling things. Above all, a long, long invocation to the Great Serpent of life and death, who would not come and would not listen, though I called and chanted through the hours of the night until again the bronze clanked and a moaning went through the row of priestesses and I rose. Finally the closing of the door and a prayer at the shrine in my chamber. I heard Minos enter silently and pause when he heard my voice. I stood and knelt, stood and knelt, abandoning the prescribed ritual and responding only to the fatigue in my knees and arms, counting on Minos' ignorance. My mother had been careless of all other rites, why not of this one as well? On and on I went until I heard behind me again the impatient voice of metal. Then I began the Sacred Dance. Tiles twirled beneath my feet, and I let my voice rise until it hit that tone that carries to the sacred grove and beyond. I tried to imagine what would stir in the minds of those who heard. Pharos, if he lived. Korkyne. Any of the mountain people who might flee back to Agriope and lay my cry at her feet.

Light was beginning to show behind the pillars bordering my court. I was tired, but not so tired as the one dropping to the bed behind me. As I twirled, I planned. By the time I was sure that the loud, even breaths meant deep sleep, the light was full and the twittering of the birds had softened into the daylight hum. I opened the door and my priestesses carried Minos, sleeping heavily, into the antechamber. I appointed two of the women to watch at my door. Then I went back to my bed alone and slept soundly, not dreaming even of Pharos.

The next night the scene was repeated, and the next as well. On the fourth night Minos protested after I had danced only an hour. I dropped my arms at once and stood still as if listening to the earth. Minos listened as well. What fear there must be in him to make him so patient here where he has all the power, I thought. I raised my arms again and looked around from one side to the other as if watching someone move. "The spirit of Pasiphae will not concede," I whispered. Minos turned away irritably as I began again to dance. Round me the fresco ladies twirled, rose, and fell. The mosaic underfoot gleamed in the light of the altar lamps. I heard Minos moving restlessly about the room. Suddenly he grabbed my arms and stopped me. I moaned and turned my eyes wildly from one side to another, mumbling my mother's name. But Minos held on. Finally I let my body go limp and I almost fell from his arms. As he was bending toward me, I opened my eyes very wide and said in a clear sharp voice, "Yes, Mother, the offering." Again he let me go and stood silent while I prepared the libations. The first for the Mother, the second for me, and the last for him, all from the same *rhyton* but poured into different cups. And in the bottom of Minos' cup waiting for this moment, a sleeping potion. It worked almost at once. Again I had him carried away.

On the fifth night, Minos would not let me dance, saying it was enough, the Mothers would have to be content with the ceremony already done. "Perhaps they will be," I said and started again to prepare the libations. This time he would have none of it but took me at once to the bed and began pawing at my breasts and tearing at my girdle. For a moment, I looked at him as if in sympathy. "What a tragedy that the Mother's will is against it," I said loudly. I could feel his body sag, but he roused himself again, tore off my skirts and threw himself upon me fiercely, his face contorted as if in pain. But for all his writhing and puffing, his snake remained limp as a worm. I lay still waiting for him to tire. When finally he did give up, he took my clothes, threw them violently at the wall, and collapsed upon the bed. I rose naked and unviolated, pulled on a white ceremonial robe, and continued the dance as he wept into the pillow. Later, when he slept, I had him carried out again, but he woke when they put him down and strode fiercely back into my room. I stayed at the altar, praying, and finally he went back to sleep.

In the morning word about Theseus' arrival came. It meant nothing to me then. What still sticks in my mind is the face of Daedalus as he entered the room and saw us. Daedalus, that hard bright man with eyes as wide and clear as the sun itself, looked at Minos and hated him. There was no mistaking it, though no word defined it. At that moment I knew his skills were still there for me to use.

DAEDALUS:

There was no sign of Ariadne or Minos for days. No sign of a revolution either. The palace people straggled back. Guards and warriors were everywhere. Common people kept to their houses. Slaves and artisans went on about their work.

On the fifth day a messenger arrived from the port. Why they brought him to me, I'm not sure. The guards said they had found him in the corridor near the Great East Hall. He wanted to see Minos, he said, but they brought him to me. They didn't want to make a decision, I suppose. What was his message? A ship was approaching, Asterios' ship. That would be the arrival of the Athenian hostages. I dismissed the man with a wave. But there was something more he wanted to say. He started to speak, thought better of it, looked around, would not leave. His orders were to see the king, he said.

I had no more desire than the guards to interrupt Minos at his pleasure, but this sounded like news he would welcome. I sent a slave to tell him. They knew well enough where he was; you can't hide from slaves. "Come," was the reply. To Ariadne's *megaron*.

The messenger went in alone but came out almost at once to say I was wanted also. They were both there, Minos sprawled on the bed, Ariadne a dark silhouette against the doorway to the balcony. I could not see her face.

"Repeat your message," Minos said, and the Cretan boy looked at me with a kind of scorn in his glance. "One of the hostages," he said, "is the Attic prince, Theseus."

The words dropped like ice into a chasm inside me. I am not an emotional man, nor given to much solicitude for a state that had sent me into exile. But no man wants his native city to perish utterly, to be wiped back into the maternal mud. I had watched Athenian slaves brought in, worked like animals, made into foppish bull dancers, killed—all with equanimity. But the vision of a prince of Athens, Aegeus' own mythic son, forced to grovel at the feet of this malevolent, incestuous Cretan—it showed on my face, I realized, as I saw Minos watching me. He paid no attention to the messenger, merely waved, and without rising said, "Tell them to wait at sea tonight and dock in the morning." It could have been spoken through a closed door. He had wanted me to see them together there. He had wanted to see me as I heard the news. Why bother to impress an Attic slave? Or was it another way of showing the impotence of Athenians?

Ariadne said nothing.

# 5

DAEDALUS:

IT WAS A FLASHING DAY, sun in and out of clouds, sea roaring. White waves seething out of gray water drove the ship in fast. The huddle of white at the bow, hemmed by an intermittent glint, became, as they neared, men and women, swords. At last the ship knocked against the dock, and the hostages clambered up the rocks, agile and young, tribute of Attica. I heard Minos take in a deep breath. He seemed to shiver at the feel of his strength.

Asterios led the captives. As he climbed up to Minos' perch, the people on the shore, noble and common, warriors and artisans, all applauded him. Minos looked at them irritably. Asterios was vastly pleased. The hostages stood, taller than their captors, in a line on a level just below, girls and boys intermingled. They were shockingly young. The girls backed up suddenly as if at a word, though I heard nothing, and from the row of boys one stepped out. I heard Minos' smothered laugh. This would be the Attic prince, then. He was taller than any man I had seen, and, for one so young (eighteen at most), broad in chest and shoulder. Hair fiery when the sun gleamed out, face proud as a god. The voice was deep. I felt it in my chest, vibrating there as if I'd breathed it, and so I lost the words. They seemed to concern one of the girls. Had Minos asked for her? I must have missed an order. His men were already dragging her forward when Theseus (it *was* he!) stopped them. The swords flicked up fast, ready to slice, but Minos put out his hand. A game with a princeling amused him, no doubt.

But it was not amusement on his face that I saw as he drew a ring from his finger. I couldn't hear what he said. The wind tossed their voices about like dice. "Poseidon," I heard Theseus say, and then Minos' face closed and he threw the ring as far out into the harbor as he could fling, saying something else that was lost in wind. His face was full of scorn. The ring arced and caught the sun's glint once before it disappeared into the green. Theseus, too, caught the sun in his hair in a regal, arrogant pause before he dove expertly into the waves. We all watched, slaves and rulers, as the water closed over him. Ariadne leaned out of her litter to look over the wharfside, her face a riddle, even to one who had learned to read monarchs like papyrus. The Athenian hostages seemed to have shrunk in their waiting crouch. Anyone could see how they depended upon this prince, were nothing without him.

There was time for the ripples arising from his dive to reach the wharf and break, for the crouching hostages to droop their shoulders, for Minos to settle back into his chair and drop his hand, for me to compute the loss to Attica of this presumptuous youth, before the water broke upon his drenched gold curls and he swam with strong even strokes to the wharf, pulling himself up with a flourish as if it were no feat at all to have stayed so long out of the air. How I envied that gesture. It was as if he had communed with some divinity. He seemed like a young lion as he leaped back to Minos. The ring was on his finger. Slowly he drew it off, extended it, and, as Minos reached out to take it, suddenly threw it out again in a wide arc back into the waters of the harbor. Minos' face darkened and the swords of the guards rose up, but Theseus was already at Ariadne's side. There was a length of seaweed in his hands fashioned into a circle. He laid it before her as if it were a crown. She placed it upon her head, wet as it was, and smiled. I think she said something, but it was all lost in Minos' sudden shout and Asterios' order, the flash of swords, a whip's lash along the ground not two inches from Theseus' foot, and the swirl and movement of everyone departing. As Asterios herded the Athenians up the path toward the palace, the people watching applauded again, but it was not clear whom they were praising, captor or captives, all walking proudly as rulers.

Now the world held an excitement for me that I had forgotten. Outwardly I went on solemn, serious, a devoted subject of Minos. Architect and engineer in the daytime, physician at night. He wanted ships; I built them. He wanted aphrodisiacs; I found them. The night calls ceased for a short while, then were renewed. Sometimes I was summoned to Ariadne's *megaron* again, more often, to Minos' private quarters in the little palace. The Egyptian and I conferred. We even asked the herb women, the priestesses. Our requests were veiled, and they took great care to make the answers equally ambiguous, but the matter was clear enough. Minos was impotent. Was it Ariadne's doing? I could see her great uncompromising eyes bleakly assessing Minos' rise to power. She seemed helpless at times, but omnipotent at others, in the Great Mother's direct line. Minos must fear her then, for one could tell that he had never thrown off the old religion completely. It raged against his hand even as he lifted his sword.

Yet in the arena, all was serenity. The Athenians trained as mountebanks, learned tricks in bull handling for the next ceremonies. I went to watch their training and saw Theseus springing from the stuffed bull like an athlete, but he was not as skillful as some of the others. He would be a good bull dancer, likely to escape killing for a season or two, if his luck held. No more than that. But there were exciting rumors about him—of his having taken Ariadne's fancy, of secret meetings in the night while Minos raged for the return of youth. Perhaps they were true, I thought, staring at the public mystery of her face, though I knew nothing about it, nothing at all.

Months of this. Then suddenly Minos announced that he was going out on another voyage to get more hostages. "More kings," he said, sweeping his arms across the horizon as if gathering them in (and all the while calling each night for help against his nightmares). Asterios was more sullen than ever and let it be known that the role of gatherer of tribute belonged to him. But Minos was adamant. He was jealous, perhaps, of the adulation laid at Asterios' feet as he paraded his captives and made them do their tricks for the populace. When a man feels his power slipping away, his judgment slips with it; he becomes a fool. Minos would not have listened to me, had I wished to save him. Far from that, I was dreaming— every hour he let me sleep—of Attica. When he told me that only the Egyptian physician would accompany him, I saw that he had read my thoughts. As for Ariadne, the idea of the journey was, I think, hers. At any rate, the very night of the day that Minos' sail slipped away to sea, there came a summons from the queen. It surprised me as I stood on my balcony trying to see what was causing a riot of sounds in the central court.

Now, let this be clear. It is true that I had some affection for this woman. I had watched her grow from barbaric child into queenhood. What is more, I had seen her learn to think, which is something none but a few in any age can manage. This, too— though she had taken my son, I did not believe she had willed his death. Still, she was Cretan all through, bred that way, and no one can escape that breeding. Above all, she was mistress of a foundering ship on which I was, at most, a favored servant. Besides, there are winds that rise in the world that push us whether we wish it or not. I am not a liar. I am not a brute. Yet one is not called upon to yield all he knows, nor to work against himself.

# 6

ARIADNE:

LIES LEAPED ABOUT ME like hierophants in the old confusion of shadow and flame. Athenians are liars. I saw the shift of vision and the too-steady stare and the pauses before answering. But I did not know how much they lied until after the Mother had spoken.

Theseus. Like a plummeting hawk he fell into Knossos. My plan demanded a man of blood. I saw it on his hands, washed though they were with sea water, flinging Minos' ring into the sea and bringing me a crown of weed. When a slave laughs at his captors, look for a man of courage. It was what I needed.

The first night that the old king gave up his futile attempts at my seduction, I had Theseus brought to me through the secret route Daedalus had built for my mother. Minos was busy weeping in his little palace and calling for his physicians, poor fumbling fools, a thousand years more ignorant in those things than the youngest priestess at the mountain shrine.

The prince wore his chains like jewels. I had him stripped, but even then he stood without shame, though one could see his pride was on the line. I ordered my slaves to bathe and annoint him. When they brought him back I sent them out to guard, and I fondled him, testing his manhood, watching his eyes. The chains were gone, but I could tell he distrusted me, was not sure we were really alone. His chest was broad and covered with fine golden hair, curling and wiry to the touch. His throat was strong, his head small and capped with that same sunborn curling hair. His shoulders and arms rippled with muscles, gleaming in the oil. His hands were calloused, fingers rough at the tips, nails torn short, knuckles scarred. The pulse at the wrist beat heavily in spite of the impassive blue of his eyes. And when I touched his snake, it rose obediently as if obeying another law than that held so steadily in his firm lips. I turned from him and lay down on the bed, but he did not move. He was very large. Much taller than Icarus, much broader. I felt my loins throbbing. Perhaps I smiled, because suddenly he laughed. That laugh rushed over me with the coldness of a mountain torrent. I could hear the Angry Ones whispering in my ears. As he came toward me, I stood. For a moment I paused, listening back through centuries. Then I called my guards and they chained him again and took him away.

I walked about all night. It was the time of the full moon. I stood on my balcony and watched the gold ball move through blackness, rise above the horns on the roof into the broad deep night. I must have stood for hours, my hands pressed tight against my mouth. I felt Korkyne watching me the whole time, but she made no sound. Finally, the sky lightened. I felt the stiffness in my arms as I dropped them. A pain ran down my spine and forward into my groin. Korkyne came and helped me bathe. As I lay down upon my bed I found her message. "Not this one. He is death." I crumpled the note and burned it.

The plan required a man willing to kill and skilled in it. One who needed Minos' death and had the courage to undertake it. One who could lead the slaves and command respect of the nobles. The son of a queen with the authority to make agreements binding upon his country. A man worthy in the eyes of Cretans to be my consort. For weeks I studied Theseus. The story of his capture was all over Knossos. Asterios had told it again and again to anyone who would listen. Even Minos reveled in it and threw triumphant glances at me as if to say, "See how powerful I am, even though—" I called in old Thonos, whom Korkyne trusted, and had him check the story with members of Asterios' crew. They confirmed it. This really was Aegeus' son caught in the hostage lottery. The old king had wailed weakly and fallen to his knees at Asterios' feet like any slave. But Theseus raised him up brusquely and spoke, more to the Athenians than to his father, they thought. They could not catch all the strange accent, but it had to do with honor and courage and the will of Zeus. Thonos grimaced here.

I asked Daedalus also, but he seemed to know very little. My old tutor still had the power to make me believe his tongue was honest. Menor was fearful, and also Korkyne, but they spoke against Theseus without knowledge, I thought. The stories they had heard were phantom tales, laced with old superstitions—nothing of substance. Nothing reported by someone who had even seen Attica. And they all agreed that he was indeed the son of Aethra, High Priestess of the Triple Goddess and Queen of Pitthea.

"Test him," I said.

"Test a slave?" Menor was a man of honor, dependable as anyone upon this shifting earth, but he had no imagination.

"A slave is one who has been conquered," I said. "Theseus is not a slave."

It did not illumine him.

"You're a warrior," I said. It was true. He had come down from the mountains years before to follow Minos on the sea. Only in his old age had he given it up to return to his family. Only in his old age had he come to see how Minos threatened the old values. Even now, Minos trusted him with the training of youths who aspired to soldiery, trusted him even though he was kinsman to poor Pharos. "Devise a plan for revolt," I said. "Tell him of the hatred of Minos shared by the mountain people. Ask his assistance in organizing the slaves. Ask him for counsel. Test his skill."

"And if he should prove untrustworthy?"

"Oh Menor, the world depends upon men like you, yet you are timid." I laughed. "How can he harm you? A slave? If he denounces you, you will deny it. Whose word will Minos honor, do you think? But if you're afraid, you needn't be involved. Do it through someone else—a boy from your village, someone like Pharos. There are plenty of them who would offer themselves gladly."

Menor was offended. It took me some time to win him back to humor. Finally he agreed to try.

He did it himself; his pride demanded that. I don't know how he presented it, but Theseus took up the challenge, laid out a plan, talked with the Attic hostages, the slaves from other colonies, went beyond that—mapped out a strategy of assault upon Knossos by the mountain villagers that showed an amazing knowledge of Crete. Who knows how he had come by it? Menor thought it came partly from his working for various members of the palace guard, because Theseus made a list of those whom he considered sympathetic to the cause. He frequented their homes often. He was a kind of celebrity, a prince and a champion bull dancer. The nobles enjoyed showing him at parties, though often they must have thought of him as not quite human and talked more openly than discretion should have allowed.

Menor came back to report within a month. He was jubilant. Theseus had knowledge of the inhabitants, skill in military tactics, a vision of the future that excited any man. Yes, he had passed the test. This was a man he could work with, could follow.

The surety in his eyes almost deterred me. I would have preferred less enthusiasm. I remembered the chill I had felt when Theseus laughed. But then I pushed the memory away, back into the muddy cave littered with dirty rags, golden bowls, and death.

I had him brought to me again. I see him still in dreams, coming through the door with guards on each side, pausing as they unshackled him, pausing again after they had left, head slightly to one side, chin lifted, eyes alert. Determined this time, perhaps, to be scornful to the end of a slave's endurance.

I told him what Menor had reported. His eyes were wary. This was a man who had seen a trap before. He paused before committing himself, but then he did do that, having assessed me as honest, I suppose. We were peers. No doubt he knew something of the jealousies that afflict all royal families. No doubt he felt he knew me well enough.

We talked. He explained his plan. It was true, his knowledge of Crete was admirable. And he spoke with authority of methods of deceiving Minos, ways of deploying Asterios' troops on fruitless missions, plans for gathering the mountain people at key locations where they could descend upon the palace at a moment's notice, take possession of the arms, the ships, decimate the guard, trap the warriors. It was a language I knew little of, yet it convinced.

Perhaps, *therefore* it convinced. Yet Menor, the warrior, had also been persuaded that this man would serve us.

Still, as he talked, it seemed to me that I was watching a child. He was so sure of everything, so positive that the future was in his hands. Daedalus would have smiled. However, I reasoned to myself, each of us need not be all. Each has a place. Even the Mother has need of a protector. There are those who envision and those who act.

Earnestness became him. There was a flush of pink in his cheeks as he strode about the room, showing me the way it would be done, acting out the battle, straining almost as if his adversary were there pushing against him, invisible but strong.

"Let's make a pact," I said. And we did, touching hands as our seal. We were alone, the prince and I, except for the Mother's emissaries, breathing inside our breaths, willing us to act without our will.

He paused as I came to him and caressed him, as I disrobed him myself and bathed him in scented oil. He paused even while his snake lifted, even as I pulled him down with me to the bed. Until at last . . .

Should I have known then what lay ahead? Why was Korkyne's vision so much clearer than mine? Even now, I think that for a while there was only love between us, only a tumble of movement among the soft blankets, the world abolished—swords, plans, thrones, all abolished. Korkyne smiles bitterly and does not believe. But Theseus was man as well as monarch. The surging of the Mother's will stirred in him as well as in me, I believe. I suppose I should have known by the brutality of his thrusts, with no thought for my pleasure. But my pleasure was there without his thought. It sickens me to see how even now I want to feel that he loved me. The old lie of the loins, put there by a whimsical goddess to mock our minds. Well, whatever was in his mind, the act was love at that time, and I at least forgot the world.

Even when I remembered, there was no need to give up Theseus. Minos spent his nights now crying for Daedalus and the Egyptian. Or he would go up to Iyttos and pray to Zeus. Sometimes he called for a priestess, but he would not come near me. The Evil Ones assaulted him in dreams, Korkyne said. Someone had seen my mother rushing down the Royal Way to his little palace, carrying knives. Strange black birds beat about her.

Asterios ran from one shrine to another without Minos' prompting, as though a lust for the blood of priestesses absorbed him. Again and again he returned with the pitiful raving captives. Never did he bring the kind of priestess who had been with me on the mountain, solemn and strong. Those must have been killed on the spot. The ones he brought to display in the courtyard and in the streets were those whom he had already driven mad with his drug. He would parade them, chained, between horses, then beat the animals to make them pull apart, stretching and tearing the chained arms, or to make them crowd together, trampling the victims. When he had no fresh captives, he would bring out the bull dancers into the courtyard and set bulls upon them, but not in the manner of the ritual where a team of dancers confront a single bull and perform the sacred movements and, often as not, escape to dance again. Asterios would single out one dancer and loose several bulls, taking care first to madden them with pain by stabbing their sides until the blood ran down and covered them. Then, often, the dancers would be killed. Theseus writhed at this, hated Asterios more than Minos. But Asterios never chose him for this game, preferring to parade him on the streets tied between horses.

Sometimes a murmur would go through the crowd. Once in a while some fool would applaud Asterios and rush forward to grovel at his feet. Perhaps fear drove him, or some awaking savagery. But for the most part the people were silent. They watched. Sometimes I found them watching me.

Minos watched too, but he never looked in my eyes. When he watched Asterios, he applauded, but it was easy to see the envy in him. One morning he announced that he was going on a sea voyage and that he would return with not one prince, as Asterios had, but "with twelve kings and twelve queens." As he spoke, his cheeks shook. He was fatter, it seemed, and yet he looked ill. The guards applauded. Asterios looked glum.

But Minos did not leave at once. Weeks went by and the royal ships remained in dock. We had time to plan, though we sensed a greater need for secrecy than ever. Theseus knew strategy. It was easy to see that he had fought many battles. The task suited his talent. A kind of mask fell upon him when he spoke of ambush and sudden stabbing, as if he moved into another being and felt more at home in it. It was an existence that could have left me out entirely had I not made the step with him. But I was not so lost in love as to forget why I had brought him to my bed. We had our agreement. He promised to restore the old religion and the full power of the queen, and I promised to free Attica from tribute. But none of this could take place until after the death of Minos. And Asterios. And whoever else supported them. We met with Thonos and Menor and planned our actions carefully.

When, finally, Minos' sails disappeared, we brought in Daedalus.

# 7

DAEDALUS:

THE MOMENT I SAW Ariadne, I guessed that she was with child again and it sickened me. But then I saw Theseus standing in a corner! One could tell at a glance that this was not his first visit to the queen's quarters. He was at home in the room. He bowed to me. "Your name is a legend," he said. "An Attic youth grows up hearing of the marvels created by Daedalus."

The cleverness of his phrasing made me smile. I knew that he himself had grown up far away from Attica. The princeling had learned his trade.

He was a joy to look at, too. The enormous muscles of his arms and chest, naked in the Cretan fashion, gleamed with oil and rippled as he moved. His dress was all Cretan now—jewelry and loincloth. Even his hair had been shaped to the Cretan style, though it had not been dyed. Except for his size, he could have been a noble of Knossos instead of a captive bull dancer. But his stance was still that of a warrior.

"Few Attic youths dream of becoming smiths," I said. "Their hearts are all with Heracles."

"Oh, where their hearts are . . ." Theseus waved an encompassing hand. He smiled, but his eyes were measuring me. "You've kept up with happenings at home?"

"Those of importance," I said.

Ariadne was watching both of us. "You have not told me about Heracles." It was not clear whom she addressed. I did not reply.

"He's my kinsman," said Theseus. "A strong man. I met him only once, when I was a child. He tossed me in the air like a toy."

"Is that enough to make the Attic boys dream of following him?"

Theseus threw me the briefest of glances. "He has killed monsters."

"What sort of monsters?" she asked.

"Thieves, murderers, ravenous beasts . . . ask Daedalus. He's a better storyteller than I, I'm sure." Theseus' eyes were fixed upon me now.

"Have I been summoned to tell stories?" I asked.

"No." Ariadne's voice was abrupt and cold. She began an intense questioning. What ships were due to return soon? When were they expected? What ships were being built? How many swords were kept on hand, and where were they? How long did it take to forge new ones? When she paused, Theseus asked more questions along the same line. It was obvious that there were plans well advanced.

A sudden sound in the outer chamber stopped all talk for a moment. Ariadne's woman, the tongueless one, poked her head in, signaled, and left at Ariadne's wave. Then in came two Cretan nobles I knew slightly: Thonos, a solemn, religious man, no lover of Minos and shocked at his incestuous blasphemy, and Menor, from the mountains, a kin to that boy Minos had blinded. They had questions too, all regarding military supplies. I answered them in a daze. Without having been asked, without having given my consent, I was part of a conspiracy against Minos! And they all addressed me as if my sympathy for their cause were taken for granted. It must have been Ariadne who had guaranteed my allegiance. I tried to catch her eye, but she was all business, lucid and cold as any commander, for all the swelling of her abdomen. However, it was Theseus who knew strategy. One could tell he'd been on the battlefield. Their voices were soft. Occasionally they would stop and listen. Now I understood the earlier sounds I'd heard in the street. They must have been soldiers rushing down the Royal Way and into the mountains. A diversionary tactic planned deliberately to get Asterios and his men out of the way. Still, there was need for caution. Certain slaves, certain artisans had been posted outside to watch and warn. A thrill rushed through me, I'll admit. At my age, when life could be expected to be calm, I was immersed in revolution! At the same time, I was annoyed at being taken for granted.

The nobles finally left. Ariadne detained me. "You should not all leave at once," she said. "It would arouse suspicion." The room was quiet. I sipped the wine Ariadne had offered and waited for my orders to depart. She was writing quickly as if catching ideas on the fly. Theseus had gone to the door of the light well as if to seek air. He stretched his arms and yawned. Then he turned suddenly to me. "My father told me to tell you that Attica yearns for your return. The matter of the apprentice has been forgotten. Aegeus would be honored to have your service."

My head spun like a toy. How easily he had made sure of me. Like a fool, I begged, "You would give me passage there?"

And Theseus nodded, like a king.

# 8

ARIADNE:

HOW MANY WEEKS WENT BY THEN, I cannot remember. I was living on many levels, like the palace. On the topmost layer of my mind, like the highest balcony from which I watched sea and land, walked death. I had good advisors there, more expert in slaughter than I knew, but I was with them gladly. Too gladly to analyze the silent exchanges I intercepted between Daedalus, my sword maker, and Theseus, my sword. As the sun comes directly only to the unroofed balconies, so far only into my being went my daylight mind, though at that time I thought it filled my whole habitation.

In the shadows of my quarters, I moved in another dance. There I was filled with Theseus. There never was such a lover; I say that even now after all that has happened. The Goddess cared nothing for our plans. The throne of Crete hung glowing in Theseus' mind and in my own, but it was an illusion She allowed us, so long as the movements of our dance followed Her order.

Only in the depths of the palace, in the darkness of the pillar shrine, did I come close to the Mother. I was pregnant with Theseus' child now. The flow of the Goddess had stopped within me, had begun to pulse and swell. I felt the movement in my womb, as I waited in silence at the cold pillar. But only there. All motion seemed to cease when I talked with the assassins. Every day I climbed through all the levels of my palace and myself, but it was the sun that spoke most to me. Death, it whispered.

# 9

DAEDALUS:

TIME SEEMED SUSPENDED, and within it, a seethe of deception.
Asterios was kept running back and forth, to the mountains, to
the coastal caves, to some obscure house in Knossos, to the
mountains again. And with him went his great gang of blusterers.
Sometimes they found nothing, sometimes they fought at shadows
that seemed to disappear into stone and night. Sometimes they
returned with captives or the remains of captives, which they
displayed in the streets and then threw casually into a chasm. How
many half-crazed creatures gave themselves as sacrifice, I don't
know. Many of them, I'm sure, knew nothing of the plans, were
simply swept up in the fever that raged throughout the island, a
fever bred of longing for an idyllic past they thought had been their
heritage, of disgust for Minos and his minions who had now openly
set themselves against the rule of the Mother. Many of them hated
Minos for bringing in so many foreigners. Others, perhaps, were
merely hungry and thought they had nothing to lose. I didn't care.
I was never so little a Cretan as then. All I felt was the wind
gathering in Athens, a wind held in the power of men like Theseus,
whose strength could be made to open the earth, rip out her secrets,
lift men to the stature of gods. And, of course, get me back home. I
must admit that I did not care what would be destroyed in the
process. I did not even think about it.

I did my job. I built the ships and the weapons they wanted, all
under the guise of Minos' orders. It was not difficult. I'd been in
Crete so long, they seemed to have forgotten my ancestry. People
have short memories. Even Asterios did not question my word, but
then, he was not hard to fool. A suspicious man, but placated by a
show of concern for Minos, for naval strength, for law, for Crete. A

simple man, in whom there lay few shadows and those only the silhouettes of power.

Minos was still absent, chasing after phantoms of youth. Ariadne, I saw daily. We talked of the plans. Why should we have talked of anything else? What more could she have expected of an Athenian? She questioned me about Theseus again. "What do you know of him?" she asked.

"That he is Prince of Athens, son of Aegeus," I said. And lover of the Lady of Knossos, I might have added. She frowned. It was not the time for games. I hurried on. "I don't know him," I said. Her eyebrows raised skeptically. "You forget that I've been in Crete almost as long as you. We met the prince at the same instant."

"Will he make a good general, do you think?"

"Oh yes, no question of that."

"As good at killing as Asterios?"

"I should think so, yes. Haven't you watched him work the bulls? He has agility, precision of movement, muscles." She was looking at me, but her mind was elsewhere. "They say he's equal to Asterios as a spearsman. He's more intelligent, too, and younger," I said.

She was seated across from me at a table, but I could see by the movement of her arm that she was pressing her hand against her belly. "And of course, he's much handsomer." I smiled.

She stood up angrily and walked to the far end of the room. "I'm aware of his physical attributes," she snapped. "What I want to know about is his reputation. What has he done to make him a hero before he became a prince? What did he do on that journey from his birthplace to Athens?" She whirled about and glared at me.

So, then, she distrusts his story, I thought. Just as well. But I had little information to offer. "They say he cleansed the outlands of thieves and ruffians."

"What kind of thieves?"

"Those who steal another's birthright," I said. "Usurpers."

She studied me for a moment in silence.

"Such men as Theseus are useful," I offered. Another long moment went by.

"And who is Heracles?" she asked.

"The same sort of man. Older. More famous. Much admired in Attica for his fighting skill. For his aid in defeating their enemies. A hero."

I thought she was about to question further, but she gave it up. Apparently it was enough for her. She returned to the plans.

It was not enough for me. I wanted to know more of Theseus. I had him brought to my quarters along a hidden route that I had built to my own room, telling no one, not Minos nor his daughter-queen, nor anyone save the slaves who had hauled the stones, and they were long gone. Now only my body servant, Pholus, a Sicilian, knew the way. I cannot forget the night he brought Theseus, his bull-dancer jewels concealed under a large cloak. The moment Pholus was gone, Theseus stripped them all away, cloak, jewels, loincloth—all flung with a scornful gesture into a pile at the door. He stood before me naked as a god. Had anyone been watching, they would have thought he was courting me in the new fashion. But it was not that. It was truth he wanted to reveal to me, and a feeling of oneness in love of Attica. So he said.

He asked for a basin of water and washed away the Cretan colors. Then he asked me for a covering. When I gave him an old cloak that I had brought from Athens years before, he smiled eagerly and embraced it as if it were a friend.

I brought wine. We drank. We talked into the night. He was as full of himself as a gander, but the backwoods boy showed through. His eyes were still popping at the gold-encrusted swords, the maze of frescoed halls, the gilded furnishings, the jeweled, half-naked women, the gorgeous slavery of the bull dancer's life, the fondling of the queen—more than he'd dreamed, more than he'd dreamed. Yet he seemed to feel he had it coming all the same. He was comfortable now, assured of my allegiance, lounging on pillows, wineglass in hand.

"I've been waiting for this," he said, waving his hand to include much more than my meager quarters. "It's my first really big chance. The Cretan adventure, I call it. Set up for me as if I'd been born to it. Which I was, you might say. It's a job that has to be

done, that's clear. Just waiting for the right man to come along."
The shift of his shoulders settled the mantle of rightness.

"I wasn't caught in the lottery, you know. I volunteered." He
paused as if for applause.

I gave him my warmest smile.

"All along the coast they've felt the sword of Minos," he said,
"but not here so much as in Athens. Its youngest, best blood has
been wiped out every few years; did you know that? It's made them
a race of slaves!"

It was clear that he did not include himself. Of course, I nodded.

"We'd heard about it at Troezen long before I left. What started
it, I guess, was the death of the Cretan prince years ago at the
games. You probably know. Hell, he asked for that, the way I've
heard it. But Minos took the opportunity to sweep down like Zeus
himself. And Aegeus bowed down to him, gave up, sold out. Now,
how can you respect a man like that? It makes my blood boil when
they say he's my father. I don't believe it for a minute. It's just the
wishful thinking of an impotent old man, blind drunk, probably.
Of course, my grandad swears to the story too. But then Grandad's
got his own reasons. I let the story stand, though. Who'd throw
away a kingdom, even a conquered one?"

"Indeed, who would?" I refilled his glass.

"Naturally, I prefer to encourage the other story of my birth, the
one my mother hints at, the visitation of Poseidon. That's better for
my reputation, and likely enough considering my build and skill.
You can't tell me I got these shoulders from any ordinary father. So
you see, the thing I planned to do from the start was to claim my
birthrights, all of them. But first I had to make a name for myself."
He laughed. "I wasn't sure about your sympathies, you know, until
you mentioned Heracles."

It was a shrewd eye appraising me. He's not a fool, I thought.

He leaned back and looked at the ceiling. "I'd studied Heracles'
career ever since the time I sat at his knee, breathless, listening to
the stories he told my grandad. I was just six or seven, couldn't
have been more. We hit it off right away because of that lion skin

[ 188 ]

episode. He always wears it, you know, and has ever since the Nemean adventure. It was his signature, you might say. Well, anyway, first time I remember him, he'd decided to play games with me and my cousins. My grandad was in on it, I guess, though it doesn't really fit his style. He's much too serious. It had to be Heracles' idea to drape the skin over a stool so that it looked like the live beast, gnashing its teeth and ready to charge. In we came from play, three or four of us, eager to meet the hero. Tumbled into the hall laughing and charging around and almost fell on the damned lion skin before we saw it. Then there was a screaming, you can bet, and they all went blubbering around to hide behind the pillars or the skirts of my mother who'd just come in. All but me. Oh, I was fooled too, especially when my mother shrieked. But instead of running out, I grabbed a sword I saw lying on the bench—Heracles' sword, no less! I recognized it from the stories—and I charged at the fierce thing with all my baby might, ripping the skin down the chest and sending the stool flying and myself as well. Then in rushed Heracles, naked as a stallion and whinnying with laughter. He seized me round the middle, threw me into the air, and caught me. And all through that, I wouldn't let go of his sword. Very nearly took his head off."

He was pleased at my laughter. He stretched out comfortably.

"Heracles loved it. Said he'd never seen such a lad before and I was sure to be the greatest hero yet, maybe beat even him, if he didn't watch out. Damn, but I'd never felt so good before—all the boys peeping around and envious, even my mother smiling now that the excitement was over, and old Grandad standing there proud and solemn as if I'd just been dedicated to Zeus.

"I learned then what I had to do. You've got to train first in the country, the more remote the better. The farther a story drifts the bigger it gets, that's what Heracles said. Mountain people can't tell the difference between a monster and a shadow. Besides, it gets you into condition for the big challenges.

"I'd already found out what I had in me. I was always a head taller than the local kids as far back as I can remember. I could wrestle them twice my age—and had to. 'Look at the big stallion,' they'd say when I came in. They learned to shut their traps, though. Put up or shut up, I say.

"But I had a lot of growing left to do. I trained night and day in the fields, on the mountainsides. The mountain boys would come down and watch. Then the biggest of them would challenge and they'd all close round, half-scared, half-eager to see the big horse get it. But I never lost. It wasn't only my size, either. They thought the gods were with me. You could see it on their faces. If they hadn't been so scared, they might have downed me sometimes. Because they taught me something too. Holds and twists I didn't know about. I'll show you if you like. But I invented new ones. I have a gift for it."

Again he shifted his shoulders and got up to stride around my small room, dwarfing its proportions with his bulk.

"But it wasn't enough!" He swung his arms as bull dancers do just before the animal is released, to stir the blood. The gesture was graceful as a lion, but too large for a dancer. They should have had him wrestling bulls, rather than vaulting them, I thought.

"Besides, I had to get away from my mother."

I suppose my amusement showed. For all his size, he seemed suddenly to be a child. An angry child. He whipped his hand down as if striking a blow, but it closed on nothing. "Do you know Troezen?" he asked fiercely.

"Not well," I admitted.

"A backward place, run by women!"

"But I've heard of your grandfather's library," I said. "And his wisdom. Surely—"

"Pittheus is a book fool! He reads while my mother runs the land. It may be changed by now. It certainly would have been if I had stayed, but I had bigger plans. But even there, even in that backwater, the men are restive and balk at being held back, while a woman gives the orders. They know what's happened in other places. We saw to that, Connidas and I. Connidas was my tutor. He read a lot, too, but he was no fool. And he'd been places and had seen the changes, the old religion shoved out of the palace and back into the woods where it belongs, catering to women and doddering old men like my grandfather, senile, living in the past. I can't stand old men!"

He took a big swig of wine and measured me again with his eyes. I could see that he felt embarrassed at his last remark and didn't know how to withdraw it. He had been carried away by his story, by his pleasure at talking freely to a fellow Greek, by the wine. "Damn, you're not old," he fumbled finally.

I nodded in gratitude for the lie and changed the subject. "Tell me how you left Troezen."

He went on for hours. It was a braggart's tale, enlivened with much muscle flexing, swinging of arms, demonstrations of wrestling holds, fighter's tricks. I'll admit I plied him with wine. You can find out a lot about a man when he's in his cups. This one wanted to be a hero more than any I've ever met. That visit of Heracles stayed with him every minute. How much of it was true, I don't know. The way he told it, he had cleansed the whole countryside between Troezen and Athens of thieves, murderers, and monstrous beasts—the same story I'd heard before. But as I questioned him more closely, it appeared that some of them might have been described in another way. Periphetes, for instance, the Epidaurian, was a craftsman and a cripple like me, lamed purposely in childhood to make him stick to his trade, as is still the fashion over there. He had invented a club inset with metal spikes that Theseus wanted. But Periphetes wouldn't give it up, grabbed hold of Theseus, and tried to stop him from—but here he stopped and would not say just what it was that he had been about to do. So Theseus ripped the club out of his hands and killed the craftsman with his own invention. He carried the club about with him for months, flourishing and maiming until the Cretan ship came into the Athenian harbor. Then he hid it carefully where he could find it on his return from vanquishing Minos. Oh, if he only had it with him this minute!

I had heard of a Periphetes once when I was an apprentice, a pious fellow and a fine craftsman, devoting his life to service in the old religion. I didn't mention it. I doubt that Theseus would have listened anyway. He was rushing on to the next exploit.

"What a woman, this one. Stately—twice the size of your Cretan girls. Beautiful, with white hair streaming down her shoulders and a skin like cream. Young, ignorant—a worshipper of shrubs and grasses. And frightened as a fawn. But she liked me well enough when I took her. Screamed but hung on. Cried, but you could tell she liked it. Would have come with me, said she would, I swear it. Would have, too, if it hadn't been for the other women wailing and pulling at her, I could tell. Agreed to meet me at a certain place in the woods. But when I went there I found her dangling at the end of a rope strung to a branch. I cut her down, but she was dead. What a waste of a woman. Her name was Perigune. Daughter of the North Wind, she called herself. A priestess."

He looked to see how I was taking that. I made my face as noncommittal as possible. Certainly I was no defender of the old religion, whatever my allegiance to Ariadne. But mainly I thought of Attica. This honking gander was my only hope of transport. I nodded.

He seemed reassured, took a deep breath, and spread out his legs. "If you want to know, there were plenty of them. A priestess makes a good lay. She's used to it, has all kinds of tricks. But watch out, or she'll bed you down for life, which may not be all that long if it's one of those tribes where the king lasts only a year like Perigune's. I had some trouble getting away from that one, I can tell you. I hadn't had much experience then, and she really was a beauty. Well, if you want to know what really happened . . ."

He filled his glass again and settled in for the true confession. By now he was quite drunk. "I could have got away many times on my own, but I wanted her along. I can't say she consented; she never did talk much. But she would have come, she'd have got used to it. Her women wouldn't hear of it, of course. And her father, Sinis— One night, I caught him sneaking into the cave where I'd bedded her, a knife in his hand. I killed him on the spot. But then she woke up and cried, and I knew I had to get out of there fast. I told her to get ready and meet me at a big pine where we'd sat and fooled around. She agreed and I left to get my things together. I should never have left her, I know that now. Well, it didn't take me long. Soon enough I was on my way to the pine. The moon was full, I remember, a bad time for running off unnoticed. You could see a good fifty meters away. But there was no one around to stop me. I headed for the pine, and still there was no one in sight. Well, she's late, I thought. Fussing about the things she wants to take with her. I should have grabbed her and hauled her off with me as she was, but damn it, I guess I wanted to please her. I sat down to wait. That was when they jumped me, a horde of women and old men. Lucky I had my club. First to get it was old Polypemon, her grandfather. Procrustes, some call him. Well, he got what he gave, and more. So did the rest. They weren't used to fighting, you could see that. Some went screaming off into the bushes, some clawed my face with their nails and kicked. But my training saved me. And they had no weapons to match my club. I killed most of them with it, even Perigune, if you must know. You can't let a woman get away with betrayal. But I didn't kill her until I'd had her one last time, and right in the shrine where she hadn't let me even peek. Then I strung her up and set fire to the brush. That was some blaze, I can tell you. But I didn't stick around to watch it long. I was disappointed, for one thing. She really was a beautiful bitch. Then too, I thought the villagers might get excited about it when they found out. The cult was pretty popular in those parts. Also, Sinis was a relative of my mother's, which would upset a whole lot of people."

There was no sign that it had upset him to any great extent. He leaned back on the couch and hummed to himself, as if remembering pleasant times. I thought perhaps the recital was over, but no, he had more to tell. More heroic exploits. Against the Crommyonian Sow, Phaea. I was aghast. "Phaea, the Shining One?" I shouted. Had he been sober, he would have noticed.

"Right," he said. "What a woman! A real fighter. Have you heard about it?"

"Maybe it's not the same woman," I said. "This one was older than I am. Brilliant. Learned in ancient lore. A prophetess."

"That's her," he said. "What a battle she put up. Took me weeks to track her down. She was always one step ahead of me. But I cornered her finally in a cave. There she sat in her rags, pouring wheat and honey into a pot, skinny, old as death. And I came up quiet across the moss and grabbed her. How she tore at me. Slung the gruel in my face and blinded me for a moment. Grabbed a hatchet and whipped it at my head. See? Here's a scar. Then she went for the pot of water boiling over her fire. But I got there first and tipped it onto her. She missed her footing and fell backward into a ditch. I had her then. Gave it to her any way I could. And when I was through I spiked her on a pole and left her as warning to any of her friends who might have scurried off into the hills."

I am not an emotional man. But there are times when the pain of living seems to overwhelm all memory of joy. How I wished Theseus would leave! But he went on and on.

Sciron thrown into the sea. (A mistake, that, he admitted. Turned out to be a decent man and a kinsman. Well, no help for it. Mistakes are made.) Then Eleusis and the wrestling with Cercyon. The first really big victory, that, the downing of a famous wrestler, the crushing of his ribs, the howl of the dying man. And then the sweet, sweet aftermath. His daughter, tiny as a fox, with sloe eyes and soft down between her legs, his first real virgin, the blood proving it.

I listened with half my mind. I was thinking of Phaea. I had heard her speak when I was a youth. She had been the first to awaken me to the poetry of the ancients. Inside my memory I could hear her saying, in counterpoint to Theseus' tale:

> *Oh my Lady,*
> *At the sound of your voice,*
> *The trees bow down.*
> *When men appear before you, weeping*
> *For what has come from their hands,*
> *They receive from you*
> *What they have earned.*

I was relieved when Theseus finally dressed himself again as a Cretan and left. I roused Pholus from his cot in the antechamber to guide him back to the slave quarters before the night watch had gone and sent along another gold seal to make sure of secrecy. Dawn was about to break. I went out on my balcony to watch. My eyes felt as if somehow I were stretching them to gather in more than they could rightly see. Oh, my Lady, when men appear before you, weeping for what has come from their hands. . . . But I could not imagine Theseus weeping for what he had done. There was no sense of guilt in the man, though he had violated the greatest taboos. He merely put them aside as if they were clothing he could take off at will. He was the first truly free man I had seen. It was as if he had just been created whole with no woman's help. He seemed to owe nothing. Thus, all was open to him.

If only I could achieve that, I thought. Drop the allegiances to the past. Drop them out of my mind completely. What exhilaration I would feel. Such freedom gives buoyancy to the spirit. I felt as though I could fly from that balcony all the way to Athens and beyond if I had that freedom in me, in spite of all my age and lameness. Bolts of excitement struck through me as if Zeus had opened the skies.

What Theseus severed with his rough tale was the long umbilical cord that had leashed me to the Mothers. Even after all those years of mind work, they were still binding me, holding my hands. No, said Theseus, I will *not* take care. Let the Mothers weep. I will show them shapes of living never dreamed of. Not that he ever said it. Men like Theseus do not say important things, not in words. Their movements make their memorial. A writing of muscle and bone.

Of course, he's a brute. But brute work must be done. If we are to be free of the stones of the past, someone must kill the demon. Let it be those who have the hand for it, who seem to be able to wash away the unfortunate blood with a quick cold plunge into the clear sea. The bravura of that dive! And the presumption of his offering! A crown of weed to a Goddess! And the consort's ring tossed back scornfully into the water by a slave! Did any action ever spell so clearly a severance of bondage?

I decided to put myself to school to this boy who reasoned with his club and his snake. From his movements I deduced: (1) that the Mothers are not all powerful (if, indeed, they continue to exist), and that the vision of things they have provided is inappropriate to the time, is incomplete, is essentially a woman's vision, therefore *not mine!* and (2) that, given sufficient strength (and for those who can see, the sinews of the mind ripple even more beautifully than those of the body), one can sever the dominance of shadows and climb step by luminous step the orders of the intellect. Who can tell how far the stairway leads and to what new vistas? Each morning I was higher and the light shone farther. Oh, my Lady, the sound of your voice is fading.

I marveled that this ignorant young man possessed such power to move me. Freedom, then, was what he had learned on the road to Athens. This freedom was there for me.

The night was gone. I had not slept at all. I felt as though I would never need to sleep again.

I did not tell Ariadne what I had learned from Theseus. Should I be condemned for that? Who would expect me to tell her?

# VI

*Unwilling I reveal a loftier mystery—*
*In solitude are throned the Goddesses,*
*No space around them, Place and Time*
     *still less;*
*Only to speak of them embarrasses;*
*They are the Mothers! . . .*
*Delve in the deepest depth must thou,*
     *to reach them:*
*It is thine own fault that we for help*
     *beseech them.*

GOETHE, Faust

# 1

As for the rest, well . . . it should be recorded that the ambush took place in Ariadne's court, as planned. Theseus had charge of it. The day was bright and hot. Ask someone else to describe the details; ask Theseus. I was not a witness, having no taste for such things. I stayed in my room. After all, I had done my share.

*Over and over I see Asterios coming up the stairway to my* megaron. *Face dark with heavy beard. Eyes set unevenly, one lower than the other. Feet heavy on the steps. Body broad. As he comes close to where I sit, there is the smell of bulls.*

*"I have had a message," I say. "Minos is dead." His face changes. He does not know whether or not to believe me. Perhaps he wishes to. He has been a good tool, but surely he longs to be master. How should he read my sending for him? We are alone, it must seem to him. The room is empty, my guards have been sent away, I tell him, to allow us this moment of secrecy, this revealing*

*of an awful truth that will turn the palace on end, will send hordes running through the streets. He studies my face. I am not weeping.*

They pulled it off. That's the only thing that counts. And they had surprisingly little trouble, it seems. Of course, the country was ripe for it.

*"Minos is dead," I say again. He studies my face. I know he is wondering why the messenger has not come first to him. "The ship came in an hour ago. You were in the mountains," I say. It is true. And I have had a messenger. "The ship bearing his body follows," I say. "We must prepare the rites." His eyes soften. "The ritual games," I say. He puts down his sword and walks thoughtfully toward the pillars of the inner court where the anemones are flaming.*

Thonos and his men had control of the palace guards. Two-thirds of them were with us anyway. They hated the warriors even more than Asterios. Because they were foreigners, no doubt. They lined up all those of the enemy that had escaped the ambush and killed them. I was not a witness, that's not my specialty. I'm not sure how they could kill so many so quickly. Of course, they had opened the prisons and the slave quarters, freeing hundreds of killers.

*And then they are upon him, Theseus and Menor. The swords come down and the thick neck opens weakly like a mouth and everything becomes red, the anemones, the shining blue tile, all the bronze. The feathers of his helmet all red. Only the face above that second mouth goes white, and the eyes, they too become white. Now there is crying everywhere. It is Theseus' voice that comes from every doorway, so loud that my hands fly to my ears, but the voice comes over and over in echoes from above and below. Theseus is all blood. He fills the room. His sword slashes the walls of the palace and they tumble around him. I hear laughter. I cannot believe that it is my own. It follows after Theseus' shouts like the tremor of a harp string. In the crimson din, I stand still and laugh. I feel the dais trembling.*

They broke into the warehouses and armed themselves. That's when the house slaves rose up too. These affairs are necessarily violent. Finally word came in from Menor that they had secured the ships, and the thing was done. It had taken no more than half a day. Can a world die in that time? If Theseus had described it, it would have more substance.

I thought of Minos sailing somewhere in his dream. It would take longer for the news to reach him than for his decayed empire to collapse. I sat in my room, reading the same lines over and over. As I recall, it was a lamentation from Sumer—about the destruction of Ur. "O Queen, how has your heart led you on, how can you stay alive?"

*To hold the knife in one's own hand and press it down into the smooth skin, making a thin line, so thin that it is almost invisible between the beads of blood, and then to plunge the blade with all one's strength into the chest, to feel it sink with surprising swiftness deep, deep into the flesh, to see the face turn color and the lips sag, the eyes turn to crystal as they look into one's own . . .*

I stayed in my quarters until they sent me word that it was safely accomplished. For an eyewitness account of the activity, consult those who specialize in it.

*Theseus is holding a priestess. It is Thera. "Kill her," he says to me in that voice that sweeps all other sound away. Years go by, swelling and dying, before my hand comes up slowly as if in blessing. I see that I am holding a dagger. Theseus is shouting, but I cannot understand his words. His hands have smeared her arms with red. His fingers dig deep into her skin. I see the slimness of her shoulders held against his sword. Her eyes stare into mine. I think she is speaking but I cannot hear her. I see my dagger slice a thin line across her left breast and the red beads bloom against the white skin. Then I feel the plunge of the dagger and my hand on the hilt comes down upon the soft, tearing flesh. I see Theseus fling her body across the room as easily as if he were throwing a spear. All the walls of the hall are covered with blood, all the pillars are dyed with it. The light well is piled with bodies, all red, and through every corridor rings the voice of Theseus and the clash of his sword.*

We met for an hour or so in the Great East Hall. Ariadne was ecstatic. Theseus strutted under the gold *labrys*. Thonos talked incessantly as he had never done before, telling the same story over and over, like a litany. His lieutenants, too, could not stop their retelling of the events. We did this, and we did that. As they talked the happenings grew to god-size, until I wondered how they could have waded through the blood in the streets. How had they had time to haul off the mountainous heaps of bodies?

In the central courtyard, a chanting started as if someone were praying. It was a single voice at first, but shortly another joined, and then another and another, until the stones rang with voices. We went out on the balcony. The courtyard was full of shouting people. When they saw Ariadne, they cried louder. The new gold crown that I had made for her at Theseus' order shone splendidly in the sun as she smiled and waved blessings into the din. It was a magnificent sight.

When Theseus appeared beside her in Attic clothing, the voices stopped. There was total silence for a moment. Then a murmur arose. It was clear that the people were not sure what they had got themselves into. Ariadne spoke to them. A treaty had been signed, she said, between Crete and Athens, between Crete and Pitthea. No more hostages would be taken, no more piracy allowed. Gold seals would be exchanged for grain. There would be peace between nations, food for the hungry, no more war. Phaedra and the child were brought out, and Ariadne waved her hands as if gathering in the whole of sky and earth to comfort and protect. The people loved it. They crowded into the Great East Hall to celebrate.

*I am in my gold dress and my new gold crown, and Theseus is all in gold, pausing as if for display under the gold labrys. The hall is swathed in gold. Korkyne is at the side, near the altar, in a gold robe, Deucalion in her arms, wrapped in a gold shawl, and Phaedra in gold skirt clinging to her as if in love or fear. Now all of us are gold and shining in the sun. And I am laughing. I look down from my balcony into many faces, all laughing, though without sound.*

It was during her speech that I felt the first shudder in the earth. There was a pause in the crowd noise, then a resurgence. They seemed to be too excited to see the sway in the trees, the door swinging. A flock of birds swept upward from the roof, wheeled above the palace, and flew away toward the mountains. A sound came up from the earth like the heavy groan of a sleeper. Ariadne was looking at Theseus and he was lost within himself. Neither of them seemed to have noticed the unusual signs. A flute started to play, then a drum. It was the beginning of a ceremony, I presume, though not a solemn one. There was no solemnity in them.

I am not sure why I left the balcony—left the palace, in fact—grabbed Pholus and ran all the way down to the wharf. I don't believe that I was frightened. It was nothing so clear as that. I thought it was just to see whether all was well in the ship that had been promised me. I could not wait to leave Crete. Every moment for weeks I had felt Minos' mast rising out of the sea to prevent my going. Later, there certainly was fear. I remember seeing the Sicilian's face bobbing along beside me, his lips drawn back in a grimace. Suddenly a ridge ran down the street like a wave. The cornice of a building splattered at our feet. Stones, brickwork, tiles crashed about us. The groaning sound from the earth grew louder. Pholus was shouting at me, but I could not hear him. He pulled me into a building, but I fought with him to get out again. All I could think of was my ship. I dragged him along with me through the crumbling walls. There were open cracks and broad wavy folds along the Royal Way. The sky was dark. There was a smell of sulfur. I did not notice ash in the air until I saw Pholus' hair become white as if he had aged in a few moments. Underneath, the ground shook and turned upward. I felt dizzy. The air burned my throat.

*The fire of the torches turns red, and all the gold turns red, as if blood were falling from the sky and covering everything. And the shaking of my laughter creeps out into the whole palace. All the walls begin to shake; the floors rise and fall with laughter. The pillars tremble. The torch fire goes everywhere, along the floor, up the walls. The pillars are burning. The oil at the altar is burning. I feel the fire running along the rugs at my feet. The hair of a priestess flames up like a crown. I see Korkyne running, running, but I cannot see Deucalion. Phaedra stumbles forward with hands outstretched. I am all red, all aflame. The tremble of the laughter goes on and on.*

There were screams all around. I saw people running, a woman dragging a heavy bundle of clothes, a child caught under a rock. The noise of the earth grew, blotting out any sound they made. Their eyes rolled, their hands rose and fell as if they were puppets. I could hardly breathe. Flames broke out suddenly in a building and singed us before we could get away. I stumbled over a rock and went down on my lame leg. Pholus looked at me, ran on for a few feet, then came back and pulled me up, half-carried me on his back. We were at the wharf, but the sea was not in sight. It had drawn back as if sucked into a great mouth. Dead fish lay upon the sand. Ships keeled over sideways in the dry bed. Then in the distance, toward the northeast, I saw a mountain of flame rising out of the dark water. By that time the sky was as black as night. Only the monstrous fire with its shooting ribbons of color could be seen. Hot cinders were dropping upon us. Suddenly a deep trench appeared at our feet. I fell and felt Pholus' body crashing upon my back.

*Someone is beating out the flames. Theseus? I think he has carried me somewhere. It is all shadowy as if the sun had died. Everywhere is movement. Many people are running. Walls lift and bend. Streets twist. Trees burn along the road like mammoth torches. Fire falls from a black sky. I am still laughing. Or perhaps it is someone else laughing, perhaps the Goddess Herself. At some point, it turns into weeping.*

*I am lying on the ground and the ground is shaking. I hear Theseus shouting and I call to him. There is pain all around me now, as if I lay in a pool of pain. I can feel the birth beginning. I call and call but no one seems to hear me.*

I woke on a ship. We were out to sea. It seemed to be night. The ash was still falling. In the distance, red and yellow ribbons shot up into the sky again and again. A stranger noticed that I was awake, ran off and brought another who examined me, bathed my face, wrapped my leg. They seemed to speak no Cretan. Nor Greek. But then I recognized a Sicilian phrase I had picked up from Pholus. They were all his countrymen—slaves, taking the opportunity to escape. My proper comrades, I thought. But I could not see Pholus anywhere. I asked about him. It took a while to make myself understood. When I did, the news was bad. They had left him for dead. Why had they taken me? Perhaps in the darkness and chaos they had thought I too was Sicilian. When they were able to see me clearly, they were probably far out to sea, eager only to get as far away as possible from the turbulent waters. None of them seemed to know who I was. I decided to remain quiet. When they asked insistently I pretended to faint.

How many there were aboard that ship was never clear to me. They tended to me well enough, as well as they could, no doubt, for they were constantly battling a vicious sea. The rolling of the ship added greatly to my pain. Like many other Athenians, I have never been a good sailor. Two or three days went by, I think, before it was really light again. Even then, the ash kept covering us like snow. On about the third day, a man came and stood over me and said, "Daedalus." He looked somewhat familiar. A palace slave, perhaps. I wondered what they would do with me now that they knew who I was. But I had no cause for fear. The man's manner was reverent, almost worshipful. He brought a blanket, a handful of grain, and a bottle of water. He did not speak further but sat with me as if he were on guard, brushing away the constantly falling ash.

All that time, I seemed to be thinking of nothing. As if my mind had been seared by the flames, as if they had burnt away my memory, I did not think once of those still in Knossos.

*Korkyne found me with the dead infant between my legs. A girl. The future Queen of Knossos. Her skull had been crushed.*

*It was Theseus' doing, Korkyne tells me. With a strange lack of surprise, I recognized that it was what he would have had to do. Had the child been a boy, he would have taken it. But he would not have taken me. He must have thought I was already dead, for he had raised the rock again, this time above me, then put it down. Korkyne saw it from where she was crouching with Deucalion in the bushes. Then the boy gave a cry and she was discovered. She ran, carrying him, but Theseus caught her, grabbed Deucalion, and pushed her into a ravine. The branches of a tree caught her and she did not fall far. When at last she climbed back up and came to me, no one else was anywhere near.*

*I tried once to get up, I remember, but pain held me to the ground like a net. Korkyne's face appeared above me at times and disappeared, but it had no more substance than the faces of all the dead ones who came and went above me—my mother, Icarus, Merope. But mostly the priestess whom I had killed, Thera. I looked down to see whether my hand still held the dagger, but I could not tell.*

*Much later I found myself in a cave, and there were women all about. One of them was pouring herb water on my face. It was not so much pain that I felt then, as death. It seemed to have come up from the rock and surrounded me.*

*But death does not come at a wish. I still live, though my mask is changed. The flames licked my hair and my face and took away whatever beauty I once had. Even Korkyne might not have known who I was had not the remnants of my gold dress still clung to my burned skin.*

# 2

DAEDALUS:

IT TURNED OUT FINE, in the end. I couldn't have wished for more, if I had planned it. Cocalus. Now, there's a king! Let the ages take note. This is how it's done. Number one, he provides me with all the materials I can dream of. If he doesn't have them here in Sicily, he sends out a pride of lions to capture them. They do. They've been trained to fight with spear, club, arrow, dagger. Like Theseus. It's caught on all along the coast and the Sicilians have a knack for it that only needed awakening.

Number two, I have the princesses vying with one another for my love pats. Well, why not? I give them temples, one after another down the bleak coast and stretching back into the lush foothills. Now, these are monuments that will last. None of your Cretan clutter. These columns rise two by two, balancing the roof, the power of the stone, the forces of wind and earth. Balance is all. Nothing too much. The best of the old, the best of the new. I've found it. Beyond my dreams, I have found it.

Cocalus knows how to handle things. There is no question about where the power lies. Men must rule, that's clear. Women can't fight as well. But Cocalus knows the need for the old redemption. Too much blood and we all slide into agony. We need the Mothers to comfort us. And so he allows his daughters full rein to salvage the wounded, the dying, the wrongly born. They adore it. It endows them with lost deity. Oh, Cocalus, I didn't know you were the ruler I had waited for.

Crete? Well, that's a nightmare. Fortunately, I'm awake. I had forgotten it, if you must know, until Minos appeared. The stories came down the coast ahead of him. He was a ragged apparition, they said. A few men clung to him, who knows why? Their youthful dreams haunting them, I suppose. He was stalking me, they said, was obsessed with finding me, thought it was I alone who had changed the world and turned him out to wander, hungry. He carried with him a triton shell and a string and thought only Daedalus could thread it.

Cocalus' daughters knew what he was up to at once. Sciacca told me, bless her. Her hair shone, her breasts trembled, her lips were dry. "The demon is here," she breathed.

"What demon?" I asked.

"The one who pursues you."

"Many demons nip at my ankles."

"This is the one whom the fiery tongue of the Mother seeks."

"Minos?"

She clung to me shivering. I placed the toy I had been constructing on a table and drew her close.

"Does he ask for me?" I said.

She shook her head. "He only says, 'Find me the one who can solve this puzzle, and I will reward him.' And he shoves the broken shell into our faces. And the dirty thread. 'Find him, find him!' He trembles upon the words. His voice strings out into air. His breathing is like wind through reeds. My sisters look at each other and whisper. 'Where is he?' Minos says, watching them. 'The Mother needs him,' he says. 'The Goddess-on-Earth needs him,' he says. 'I will give you gold for your temples, if you will tell me.' And they look at each other. They love you, but I can see how they are thinking, maybe he has hidden it somewhere. The Mother loves gold. With gold the hungry are fed."

"They have told him?"

"Not so easily as that. They love you. And they know how the Mother's fire has followed him."

"They've sent him away, then?"

"No. He rests in a chamber near the baths."

"The Goddess has sought him for a long while," I said. "Perhaps you should help him come to Her."

"I know the plan," she said and ran off.

I don't know exactly what she did. I don't want to think about it. It's a new world, and it suits me. Minos should have seen that. He should not have come here.

There was some screaming during the night, but I did not leave my room.

Finally Cocalus sent for me. "Look at this," he said. There was a covered object on a bench. He insisted that I look at it. A slave drew back the coverings. The corpse of an old man lay there. The skin had swollen and burst. The flesh was gray. There were no clothes. A gold belt engraved with spirals had been thrown across his waist. Over his eyes lay a gold mask embossed with a double axe.

"Is it he?" said Cocalus.

Who can tell the identity of the dead? Their records are in another language. But the features were those of Minos.

Cocalus brought me to his quarters. "He wanted to kill you, you know."

I nodded. What was there to add? I thanked him for saving me again.

He waved it aside. "It was the women who did it." He sipped his wine and studied me. "Be glad they love you," he said. Suddenly he doubled up in laughter. His wine spilled into his beard. He choked, laughing, threw the glass across the room, and fell back in his chair, sputtering. When I tried to assist him he waved me aside. "Drink, drink," he said and convulsed again into laughter. It was too much for me. I drank his good sweet wine and laughed with him until I was weak, though I was not sure what we were laughing at.

Finally Cocalus fell silent. His eyes were wary. "Sciacca says you tell stories."

"Not so well as you," I murmured.

"The bull mounts the heifer in Crete, she says."

"As everywhere."

"But the heifer in Crete is the bull's own child, she says."

"It has happened."

"That breeding, though sweet, leads to madness, she says."

"Or death."

"Ah, all breeding leads to death." He looked at his hands. The veins protruded. They were the hands of an old man, not unlike my own. "Sciacca says a man may be scalded to death as he sits in his bath. Or so you have told her it has happened when the gods will it."

"Sciacca is a priestess. She knows more than you and I of sacrifice."

Cocalus looked at me for a long time in silence. "Is it true that Minos slept with his daughter?" he said at last.

"He was her consort."

The shadow of the courtyard wall had moved across the floor. Cocalus noticed it. "The hours are drowning," he said in a mournful tone. Then suddenly he collapsed again into helpless laughter. Spasms started inside me, too, but this time I did not succumb. Cocalus slid out of his chair and lay upon the thick rug, his shoulders heaving, tears streaming down his cheeks into the beard. Finally he was quiet. "We will build him a tomb," he said somberly.

"Minos?"

He nodded.

"They'll object."

"You'll see," said Cocalus.

And so I ended up building a magnificent structure for Minos after all, to house his incestuous bones. The women did protest, but Cocalus won them round with plans for new temples and baths. Lucky Cocalus, inheriting his throne, the blood all safely in the past, the queens all dead, except for these young, ignorant daughters whom he loved, but not too well. In the building of Minos' tomb, he restrained me only once. Cut the size by a third and deleted the gold ornamentation on the walls. "One must not go too far," he said, "for those who have gone too far." Cautious Cocalus. I accommodated him. Why not?

This I know how to do. Pile stone upon stone until the earth threatens to reclaim them. The higher She lets you go, the more hope of Life. Each block the same size. Rectangular blocks. Separated by lines intersecting at right angles. Clean, clear lines. Symmetrical. One day the world will chafe at any other design, will look to these monuments for the secret of building. Will remember Daedalus. Not the warriors, not the women, not even Cocalus, though he doesn't know it. Only Daedalus. Only the Builder.

Akragas, most beautiful of mortal cities, your walls will never fall, I swear it.

How do I know what happened to Ariadne? There was an opening of the earth, and fire consumed everything. Did she die? I suppose so. I don't know. Theseus didn't die. You've seen what he's done in Athens. Theseus is a leader. He knows how to change things. We'll all be the better for it, I've no doubt of that. Cocalus has signed a treaty with him. That's what we need. Agreements. I will not kill you and you will not kill me. It lasts long enough to forge more swords.

There was a time when I thought perhaps the rising of the mind from the earth would have saved us all that. Dreams, dreams. I am concentrating now upon fortifications. Kamikos wants them. Cocalus says, give them to him, he is a general, he knows our needs, he knows how our enemies will attack. Even Sciacca says, give them, it's of no consequence, but don't forget my temples. I don't.

Cocalus has just given me a manuscript that he says he got from a shepherd many years ago. The man had found it in a cave. Cocalus could not read it, so he put it away and forgot about it until now. It's quite soiled and torn, but some of the lines are clear. The script is similar to that of ancient Crete. It seems to be a kind of primer for novitiate priestesses. Whether or not it is genuine, I cannot be sure.

1. *She who watches is herself watched.*
2. *She who wills is herself willed.*
3. *She who is barren becomes fruitful; she who is fruitful becomes barren.*
4. *She who climbs to the top finds herself in the depths.*

They all seem to be paradoxes, leading to the same dismal observation—the cycle of birth and death, the old generational trap. I am impatient with them. Their wisdom is minimal and all designed to teach submission.

There is another section, however, that I find fascinating.

> *If a straight line continue far enough, it will*
> *join again with itself.*

An additional paradox, perhaps. One could read it to be still another statement of the cycle, though it does not follow the "she who" form that is so clearly a command to resign oneself (herself) to helplessness. Also, the figure of a perfect circle accompanies the statement. The fact that it is just a circle and not the familiar symbol of snake swallowing itself is what interests me. It seems more likely to be mind work. The problem of a straight line is one I have puzzled over before. There is no question that a line leading directly away from one on a plane eventually disappears. Like a road on flat land. Or a ship moving out to sea. It's a failure of the eye, presumably. The line does not really disappear. The road goes on. The ship reaches Athens. Furthermore, some people can see it longer or farther than others. But who could travel so far as to test whether it would join again with itself? What an enormous circle that would have to be.

No doubt I am reading more into this statement than I should. I suppose it's merely the same dreary old cycle.

However, the following one does sound quite a different note:

> *All souls revolve like the stars.*

What is particularly frustrating is that a design of some kind apparently accompanied this statement as well, but the manuscript is badly damaged at just this spot, and I cannot tell what it was. What can this observation mean? The stars do not revolve. I wish I could have discussed it with Ariadne.

There has been a distressing occurrence, not on the battlefield, but right here in the palace, and Cocalus does not seem sufficiently disturbed. I would not have expected this mild man to accept it so calmly. It must be that he, like everyone else, is under the spell of Heracles. The great hero has been our guest for some time. Everyone flocks to see him. He's aging, but is still a magnificently strong man, with a manner that sweeps everyone into vassalage. I can see why Theseus idealized him.

But after what happened yesterday . . . it's hard for me to understand how they can accept him in the same way after that, especially Cocalus.

What happened is that two heralds from the Minyans were on the way here to collect a debt that Cocalus had agreed to pay them after the last fracas. Heracles met them on the road. What ensued then is not clear, but they offended him somehow and he attacked them. Now, that's a betrayal of an honorable trust. True, they were from the enemy, but a treaty had been made.

And then, how he did it! He cut off their ears, noses, and hands and sent these back to the Minyans, tied around the victims' necks. Heracles described it himself, bragged about it, seemed to enjoy our horror. None of us spoke, not even Cocalus. At last the hero's wife (brave woman) came forward timidly and reproached him ever so gently. But just that tiny rebuke sent him into a horrendous rage. He whipped out his sword and killed her on the spot. Then he killed their children, his own sons and daughters! I saw it myself; it was in full view of everyone. And no one said or did anything.

It was just a fit of madness, people say now. Heroes are subject to that. He has regained his sanity, they say; he sat in a dark cave all night, mourning, and today he's sane again. But surely this was the act of a monster. And when he will start to rampage again, who knows?

People are frightened of him. They hide when he comes near. Yet they peer at him round corners, fascinated. Cocalus, as well. He cannot take his eyes off the man, fairly fawns on him, offering lavish gifts, even one of his own daughters! In private conversation last night, he was willing to admit that there is danger in cultivating power without restraint. But then he shrugged it aside almost at once. "We need him on our side," he said. "The Minyans will be sure to attack." And when I could not stifle my protest, he said, "This is how power is held. The state depends upon it." Cocalus is so sure of this, he will not listen to my reasoning. To whom can I apply, if even this moderate king will not listen?

I think it may be time to move again. I had not wanted to. It has been pleasant here. I've built structures I am proud of—the fortifications, the reservoir, as well as the temples. And I have enjoyed Cocalus' conversation. I'm comfortable and I'm old. But this outrage of Heracles' has disturbed me deeply. Perhaps it is *because* I am old that I am so disturbed, as Cocalus says. After all, I have seen worse things in my time. But it seems never to end. And this brute is lauded by all as the greatest hero the world has seen.

There is a problem here that Cocalus hides from—the problem of balance. It cannot be evaded in the state any more than in the structure of a building. Both will fall without it. Just as by learning the nature of stone and the necessary symmetry of form one can achieve the balance of a column, so by learning the nature of a hero and the necessary control of his strength can one achieve the harmony of a state. This, Cocalus agrees to.

"But how is it to be done?" he cries. "No one controls a hero. The Mothers are dead!" And then he starts laughing and will discuss it no more.

But an answer must be found.

A messenger has come from Sardinia. The king wishes me to build a palace for him. Cocalus is sad, but he will not detain me. I think I have the strength for one more construction.

Maybe there are no heroes in Sardinia.

# 3

LIKE THE SCATTERING OF BEETLES from a broken mound, everything fled from the palace, drifted outward, many feet running, cries rising like smoke, rubble and shattered flesh disappearing into earth. Pillars burned and all the dead came forth. Some say that Pasiphae went chanting and dancing through the rooms, bathed in fire, until the winds picked her up and held her, screaming, above the crumbling palace, then dropped her into the mountains where she remains, guarded by beasts and birds. Others say that as she stepped into the great courtyard, a moan rose up out of the ground. The palace guards approached her with raised axes, screamed when the wind from the flames whipped open her cloak and displayed her jewels, her breasts, her rich golden garments, and fell upon the ground, putting the axes in front of them as in the ritual. Many people seeing this started to follow, hoping to pacify the anger of the Goddess. But the flaming wall collapsed and shattered down upon them. Others say the ground opened with a hiss beneath Pasiphae's feet and engulfed her. Still others say that in the smoke and confusion she escaped to the high places, but the mountains would not accept her and now she runs wildly from peak to peak with fire streaming from her hair like a burning crown.

Some say it is not the old queen, but Ariadne.

*　*　*

She is neither dead nor mad, though she cannot move without pain. Though she does not look in mirrors. Though her people stand at a distance and cover their eyes so that they need not see her face. Though there is nothing, nothing in the world.

Pasiphae was wrong. One cannot steal what is intended for sacrifice. If the pure spring water of the offering is left unguarded for a moment in the fire dance, a masked *kourete* will slip in the drug. Pandareos' minion. Or Minos'. Or Minos himself behind the mask. Then the drink is taken, and there is a closing in of dancers and of sound, lovers fall upon each other like dogs, torches flicker and go out, and darkness covers the writhing, pumping bodies, darkness in the minds of dancers and of lovers. Of all except one who waits, clear-eyed, watchful, for the inevitable sleep, then takes Icarus, limp and dreaming, and drags him to the cliff.

It was Theseus we should have killed. Now he has taken everything.

"If there had been no Minos, what I could have done!" shouts Daedalus' daughter. "I would never have killed Icarus, not even if he had offered it. There would have been *no* killing. Only seeds would have been sacrificed as in the ancient time, only gentle foods, and the Mother would have accepted. I would have built workshops for the potters and the goldsmiths. No one would have been hungry. I would have brought water from the mountains to nourish the fields. Daedalus was working on it!"

"Daedalus forged swords with delight," writes Korkyne.

* * *

We have surveyed our realm. It is not wide but deep. The entrance might be overlooked by one accustomed to bronze walls, pinnacles of gold, roofs of ivory and silver and orichalcum. The portal lies under a twig. A path the width of a viper winds up and up, a promenade for a thin queen. The antechamber is subtly curtained in leaf patterns to soften the bleak gray rock of the walls. All the stairs are carpeted in wet moss. The royal entourage watches her step.

To the left as she enters is a corridor leading to a meadow of white grass, which emits the fragrance of death. To the right is a spring that holds a strange power. If a sword is dipped in the water, fragments of metal rush to it as though they wished to be taken from the body of the Mother into the weapon. When the spring dries up, the plains of Megara are freshened. When it flows freely, as now, vines die; sheep drop and stiffen.

The queen's *megaron* is eternally dark, hardly touched by the tiny lamp. Rock curtains hang about the bedchamber and cry out, when struck, in deep sonorous echoes. Water is always trickling somewhere as though a wound were bleeding insistently. The walls slope up and up, curve inward toward the apex. There at the top is an opening to the sky. All day it is a blue eye flecked with clouds, the cold eye of Zeus. At night, it is the eye of death. The constant water speaks, but one could go mad trying through years to understand. If one were to shout or to pray, the shouts and prayers would return again and again, mingling and overlapping. There is an inner chamber, though, where a prayer can leave the throat and be lost at once in the abyss. There, a drop of water falls each hour from a high wall into clay, crying like a dove encased in rock. And if one lies prostrate against the hollow floor, a beating begins in the stone like the beating of a heart. That is the sign of the queen's existence.

Her realm is an offense against Zeus. When he rages, the sharpest spears out of the sky are flung against her portals. Anyone guarding then will die, no matter what her courage.

*   *   *

A blue haze lies over the entire country. Nothing grows. Along the paths lie bodies, bloated and black, covered with flies, torn apart by dogs. Many of them are children. We do not have the strength to bury them all.

When at last rain does come, the sky is red with mud. Ice falls. Then frogs and fish. The soil washes away down the rocks back into the sea.

*   *   *

Two crones sit in a secluded niche. One has thrown her cloak back against the rock. Its texture is rough, as is that of her dress. She wears the clothing of a slave. Both of them wear the clothing of slaves. One is shrouded close as though she does not dare show herself. A stranger coming upon them unexpectedly would have trouble seeing the face of the shrouded one. But if he should remove the head covering, the cloak, the thick dress, he would find a scarred woman upon whom fire had written a message.

No stranger comes, however. There are guards at the approaches to the niche. The two women sit in silence. One is writing on a crumpled papyrus. "The mind flays the old mysteries," she writes. "Like a warrior, it charges into darkness, flaunting arrogance. The darkness draws back from it, and the mind revels, believing it has won. But when it is tired of reveling, it sleeps and the darkness flows back to enclose it. After a while the mind wakens again. Then there is another charge, a great battle, many victims, much death. Again the darkness draws back and waits. Again the mind wears itself out and goes to sleep. Again the darkness returns."

The shrouded one reads but says nothing. I wandered through endless passageways, she remembers, shining my blind light against walls that yielded sometimes to my touch and surrounded me. Or barred my entrance and turned shiny like polished bronze so that I saw my face repeated and repeated. Or I saw that the walls were alive, pulsating like throats, the floor moving underneath, leaves sprouting through tile, water following along behind me like a dog, pausing when I paused, held as if by an invisible wall, standing upright and churning, and then turning dutifully as I turned to go. I expected in each moment that the wall would break and the water would fill all the passageways, cover me entirely, so that when it did come—

"When the mysteries are neglected, the Goddess suffers," writes Korkyne.

The shrouded one flings the papyrus on the rock. "There is no ritual I have not performed!"

"It is not that," writes the other.

"What, then?"

Korkyne encloses the shrouded woman in her arms. But the woman's form remains stiff, even though waves of compassion surge over her, and like parched earth she receives them hungrily. But like the rocks she is washed bare. There is metal in her that clings to swords. "Daedalus was right," she says. "Whichever way I move the viper will strike."

Korkyne's arms drop, and they are separate. Two solitary women, one weeping, one cold.

* * *

Achelois plays with Korkyne's child, holding her high toward the clouds. As always, this young priestess has the eyes of a worshipper. She carries the baby like an offering. She herself is little more than a child, but she has been caring for the weak for years, her mother, her little sisters. Now they are all dead and she has come to us. At night she weeps for them. But she is laughing now. The baby too. Their voices are like shining stones.

Now the little one's laugh turns to a cry. Achelois whirls with her. The baby is quieted by the movement; then she cries again. Achelois wraps a shawl snugly about her and brings her to the shrouded woman, who waits until the girl is gone before she gives the child to Korkyne to nurse. A transparent pretense, but we honor it. We are all liars here.

It must be stated now that this infant brought forth at the ceremonies after all these months is Korkyne's child, though absurd pains are taken to convince our few followers that she is Ariadne's. "They must believe that the Goddess-on-Earth has not died," writes Korkyne. Our worship is built upon fraud. Are all these evils old? Always another lurking behind the named one, an ancestor and still powerful, so that one feels the power though one can touch only a face?

Korkyne goes into herself when the infant nurses. Her form fades until she becomes, like the rock, a holding place upon which the living dance. She seems asleep; her breathing follows the rhythm of the child. Now more than ever one can feel the loss of one's children. Now one could envy the nuzzling mouth, the stillness, the compliance that knits them to time. If we are to live, it seems we must all become Korkynes, though we drown in that sweetness.

Korkyne is as solid in faith as in the beginning, sure of the Goddess' life, waiting for stones to reveal answers. "They *are* speaking," she writes.

The shrouded one sits stolidly and lends herself to the ancient rhythms, but they do not yield the same message to her. She is always removed, dangling somehow above the earth, eternally wakeful, watching the doves die. In crystalline moments like this, she knows that the Goddess is dead. All the stony martyrs in remote shrines, all the women learning how to kill with sword and arrow will not bring Her back. The mind cuts its way through any heart.

# 4

ARIADNE:

ONE MORNING, word came of Minos. A warrior brought the news, one of his own men. We waited for him in the niche. Even Korkyne was uneasy, though it was she who had told the women to bring him. She had known him long before, this Keros. "A pious man," she wrote, "wanting to return to the Mother. No ordinary follower of Minos, but a somber, loyal Cretan who took his vows as binding eternally and who would be released from Minos' service by nothing but death."

He bowed when he saw us and lay upon the earth sobbing. For which loss, who could tell? It was a long while before he could speak, but we have learned to wait. He did not look like a warrior until he stood again, face averted. Then the story came, haltingly. Months had gone by before Minos heard of the crushing of Knossos. They told him we were all dead save Daedalus, who had destroyed the palace and escaped. In a moment, Minos became old, said Keros. Did not stir for days. Then woke one morning screaming, beat his men when they paused too long at an order, and started his wandering, a weak and raving old man, looking everywhere for Daedalus, whom he named his betrayer. He was shipless, finally. His men deserted one by one, disappearing in the crowds at the sea ports, but he hardly noticed their leaving. Incessantly he wandered up and down streets, thrusting a convoluted shell and a string into strange faces that stared and turned away. "Can you thread the shell?" he would query, believing that only Daedalus could do it. His hair had become shaggy, his robes torn. His jewels had long ago been sold for food. Only a handful of followers stayed with him. At last, in Sicily, close to his prey, in the very house where

Daedalus lives *even now,* he fell into a boiling bath prepared for him by priestesses and died. Keros was silent.

"So, Minos," I said, "the Mothers have come for you at last. And no leaf has murmured."

Keros ploughed on, doggedly reaping the grains of the tale and piling them before us like an offering. "Minos' men scattered at his death," he said. "Some of them have wandered back to Crete, hiding at first in fear of punishment, for it is widely believed that Ariadne is alive. But as they come to see how things are . . ." his voice drops to a whisper, ". . . they boldly strut past the broken walls, kicking the stones. They ape the Athenians now and flaunt their swords. But if the Goddess-on-Earth should appear to them, they would cringe."

"And then?" I ask.

"And then they would kill her."

Keros weeps, this trusted warrior who stayed with Minos to the end because he vowed his loyalty and now comes trembling for the Mother's forgiveness. Shall we trust him?

There are other stories on his lips. Phaedra is in Athens. Theseus has married her and claims Crete, not knowing that the queen must never leave her land, not knowing Phaedra's right to the throne is gone. "Besides," says Keros, "the people believe Ariadne is alive. They will never be loyal to someone else."

Oh Phaedra, Phaedra. Not a queen, but a slave. Where will you find pillars to cling to?

Deucalion is there, too, Keros reports. Theseus raises him as an Athenian. He is called Minos' son now. Not Icarus'. Not Ariadne's. And he will rule Knossos as an Athenian puppet. There is no grief in me for this lost child. I will not allow it. I have no children. All my children are dead.

Keros keeps his head down as he talks to us, like Agriope's men, as though he had never left the mountain village. "In Athens," he says, "they speak of the palace as a maze, because of Theseus' stories. He says that he alone penetrated and destroyed it."

Korkyne writes. As I read her words aloud, Keros keeps his eyes averted. "It is not destroyed," she has written. "It is wrapped about

Theseus' mind. Wherever he goes will be false leads and dead ends. His goal will be always around another bend. All his earth will be a maze and he will rush headlong down corridor after corridor, circling and bending backward endlessly around an empty center. Because he's killed the center."

"I, too," I say into my shroud.

Korkyne pretends she has not heard, but Keros raises his head sharply. He says nothing. Perhaps he has not understood? Or can he see through my veil? Does he see only dark cloth over emptiness? Why has he come back to this lost worship? What has he seen that flings him backward from the free ports of the world? Korkyne is writing again, but he looks only at my shroud. His eyes are searching. They find mine.

And now I have not the courage to crush his hope. "I, too—believe this," I mumble.

Keros looks down. I read him Korkyne's new words hastily, without thought, understanding them only after I have spoken them. "Theseus does not know what he has done. The shame is greater for those who have held the Mother within, but who nourish Her slayer."

None of us speaks then. After a long silence Keros bows and leaves, picking up his sword as he goes, walking hurriedly away like the warrior he had trained to be.


At one end of the niche is a natural apiary. "A home of sacred bees," say the mountain women, "older than all the cities of earth." We stand there. The sun begins to break through the haze. The earth begins to breathe. Bees swarm around us. A voice from somewhere whispers, "Your body is pollen. The journey is forever. Be still."

"There it is," said Pasiphae. "See?"

"It is all a lie," I tell Korkyne. She smiles. "We do not hear voices," I tell her. "Words just come into our minds." She nods. "They are not the Mother's words," I say. "The bees do not speak. We dream the whole thing."

"The Mother holds us all, will turn none away, will be assaulted again and again, and will be still loving," she writes.

I am drowning, as if in honey.

In the night, I crept silently out of the cave so as not to wake Korkyne and the infant. This skill I have perfected. I can go through the world now, moving nothing, as if I do not exist, as if I am only a name. I could not see well enough to find the path. I stumbled through brush. My limbs weighed like stone. Still, I climbed into dawn as though it would enliven me, as though Merope were tugging me upward. There was a clearing at the summit. I sank into a hollow and waited for the birds to rise.

It was then I heard the moaning. I thought at first it was from my own throat, or from the ground. Only after the dawn began did I see the shadow huddled upon the rock against the gray sky. A sound came from her like wind against cliffs. As the light grew, she stood, spread out her arms, and began to twirl in a prayer dance, but the song coming from her lips was no prayer known in Knossos. Faster and faster she twirled. Then, just as the sun flashed above the mountain, she stopped, picked up a bundle at her foot, and leaped over the cliff. She made no sound, but I could hear an infant's scream falling away.

A flask lay upon the rock. I drank what was left in it. All the dead ones came to me then, Pasiphae floating in her gold mask, breasts full and sparkling with jewels, mouth gnashing; Merope dancing blackly on her rope; my little daughter holding her crushed head. "Yield to Her; you will have to, in the end," came a voice.

I stood at the cliff's edge. Let me go down now, I thought. And I felt the enormous relief of resignation.

I thought I too had fallen into the chasm, but Korkyne was walking me back and forth, holding me like a child, showing me how to move, enacting the words of the Thrice Plougher: "Honor thy Mother, rejoice Her with the offering of fruits, injure no one."

Gradually I began to feel my legs. The sun was high now. No shadows. The flask was gone.

Korkyne is gentle. Thus, there is gentleness in the world. She smiles at lies, and they become truth.

*　*　*

Keros' eyes are eternally questioning. I will not look at him. I do not look at him. But then a moment comes when our eyes meet whether I wish it or not, and the question is there. How can a man feel the current of blood that surges up from the ages and writhes through a woman, bursting with pain, with life that is pain transformed, and with death that follows, a breath away, always following, a sure follower? Any woman's first and final lover.

Does a man think that he can escape this loving? Does he feel it is only a woman's allotment, that it will not touch him, that he will rise like a bird above the swamp, wings beating, out of the reach of the downward-pulling currents? A woman feels that only as a child. The first blood tells her the number of days that will unwind before the pull becomes irresistible. The blood says, yield, there is no escape save one, the joining of bloods in the dark of the Mother. Seek a man who will join his blood to yours. Any pain is worth that, for without it, there is nothing, which is evil. How we are caught, all of us, women and men, in a stream of blood, as though the Mother needed only that, appeared for sure only in the blood of the virgin offering or the blood of birth or the final blood that leaves the dead shell.

Keros is a kind man. His mind sleeps, but his hands worship my desire. Each stroke is a prayer to the Mother.

(Will these hands, which have served death as well, return to such service?)

# 5

"**E**VERYWHERE EXCEPT HERE," says Keros, "the ceremonies have been corrupted. Now it is only, 'Lord, Lord, Zeus, Zeus.' Even the women say it. No one is allowed to study the old language anymore except priests. The people do not even seem to realize how much has changed. Or they are afraid to say." Keros is the only one now who leaves the mountain. He is silent and full of gloom when he returns, but I make him tell us what he has learned. Agriope is dead. A young *kourete* she had pitied, who had come to her shrine for sanctuary, telling her that he had run all night from the slayers, this boy whom she had fed and comforted turned upon her, raped and humiliated her, and hanged her at last from her sacred oak with an anvil tied to each foot.

I detested Agriope, but I would kill that boy with no pang. The Mother is annihilated. It is a country of priests and killers.

It was I who found the old woman collapsed against a tree like a distorted root, and the girl hidden in the shrubs—so young I thought she was a child until I saw her huge belly. Her eyes bulged with terror, but she said nothing. The old woman struggled to stand. "Ariadne," she said. "Very holy."

I cut her short. "Hurry," I said.

My hands gathered up the girl as if she were no heavier than a sheaf of grain and carried her to our cave. The old woman staggered on behind, mumbling. I thought, it's Merope come back, and I felt as strong as in my childhood. But when I had finally placed the girl in Korkyne's care, my strength drained away. I dropped exhausted upon the rock. The old woman stood above me.

"Who are you?" I asked.

"Women no longer have names," she rasped. "They are leaves gathered by men."

"The tree is the Mother's," I said.

"And the roots of the tree are Hers."

"What shall we do with this dead tree?"

"Never believe that it is dead!" Her words struck the silence like whips. Korkyne and Achelois, who was helping her, looked up. The strange girl cried out. Birth pangs were convulsing her body. One could see the legs drawn up, the hands clutching her belly.

Korkyne hovered over her as she has always done, touching, soothing, setting up the shield within which the birthing surges and ebbs, pulling one closer and closer to the Mother's source.

(But where was the shield that other time when the burning surrounded me and Theseus stood above, stone raised?)

The old woman was looking only at me. She spoke sharply. "Pray," I think she said. She began to twirl, her arms raised. I watched, immobile. Her eyes were closed. Her rags swung awkwardly, flapping against the decrepit body. The girl moaned and tensed under Korkyne's hands. Again the old woman spoke whatever syllable it was and beckoned imperiously. I felt myself rising against my will. My arms went out and my feet moved as if I were drawn again into a scheme beyond my comprehension. All the stars whirled above me, as in the old dance. I cared nothing for the chasm at my side. I trod on the girl's breaths, lived in her moan, spun empty in the silence between. The old woman twirled beside me, silent as rock. She had thrown her robe away. One thin breast raised as she turned. There was only one. The other side was flat as a man's and crossed with dark scars. I threw off my own robe then and offered my burned dugs to the descending night. The old woman gave no sign of seeing, only twirled in a rapture I had forgotten.

It seemed to go on forever. I found I could not stop while the old woman moved. Finally the girl cried out as if from beneath a heavy rock. Then she was silent. Korkyne and Achelois were bending over close to the ground, their hands busy. Suddenly there was an infant's cry. The stars came closer. The moon grew. The old woman and I fell down upon the rock and covered ourselves.

After a while Korkyne whispered above us. "A son."

In silence the old woman stood up and took the infant. Korkyne turned back to the new mother. I watched the old woman's face as she opened the shawl and examined the tiny body. Korkyne was bent over, her eyes shaded. The old woman's face was stone. The firelight flicked at its immobility without effect.

Suddenly she walked to the edge of the cliff. I saw the flash of a knife. The child screamed. I snatched him away from her. The shawl was open. His tiny snake was bleeding. Korkyne peered over my shoulder. The old woman stood immobile like the image of the Goddess. Through the night stretched the shrieks of the infant.

His girl-mother was silent. Beneath her spread a dark pool. Korkyne hurried back and wrapped her in all the spare robes we had. I clutched the screaming infant tightly as if he might, at any moment, drop into nothingness. After a long while, he was quiet.

Korkyne and Achelois and the young mother made a circle now in the light of the fire. The old woman still stood at the cliff's edge. "Yield," she whispered suddenly.

"To what?"

"The death of this child."

"Why?"

"The Mother wills it."

"I do not go with the Mother so far."

"There is no denying Her." Slowly, as in a ceremony, the old woman removed her robe once more. The scars that took the place of her right breast danced in the light of the flames as though they had not yet settled upon a design. Her voice was so low now, I could barely hear the words. "At the start of life, when all women carried the Goddess within and were worshipped . . ."

It sounded like Merope. My mind drifted away. It could never have been, I thought for the thousandth time. The dove's eye had been still as a target. "Dove," I said, to keep it from fading.

"A name to hide the void," said the old woman. Or had I said it myself? Her eyes swallowed me. All my thoughts hurtled off into chasms. "After they had killed the sacred birds, they turned their swords upon us," she said. Her breath was sour as stale rain collected in crevices. I pulled away and listened for the screams of falling men, but they did not come.

"The noblest women were slain," she said. "The rest of us who had fought them were chained to trees and the blades were sharpened on the Mother's stone." *Come in,* said the little priestess to the murderer. "Then we were taken, one by one, to the altar. The warriors held us. And after they had raped us, they took knives and cut off one breast from each woman. They laughed and tossed our bloody dugs back and forth, catching them on the points of their swords. Then they mounted their horses and rode away.

"Days came and went before we could move. Many died. Perhaps my age saved me, my breasts already so thin . . . and that child" (she waved to the girl-mother) "hardly a woman . . . In the end, only we two were left, hiding from wood to wood, month after month as her belly grew, looking for you. We asked a woman at a brook and she covered her head and wept but would not talk. An old crone propped against a crumbling hut stared at us, shaking her head. Finally a child came running and led us into a cave under a waterfall. Through the sound of the water we could hear the neighing of horses and the pounding of hooves. When darkness came again, this child took us into the forest and showed us a trail. In the night, we lost it again and again. The girl was weak. I could not lift her. Then her pain began. That was when you found us."

Her face was dark and flat, her lips stretched against her teeth. She reached suddenly for the infant but I shrank away. She laughed at that, a thin old hag shaking with thin laughter. Korkyne looked up, alarmed. When I looked at her again, the old woman's face had disappeared into her cloak. From its darkness her voice came now in a nasal croon, a mockery of a prayer chant. "In the east, they say (Gaea, Mother) that the Lady of the Labyrinth (Gaea, Mother) is a lover of killers."

All my lover-killers swarmed around me. I held the infant so tight, he wakened again and cried. "This child has done nothing," I said.

"He is male," came the thin voice.

"You will not kill him."

Her words were a low wheeze, breath through brambles. I leaned forward to catch them. They were fast, urgent. No mocking now. "They are not perfectly formed," she said. "Nothing steadies them. They are bloodless. They spill their seed upon the ground and are empty as husks. Always they are hungry to be filled with life, yet they fear it. The Mother's blood frightens them. Then they are ashamed to show their fear. Like children, they pretend to be brave. Like children, they destroy what they cannot have. The life that will not flow through them, they spill out in rage. In the old time, they were in awe and could be gentled. Now they are all killers."

"Not Icarus," I said. She did not seem to hear. "Not this child. It is you who have tried to kill him."

"The Lady of the Labyrinth knows nothing," came the scornful voice. "I have given him a sacred wound. When he becomes your consort, it will remind him of the Mother's need." She bent down to the sparse grass and collected dew on her hand, and spread it across the infant's brow. "Son of Gaea," I heard her whisper. "Return life unto life. Mournful son of Gaea, sprinkle thy seed upon a fertile furrow. Give all thou art at thy fullest, and sleep in the Mother's Womb forever."

I held the boy to the light and examined him. The cut was tiny. The little snake would rise in its time and yield its offering. Presently the old woman came at him again, but I saw that it was only an herb in her hand to stop the blood. The knife was still stuck in her belt.

# 6

Now, SUDDENLY, HERE IS Keros out of the gullet of night, breathless with panic. He has heard in the chatter of the Attic guards a rumor. A new raid, a new routing of priestesses, a new defilement of the Mother. It is our shrine they will attack, he believes. They have found us again. We must leave at once. No time for packing. We must take nothing, only flee. Abandon our writings, the ritual vessels, everything. Quickly we shove the scrolls into the crevice behind the altar. It will hold only two of them. The other two we thrust under rocks behind the spring. They will be wet. "They will rot," I say.

"Quickly," urges Keros. "I will come back for them."

The girl wakes and screams when she sees him. The old woman scurries to her side, throws her bones over the young body as if to conceal. "He is a friend," I say. The old woman shakes her head. The young mother's eyes are wild.

"Hurry!" says Keros. And he flings the young mother over his shoulder.

"She will die if she is moved," Korkyne says.

"She will die if she is not moved," says Keros.

The old woman stares. Achelois holds the infant as we belt our skirts high. Her face is buried in the shawl. Korkyne carries her daughter from the cave. When I take the new infant, Achelois kisses me. For a moment I hold her. Her face is wet. As we run away through the mountain trails like doe, I look back and see her standing alone beside the fire.

Again and again we have run through darkness. Far behind us the swords clang out of the night and men's voices shout, but there is never a cry from the women we leave behind. Someone always has to stay for the coming of the warriors. This we have learned. When they find no one, they keep searching and searching, sometimes descending in rage upon a village and burning all the houses, herding the men off like sheep to be chained to galleys, raping the women and killing them and the children too. Over and over this has happened until it seems that we have fled from every cave in Crete.

How do they find us? Sometimes a villager will speak rather than die. Sometimes even one of our own followers will break. I would break also, I think. I have broken again and again, though only Korkyne knows it. My scars burn as if in new flame when I run through the rocks and the brush, but the pain is deeper than that. I have begged them to let me be the one to stay behind, but they will not hear of it. Only Daedalus would laugh with me over this.

When at last we stop, I am trembling with pain. In the stillness, I hear Daedalus' voice going on and on. I see the shadow of his huge head moving against my eyes.

"Where is the shrine?" I ask.

"Beyond reach," says Daedalus.

"Beyond whose reach?"

A laugh follows. Or a shudder. Enters leaves like sun, flows through stem, branch, trunk, roots, plunging down, down like water sinking, blood dropping, down to where the beating begins. Stays there, still, while the wind ceases, the sun is interrupted, a pause opens in time, a gap in the mind, through which might flood any form, monstrous or noble. Once again I sink through rock into fetid earth, lie rotting in offal at the bottom of chasms into which they throw the corpses of pigs. And I hear the voice that has been speaking forever in my ears, in my blood, speaking without words so that the force comes but the sense is lost. I hear that old woman who lies under us, cynical and calm as we plan and pain.

"Say it clear, you Bitch," I whisper.

The ground heaves with her breath. Terror swallows me. I am a monstrous infant with the head of a beast. *And as the substance drips against my face, I taste honey. Come in,* says the little priestess. I have never left this place, I think. The monstrous head bobs back and forth, riding like a great ball of dung on wooden poles, back and forth into sun, shadow . . . *This is your death, Ariadne. Enter it then,*

*learn its nature, let it seep into you like sperm, let it seek out your place of*
*life and shatter you.*

"Not yet," I tell Her. I see how my arms have formed a shield around the infant. "See how these limbs will not pull apart, how the burned skin heals me into myself, holds me, holds this child. Nothing of me yields."

But something that had been me was yielding. I saw the infant's eyes sinking, the black bloodied skull falling, the tiny stone fingers losing skin, the swollen belly bursting and the rot traveling the uncut cord toward me, reaching between my legs, entering. *As they all have done. Entering, shattering.*

Korkyne tried to take the infant, but I would not let her. Keros was watching me. They were both watching. Their eyes hung on me like leaves. A breath could break them off, I thought.

The infant sighed. Then came a shaking in the earth, too fast like a fearful heart, rising through rock and root, slowing in the ascent, lifting upward into trunk and limbs, branching outward through me toward those others as far as the reach of love. It has never been outside me, I thought. It has always risen from within, and though it trembles, it has the touch of rock.

"Without the Mother, we must each of us become the Mother," I tried to say, though I felt I had no tongue. Korkyne smiled and bowed her head. Keros, too. I kissed their hair.

The old woman was gone. No one knew where she had faded into the night. The young mother was dead. Keros' shoulder was soaked with her blood. Her cloak fell away as he placed her on the ground and the dawn light showed the scars where her tiny breast had been cut away. We hid her in leaves and ran on, without stopping for ceremony.

Now, in this new hiding place, her child shares Korkyne's milk, cries lustily, does not know of death, demands our love. And I am imperfectly formed to refuse this flawed hostage.

\* \* \*

Every day new reports come in of fresh destruction of shrines, new murders of priestesses. There is no distinction between those who are drugged and mad and those who die clear-eyed on their altars. They are all called Monsters, Madwomen, Raging Ones, Wind Demons, Temptresses, Harpies, Sirens, Avengers, Daughters of the Abyss . . .

My mother is dead. My daughter is dead. Icarus, Merope, Minos. My sister is a slave. My son will be an Attic killer. And our story, like all the others, is being told by liars. That is why I must write this for you. So that you will know what really happened. So that you will listen for Her voice.

# APPENDIX I

# The Traditional Myth

THE BEST-KNOWN (and obviously patriarchal) version of the labyrinth myth goes something like this:

Minos, ruler of ancient Crete, has a licentious wife, Pasiphae, who falls passionately in love with a sacred bull and cohabits with him, with the secret assistance of Daedalus, the famed Athenian artchitect who is in exile in Crete. When the queen gives birth to a monster, called the minotaur, Minos is outraged and orders Daedalus to build a labyrinth in which to hide this shameful progeny. The monster feeds only on human flesh. Thus, as part of the tribute paid by all the city states in the Aegean over which he rules, Minos demands sacrificial victims. The Athenians, in particular, are compelled to send seven young men and seven young women each year to be sacrificed to the minotaur.

In order to end this outrage, Theseus, heroic son of the king of Athens, volunteers to go to Crete as one of the sacrificial victims and to kill the minotaur. When he arrives, Ariadne, daughter of Minos, falls in love with him and secretly gives him the clue to the labyrinth, which she has obtained from Daedalus. With the aid of this clue, Theseus kills the minotaur, frees the Athenians, and escapes with Ariadne. However, he abandons her on an island and returns to Athens to rule. Later, he marries Ariadne's younger sister, Phaedra, and rules Crete as well.

Meanwhile, Daedalus' guilty assistance to the queen has been discovered, and he has been imprisoned in his own labyrinth by an irate Minos. However, he escapes by flying to Sicily on wings he has cleverly fashioned of feathers and wax. His son, Icarus, flies with him, but he goes too close to the sun; his wings melt, and he drowns in the sea. Minos pursues Daedalus to Sicily but is killed there by the daughters of the local king.

This story is undoubtedly an example of what Joseph Campbell calls "mythological defamation":

> It consists simply in terming the gods of other people demons, enlarging one's own counterparts to hegemony over the universe, and then inventing all sorts of both great and little secondary myths . . . to validate in mythological terms not only a new social order but also a new psychology.*

I have tried here to recapture the old psychology—the voice of a woman who was taught from birth to believe not only that the Great Mother Goddess had created and now controlled all living creatures, but also that she herself, the queen and highest priestess, was a visible embodiment of the Goddess, carrying the awesome responsibility of enabling her subjects to hear the Divine Voice.

---

*Joseph Campbell, *The Masks of God: Occidental Mythology* (New York: The Viking Press, 1970), p. 80.

# APPENDIX II

# From Robert Graves, *The Greek Myths, I*

"GREECE WAS Cretanized toward the close of the eighteenth century B.C., probably by an Hellenic aristocracy which had seized power in Crete a generation or two earlier and there initiated a new culture. The straightforward account of Theseus' raid on Cnossus, quoted by Plutarch from Cleidemus, makes reasonable sense. It describes a revolt by the Athenians against a Cretan overlord who had taken hostages for their good behaviour; the secret building of a flotilla; the sack of the unwalled city of Cnossus during the absence of the main Cretan fleet in Sicily; and a subsequent peace treaty ratified by the Athenian king's marriage with Ariadne, the Cretan heiress. These events, which point to about the year 1400 B.C., are paralleled by the mythical account: a tribute of youths and maidens is demanded from Athens in requital for the murder of a Cretan prince. Theseus, by craftily killing the Bull of Minos, or defeating Minos' leading commander in a wrestling match, relieves Athens of this tribute; marries Ariadne, the royal heiress; and makes peace with Minos himself. (98.1)

"Theseus' killing of the bull-headed Asterius, called the Minotaur, or 'Bull of Minos'; his wrestling match with Taurus ('bull'); and his capture of the Cretan bull, are all versions of the same event. . . . 'Minos' was the title of a Cnossian dynasty, which had a sky-bull for its emblem—'Asterius' could mean 'of the sun' or 'of the sky'—and it was in bull-form that the king seems to have coupled ritually with the Chief-priestess as Moon-cow. (98.2)

"Pasiphae . . . is a title of the Moon: and 'Itone,' her other name, a title of Athene as rain-maker, . . . the myth of Pasiphae

[ 243 ]

and the bull points to a ritual marriage under an oak between the Moon-priestess, wearing cow's horns, and the Minos-king, wearing a bull's mask. . . . and the marriage seems to have been understood as one between Sun and Moon. . . . Daedalus' discreet retirement from the meadow suggests that this was not consummated publicly. . . . Many later Greeks disliked the Pasiphae myth, and preferred to believe that she had an affair not with a bull, but with a man called Taurus. (88.7)

"One element in the formation of the Labyrinth myth may have been that the palace at Cnossus—the house of the *labrys*, or double-axe—was a complex of rooms and corridors, and the Athenian raiders had difficulty in finding and killing the king when they captured it. But this is not all. An open space in front of the palace was occupied by a dance floor with a maze pattern used to guide performers of an erotic spring dance. (98.2)

"'Ariadne,' which the Greeks understood as 'Ariagne' (very holy), will have been a title of the Moon-goddess honoured in the dance, and in the bull ring: 'the high, fruitful Barley-mother,' also called Aridela, 'the very manifest one.' The carrying of fruit-laden boughs in Ariadne's honour, and Dionysus', and her suicide by hanging, 'because she feared Artemis,' suggests that Ariadne-dolls were attached to these boughs. A bell-shaped Boeotian goddess-doll hung in the Louvre, her legs dangling, is Ariadne, or Erigone, or Hanged Artemis, and bronze dolls with detachable limbs have been found in Daedalus' Sardinia. Ariadne's crown made by Hephaestus in the form of a rose-wreath is not a fancy; delicate gold wreaths with gemmed flowers were found in the Mochlos hoard. (98.5)

"Theseus' marriage to the Moon-priestess made him lord of Cnossus, and on one Cnossian coin a new moon is set in the centre of a maze. Matrilinear custom, however, deprived an heiress of all claims to her lands if she accompanied a husband overseas; and this explains why Theseus did not bring Ariadne back to Athens, or any farther than Dia, a Cretan island within sight of Cnossus. Cretan Dionysus, represented as a bull—Minos, in fact—was Ariadne's rightful husband." (98.6)

# APPENDIX III
# Bibliography

Alexiou, S., N. Platon, H. Guanella, and Von Matt. *Ancient Crete*. New York: Praeger Publ., Inc., 1968.

Bachofen, J. J. *Myth, Religion and Mother Right*. Princeton, N. J.: Princeton University Press, 1967.

Bowman, J. *Crete*. Indianapolis and New York: Bobbs Merrill, 1968.

Briffault, Robert. *The Mothers*. New York: Macmillan & Co., 1931.

Bulfinch, Thomas. *Mythology*. New York: The Modern Library, 1934.

Campbell, Joseph. *The Hero with a Thousand Faces*. New York: Bollingen Foundation, Inc., 1949.

———. *The Masks of God: Occidental Mythology*. New York: The Viking Press, 1970.

Cornford, F. M. *From Religion to Philosophy*. New York: Harper, 1957.

Cottrell, Leonard. *The Bull of Minos*. London: Evans, 1953.

Evans, Arthur. *The Earlier Religions of Greece in Light of the Cretan Discoveries*. London: Macmillan & Co., 1925.

———. *The Palace of Minos at Knossos*. London: Macmillan & Co., Vol. I, 1921, to Vol. IV, Part II, 1935.

Frazer, James. *The Golden Bough*. London: Macmillan & Co., 1907.

Fromm, Erich. *The Forgotten Language*. New York: Grove Press, 1957.

Gimbutas, Marija. *The Gods and Goddesses of Old Europe 7000-3500 B.C.* Berkeley, Ca.: University of California Press, 1974.

Gordon, Cyrus. *Forgotten Scripts*. New York: Basic Books, Inc., 1968.

Graves, Robert. *The Greek Myths*. Vol. I & Vol. II. Harmondsworth, England: Penguin, 1955.

———. *The White Goddess*. New York: Farrar, Straus and Giroux, 1972.

Guirand, F., ed. *New Larousse Encyclopedia of Mythology*. London: Paul Hamlyn, 1960.

Harding, M. Esther. *Woman's Mysteries*. New York: G. P. Putnam's Sons, 1971.

Harrison, Jane Ellen. *Prolegomena to the Study of Greek Religion*. Cambridge: The University Press, 1903.

Higgins, Reynold. *Minoan and Mycenaean Art.* New York: Praeger Publ., Inc., 1967.

Hutchinson, R. W. *Prehistoric Crete.* Harmondsworth, England: Penguin, 1962.

Marinatos, S. *Crete and Early Greece.* London: Methuen, 1962.

Neumann, Erich. *The Great Mother.* New York: Pantheon, 1955.

Nilsson, Martin. *The Minoan-Mycenaean Religion and Its Survival in Greek Religion.* London: Lund, 1927.

Palmer, L. *Mycenaeans and Minoans.* London: Faber and Faber, 1961.

————. *A New Guide to the Palace of Knossos.* New York: Praeger Publ., Inc., 1969.

Pendlebury, J. D. S. *The Archaeology of Crete.* London: Methuen, 1939.

————. *A Handbook to the Palace of Minos and Its Dependencies.* London: Methuen, 1935.

Platon, N. *Crete.* London and New York: World, 1966; Frederick Muller, 1966.

Plutarch. *The Lives of the Noble Grecians and Romans.* Tr. by John Dryden and revised by Arthur Hugh Clough. New York: The Modern Library, 1932.

Reverdin, L. and R. Hoegler, *Crete and Its Treasures.* New York: The Viking Press, 1961.

Stone, Merlin. *When God Was a Woman.* New York: The Dial Press, 1976.

Ventris, Michael and John Chadwick. *Documents in Mycenaean Greek.* Cambridge: The University Press, 1956.

Ward, Anne G., ed. *The Quest for Theseus.* New York: Praeger Publ., Inc., 1970.

Willets, R. F. *Cretan Cults and Festivals.* New York: Barnes and Noble, 1962.

————. *Everyday Life in Ancient Crete.* London: Batsford, 1969.